WEAVERS' WAY

A DCI Tanner Mystery
- Book Nine -

DAVID BLAKE

www.david-blake.com

Proofread by Jay G Arscott

Special thanks to Kath Middleton, Ann Studd, John Harrison, Anna Burke, Emma Porter, Emma Stubbs and Jan Edge

Second edition published by Black Oak Publishing Ltd
in Great Britain, 2023

ISBN: 978-1-9163479-8-4

DEDICATION

For Akiko, Akira and Kai.

THE DI TANNER SERIES

Broadland
St. Benet's
Moorings
Three Rivers
Horsey Mere
The Wherryman
Storm Force
Long Gore Hall
Weavers' Way

""For the son dishonoureth the father, the daughter riseth up against her mother, the daughter-in-law against her mother-in-law; a man's enemies are the men of his own house."
Micah 7:6

- PROLOGUE -

Sunday, 24th April

SAMUEL TUNK RESTED his forehead against the painted steel of his cold prison cell door. 'One more night,' he whispered softly to himself, wrapping the fingers of his square slab-like hands around its fixed immovable frame.

Drawing his head slowly back, he focussed his attention on the door, taking in its cold grey surface for what he hoped would be the very last time. As he closed his dark sunken eyes, he spent a pleasant moment as he'd done countless times before, imagining that it wasn't the solid impenetrable barrier that it was, but instead was the open window of a quaint country cottage, overlooking one of the many meandering rivers that wound their way majestically through the Norfolk Broads, a landscape he longed to rest his eyes on once again.

With his eyes remaining firmly closed, he continued with his daydream; that the room behind him was an open lounge with a cosy low-beamed ceiling, lit by the warmth of a gently burning fire.

Drifting towards it in his mind, he found his hands resting on the top of a high wing-backed chair, feeling the warmth of its oxblood leather surface underneath his coarse calloused hands. From somewhere above came the sound of a woman, laughing at something with playful delight. As his head turned to see a narrow wooden staircase, a cruel smile tugged at the corners of his twisted crooked mouth.

Creeping slowly over, he placed a guiding hand on its varnished wooden banister to climb carefully up, the stairs beneath his vast muscular weight creaking out in protest with every tentative step. The moment his foot rested on the landing above, the laughter suddenly stopped.

Glancing one way, then the other, he stared down to the end of one of the windowless wood-panelled hallways, endeavouring to determine which way the sound had come from. Then he heard it again, louder that time, fluttering through the air like a sparrow caught in a spiralling breeze.

Seeing a small wooden door, lurking in the shadows at the furthest end, he crept slowly towards it. As his hand wrapped itself around its cool brass handle, he inched it open to find himself inside a small candlelit room dominated by a large double bed, in the middle of which knelt a gorgeous naked woman, her lustrous blonde hair resting against the tops of her pale undulating breasts.

With the vaguest feeling that he'd seen her somewhere before, he watched in lecherous awe as she arched her back, her incandescent blue eyes lifting themselves up towards a series of wooden beams above. As her full red lips parted to reveal a row of perfect pearl-white teeth, she laughed again.

Transfixed by her familiar all-consuming beauty, he took a heart-pounding voyeuristic moment to take in her smooth pale skin, only to realise that she was now staring directly at him. As his face prickled with embarrassment, he heard her laugh once more, this time lifting her hips to begin gyrating them back and forth. It was only then that he realised that she wasn't alone. Lying underneath her was a decrepit old man, his hands and feet twitching with spasmodic violence as if strapped into an electric chair to have two-thousand volts driven down into his brain. That's when he saw the blood, spreading out over the bed's white satin sheets like an expanding pool of shimmering paint.

Following it back to its source, he saw a knife embedded in the man's birdcage-like chest, so deep that only its hilt remained. As the woman's undulations reached a climactic crescendo, he watched in hedonistic reverence as she prised it out to plunge back in, again and again, launching fresh spurts of blood into her sadistically grinning face. Only when the decrepit man's limbs had become still did she lever it out, lifting it to her mouth to begin licking the blood from its glistening blade.

With her eyes now fixed firmly on his, he watched her un-straddle the now flaccid corpse to skirt around the bed, turning the knife in her hand to taste the blood from its other side.

'Hello, darling,' she eventually said, running the blade down her neck towards her heaving voluminous breasts. 'Would you like to play?'

Tunk felt his heart leap hard in his throat. 'I only want t-to watch,' came his jittering reply.

'This isn't Freeview, darling,' the woman continued, slinking ever closer. 'If you want to stay, you have to play.'

Tunk began edging his way slowly back. 'Then I'll leave.'

'But darling, there's nowhere for you to go.'

When the heel of his foot caught up against something solid behind him, a panicked glance over his shoulder told him what he somehow already knew. The object he'd backed into was the door to his cell, which meant that the woman was right. There *was* nowhere for him to go.

With his heart thumping inside his chest, he turned back to find her standing directly in front of him, the sharpened edge of her knife pressed firmly against his throat.

'Are you ready?' he heard her ask, her soft warm lips brushing gently against his.

'No – wait – stop! It's not my time!'

'It *is* your time,' the woman continued, the words whispered softly into his ear. 'It has been since the moment you killed me.'

Feeling the blade open up his throat, Tunk woke with a start.

'Jesus Christ!' he gasped, reaching for his neck.

Breathing hard against the stale surrounding air, he pushed himself up to find himself lying on his bed, his eyes darting into the corners of his shadow-filled cell. He'd had dreams like that before, but nothing quite so real.

As he attempted to rub out the images that seemed to have burnt themselves into the backs of his retinas, he rested his shaved anvil-shaped head against his pillow. After another furtive glance around his cell, he focussed his mind on slowing his still pounding heart. 'One more night,' he whispered again to himself, pulling the covers up over his barrel-like chest. 'Just one more night,' he repeated, closing his eyes to feel himself begin slipping down into what he prayed would be a deep, dreamless sleep.

- CHAPTER ONE -

Monday, 25th April

ARRIVING AT WROXHAM Police Station half an hour later than he should have, John Tanner stood just beyond the main office doors to stare vacantly about, looking for someone to apologise to. It took him a full second to remember that there wasn't anyone. Nor would there be. By that time he'd been Norfolk's Detective Chief Inspector for a little over one month, making him the most senior ranking police officer there. But having spent the previous twenty something years in the Force, during which time he'd had to ask permission before doing just about anything, he was still struggling to come to terms with the fact that he was finally in a position where he could do pretty much what he wanted, within reason of course, without having to ask anyone beforehand. He certainly didn't need to find someone to apologise to for being a little late.

Allowing a smile to play briefly over his lips, he tugged off his old sailing jacket, still dripping from the rain outside, to amble over to what used to be Forrester's old office but was now his, and the luxury coffee percolator he'd had installed in its corner on his very first day.

Reaching the door he heard Vicky Gilbert's all too familiar voice calling out to him from behind.

'Morning, boss! Did you have a good weekend?'

'Morning Vicky,' he replied, opening the door to hang his coat up behind it, 'but as I've said to you before, there's no need to keep calling me boss all the time.'

'Sorry, boss,' she repeated, with a mischievous grin, 'I don't seem to be able to stop myself.'

Tanner shook his head with mild irritation as his phone started to ring on his desk. 'Anyway, what can I do you for – I – I mean – what can I do for you?' he asked, doing his best to ignore its demanding tone.

'Henderson hasn't come in yet.'

'Sorry, but why's that my problem?'

'Because, despite the fact that he's been working here for over a week now, he still hasn't been able to arrive on time, and without wishing to lay the blame at anyone's feet, you're the one who hired him.'

'I'll admit that he has been a little tardy of late, but I still stand by my decision to bring him on board. If you recall, the boy has a degree in Criminal Law, from Oxford University no less, and passed the graduate training course with flying colours. He was also born and bred in Norfolk, which as far as I'm concerned makes him the ideal candidate.'

'He may be an ideal candidate on paper, but he's a long way from being so in real life. Apart from his inability to arrive at work on time, he's frustratingly shy, socially awkward, he can barely string a sentence together, he's a terrible map reader, and has got no idea how to use satellite navigation. He can also barely drive a car, at least not safely, and is dangerously clumsy, so much so that I think he's more of a public hazard than the criminals we're supposed to be chasing. On top of all that, I'm fairly sure he fancies me.'

Tanner offered her a sagacious frown. 'Yes, I see

the problem. Maybe you should ask him out on a date?'

'If it weren't for the fact that he has the face of a deformed donkey and the body of a decomposing giraffe, I'd at least consider it, but even if I did, I doubt he'd be able to find wherever it was we were supposed to be going, not without mowing down half the population of Norfolk on the way.'

Unable to ignore the phone for any longer, Tanner reached over his desk to pick up its receiver, only for it to fall silent the moment he touched it.

Rolling his eyes, he turned back to Vicky. 'OK, look, when he does eventually arrive, tell him to come in and see me, and I'll remind him that he needs to be at work on time.'

'If you could tell him to stop staring at me as well?'

'I'll see what I can do.'

Watching her leave, he'd barely finished pouring himself a coffee when Townsend appeared in her place.

'Morning boss! I don't suppose I could have a quick word?'

'You can if you stop calling me boss all the bloody time.'

'Sorry, boss. I'll – er – remember next time.'

'OK, so – what is it?'

'It's about Cooper, boss,' Townsend continued, surreptitiously closing the door. 'I was wondering – well hoping really – if there was any chance I could maybe work with somebody else?'

With coffee in hand, Tanner eased himself down into Forrester's old black leather executive's chair. 'He's not that bad, is he?'

'No, of course, it's just – well – it's just that we don't seem to have all that much in common, that's all.'

'I'm not asking you to marry him, Townsend.'

'I know. I'd just prefer to work with someone a little more...a little more like me, I suppose.'

'Like you, as in...?'

'Someone who isn't quite so miserable all the time. He's also lazy, arrogant, in desperate need of a sense of humour and, to be quite honest, boss,' Townsend continued, lowering his voice to cast a furtive eye out of Tanner's partition window into the main office beyond, 'he's what could be described as just a little bit dim. He also drives that car of his far too fast, and way too close to whatever car happens to be driving at a more sensible speed in front of him, which frankly scares the absolute shit out of me. Worse still, he doesn't seem to talk about anything other than bloody football, whereas I'm more of a rugby sort of a chap.'

'I seem to remember you saying that you're also a glass-is-half-full sort of a chap, so I suggest you remember that whilst being grateful for the fact that you've got a job. Millions don't, you know!'

'I'm not saying that I don't want to work, boss. Quite the opposite, which is a bit tricky being stuck with Cooper, being that he seems to do everything in his power not to. Couldn't I work with Vicky instead?'

'No!'

'Why not?'

'Because she's breaking-in the new boy.'

'You mean Henderson?' Townsend continued. 'The one who never seems to be here? I'd have thought it would make more sense to stick him with Cooper. At least they'd have something in common.'

'I didn't know Henderson liked football?'

'I was referring more to their seemingly shared lack of interest in doing anything involving actual work.'

'Unfortunately, it's for that very reason that I can't put him with Cooper.'

'Then can't I work with you instead?'

'I'm a DCI now, Townsend, or hadn't you noticed?'

Townsend shrugged. 'I don't mind.'

'Yes, well, unfortunately, I do. Besides, I now seem to have found myself permanently stuck behind this bloody desk, spending every waking hour doing nothing more productive than filling out endless stupid forms that seem to have no other purpose than to help justify my job, and just about everyone else's as well. Believe you me, Townsend, you're better off with Cooper than stuck in here with me.'

A rap at the door had Vicky's mop of dark red hair reappearing from the other side. 'I just thought you should know that Henderson's arrived, and he's only forty-five minutes late.'

'Yes, and what do you want me to do about it? Put his name forward for an OBE?'

'I thought you said you were going to have a word with him when he eventually showed up?'

'OK, fine, but before I do, if there's anyone else waiting out there to see me, you'd better ask them to form an orderly queue.'

Vicky glanced over her shoulder. 'I think it's just him, boss.'

Tanner let out a deflated sigh. 'Very well. Send him in.'

'What about me?' he heard Townsend demand.

'I thought we were done?'

'Well, yes, but...?'

Seeing the imploring look stretched out over his face, Tanner offered him a frown of paternal pity. 'Tell you what. I'm interviewing someone else this week. A Miss Gina Booth,' he added, glancing at his monitor. 'If she proves suitable, maybe we'll be able to swap things around a little.'

'Sounds good to me,' chimed in Vicky.

'For Townsend, not you!'

'Fine! But if you don't sort out donkey-boy, I'm the one you'll be looking to replace.'

'OK, enough of the moaning,' stated Tanner, his voice rising with growing impatience. 'I think it's time for the two of you to get back to work, don't you?'

'Yes, boss,' they replied in unison, turning to follow each other out, only for another face to peer nervously around the edge of the door, one that did admittedly bear an uncanny resemblance to a donkey.

- CHAPTER TWO -

'AH, HENDERSON!' TANNER began, wishing Vicky hadn't mentioned anything about his face, and the animal it so closely resembled. 'You're here!'

'Sorry I'm late, boss.'

'Don't call me boss, Henderson.'

'It's just that I missed the bus and – and there wasn't another one for ages – and when it did arrive, it got stuck in the roadworks down the road from where I live.'

'Whereabouts is that?'

'Just outside Stalham.'

'But – that's only fifteen minutes away?'

'I suppose that depends on how much traffic there is, and as I said, the roadworks down from where I live have been an absolute nightmare.'

'OK, well, couldn't you get up a little earlier?'

'I thought I did this morning, but I still managed to be late.'

'Forty-five minutes late, to be precise,' commented Tanner, glancing at his watch. 'From Stalham I'd have thought you could have walked here in that time.'

'Yes, boss. Sorry again. I'll make a point of getting up even earlier tomorrow.'

'What time do you consider to be early?'

'I set my alarm for seven o'clock.'

'And what time do you actually get out of bed?'

'I – er – well – I...' Henderson began, his face flushing with colour. 'I do sometimes wake up to realise that I've managed to sleep through the alarm, but only sometimes.'

'It sounds to me that it's not a problem of you missing the bus, but more one of being unable to get out of bed.'

Tanner watched Henderson blush again, leaving him staring miserably down at his feet.

Thinking for an uncomfortable moment that he was about to cry, Tanner placed his elbows on his desk. 'Listen, Henderson,' he quickly began, before he had the chance to, 'I doubt there's a single person on the planet who doesn't have a hard time getting out of bed in the morning. I'm fairly sure that's why they invented coffee.'

Seeing just the hint of a smile, Tanner continued along the same line. 'You do drink coffee, I take it?'

The lanky young lad shook his head.

'Then there's the problem!' Tanner exclaimed, as if he'd just discovered the solution to global warming. 'I suggest you start, and sooner rather than later. If it helps, consider it to be a direct order.'

'Yes, boss.'

'And if you're late again, I'll fire you.'

Seeing him look up with a start, Tanner's face cracked into a smile. 'That was a joke, Henderson.'

'Yes, of course, and sorry again.'

'You don't need to keep apologising.'

'No, boss.'

'And please stop calling me boss all the bloody time.'

'Er...right – of course. It's – er – it's just that's what everyone else calls you, boss.'

'Despite me constantly telling them not to.'

'Should I call you sir, instead?'

It was Tanner's turn to shake his head. 'Look, it really doesn't matter what you call me, but it does matter that you're able to arrive at work on time.'

'Yes, boss. Sorry, I mean sir.'

'Maybe you could buy yourself a louder alarm clock?'

'I actually use my phone.'

'Then perhaps you could try turning the volume up?'

'Oh, right. I hadn't thought of that.'

Wondering if it may be an idea to give Oxford University a call, to make sure he had been awarded a degree from there, or anywhere else for that matter, Tanner thought he'd better wind the meeting up before he did decide to fire him. 'OK, good. Then I look forward to seeing you on the dot of nine tomorrow morning, if not perhaps a little earlier?'

'Yes, boss, at least I'll certainly make every effort to.'

You'd better do more than that, Tanner thought to himself, as Henderson turned to show himself out, only for there to be yet another knock at the door.

'For Christ's sake,' he muttered. 'I could have sworn Vicky said there wasn't a queue.'

'Morning Tanner!' came the booming, all too familiar voice of the man who used to occupy the chair Tanner was now sitting in.

As he jumped to his feet to instinctively stand to attention, Tanner stared over at the station's former DCI, bouncing his way in through the door. 'Superintendent Forrester, sir!'

Closing the door behind him, Forrester went to hang his dripping wet coat up on the hook behind it, only to realise Tanner's was already there. 'I just thought I'd stop by to see how things are going,' he continued, glancing furtively around for somewhere else to put it.

'Oh, fine. Thank you, sir.'

'I did call a few minutes ago, to say that I was coming,' he continued, his eyes searching for the phone to Tanner's left, 'but nobody picked up.'

'I seem to have had a morning spent dealing with disgruntled employees.'

'Nothing serious, I hope?' Forrester queried, hooking his coat over the back of one of the chairs in front of the desk.

'Nothing even remotely serious, which is proving to be part of the problem.'

'I assume you're referring to the fact that everyone seems to spend their lives moaning about everyone else.'

'Something like that.'

'Don't worry. You'll get used to it. Don't forget, the DCI role has always been more managerial.'

'Which was what I was afraid of. May I get you a coffee?'

'Why not?' Forrester declared, happily plonking himself down on the same chair his coat was hooked over. 'So, apart from the normal staffing issues, is there anything else you're struggling with?'

'You mean, apart from the endless bloody forms I seem to now spend my life filling out, that everyone's decided to start calling me boss all the time – despite constantly asking them not to – and that the only reason I have for leaving my desk is to go to the toilet?'

'There must be something about the job you're enjoying?'

'Well, I suppose having a coffee machine within arm's reach is a plus,' Tanner continued, passing a cup over the desk, 'and Christine seems to be enjoying having a little more money to spend around the house.'

Forrester sat back in his chair to take a tentative sip from his coffee. 'How is she?'

'Much the same as always.'

'Still obsessed with cooking?'

'A little less so since hearing that she wasn't accepted for this year's Bake Off, but only marginally.'

'And the baby?'

'Still inside her, thankfully.'

'Don't tell me you're not looking forward to being a father again?'

'Well, yes, of course, but we've both been there before, each one of us having had a similar outcome.'

'Yes, of course,' Forrester replied, shifting awkwardly in his chair. 'Sorry, I must admit to having forgotten about that.'

'Don't worry. Christine's looking at it as being an opportunity to have a fresh start.'

'And you?'

An image of his daughter flickered through his mind. 'I suppose. I think what I was trying to say was that we're both going into it with our eyes fully open. We each know the challenges involved, as well as the risks.'

'Don't worry. You'll be alright. Anyway, believe it or not, I didn't come to poke my nose into your personal life.'

'You didn't?'

'I actually came to ask if you'd heard about what happened with regards to Samuel Tunk.'

For some reason, the sound of the name jarred inside Tanner's head. 'Isn't he one of the convicted criminals whose cases had to be re-opened since Whitaker's passing?'

'One of the many. Probably the most dangerous, as well. Anyway, there's been a concerted effort for everyone to keep quiet about it, so as not to raise the alarm amongst the local community, but I thought you'd better know what's happened.'

'And what's that?'

'He was released this morning.'

Tanner leant thoughtfully back in his chair. 'Do I need to be concerned?'

'Hopefully not, but he wasn't like Jason Baines in that he *didn't* do what he was put away for.'

'Then why the hell's he been released?'

Forrester shrugged back a response. 'As you know, every investigation in which Whitaker was the SIO has had to be re-opened. Although it seems likely that Tunk *was* responsible for what he was convicted of, it was discovered that Whitaker had been stupid enough to introduce manufactured evidence to help guarantee the conviction.'

'Dare I ask what he was convicted of?'

'Ah, right, well – he started off as just your average thief, known for breaking into people's boats whilst the occupants were sleeping inside, but soon graduated up to murder when one of the owners was stupid enough to challenge him.'

'This is the man who tied up an entire family,' Tanner continued, suddenly remembering exactly who Samuel Tunk was, 'before raping the mother and butchering the lot of them?'

'I'm afraid it is.'

'Jesus Christ! That's all I need!'

'Look, don't worry. He was locked up inside Broadmoor Hospital, nowhere near Norfolk.'

'But it did take place around here, didn't it?'

'Well, yes. It was on board a boat moored up down one of the smaller dykes, but again, that doesn't mean he has any intention of coming here.'

'It doesn't mean he won't, though, either.'

'Anyway, I only thought I should mention it. We'll be keeping an eye on his movements over the next few weeks, just in case. If I hear that he *has* drifted over this way, I'll be the first to let you know.'

- CHAPTER THREE -

THANKS TO THE combination of endless roadworks and the continuing rain, Tanner arrived home from work that evening far later than he'd hoped.

Opening the door to be met by an enticing smell, he hung up his coat to make his way through to the main living area.

'Hello, darling,' he called out, finding Christine exactly where he'd been expecting, attacking some poor vegetable with a particularly lethal-looking knife in the kitchen. 'Something smells good, and I'm fairly sure it's not me.'

'Beef and barley stew with mushrooms and aubergine,' she replied, glancing up with a brief but welcoming smile. 'At least it will be.'

'Sounds good. How was your day?'

'Oh, you know. Same old, same old. Yours?'

Ditching his keys onto the breakfast bar, he perched himself up onto one of the barstools with a despondent shrug. 'OK, I suppose. I think I'm still getting used to the idea of having to be stuck behind a desk all day whilst everyone lines up outside to take it in turns to moan at me.'

'What were they going on about today?'

'What was it again?' Tanner asked himself, gazing up at the ceiling. 'Oh yes, that's right. Townsend doesn't want to work with Cooper, Vicky doesn't want to work with the new guy, and the new guy doesn't seem to want to work at all.'

'He wasn't late *again*, was he?'

'Only by about forty-five minutes. I had a word with him about it when he eventually came in, but I'm not sure it will make any difference. His first excuse was that he missed the bus, but when I found out that he only lives in Stalham and could have walked in quicker, he admitted to having overslept.'

'What did you say in response?'

'That if he was late again, I'd fire him.'

'Not seriously?'

'Yes – as in yes I did, but no – as in I wasn't being serious.'

'Did *he* know that?'

'Er...perhaps not at first.'

'You do know that you're going to have to be nice to everyone if you want them to become loyal members of staff?'

'I *was* being nice!'

'By threatening to fire him if he was late again?'

'It was a joke!'

'I've heard better,' Christine muttered, shaking her head to continue chopping up what Tanner assumed must have been the afore-mentioned aubergine. 'What else did you say?'

'I told him to buy a louder alarm clock and to start drinking coffee.'

'Wise words indeed.'

'I thought so.'

'Although, I'm not sure how drinking coffee is going to help him get out of bed.'

'It works for me.'

'I suspect that's only because you're addicted to the stuff, and it doesn't make itself.'

'It would if you made it for me.'

'You wouldn't let me!'

'Only because you do enough in the kitchen for me as it is.'

'I thought it was because you don't trust me to make it.'

Tanner glanced nonchalantly around the room. 'I must admit, I am a little fussy about my coffee.'

'It's a shame you're not so fussy about your food.'

'You know me. I'd be happy enough with baked beans on toast.'

'Then you can bloody well make it yourself!' she suddenly snapped, her vegetable chopping becoming increasingly violent.

'You wouldn't let me,' Tanner mumbled cautiously in return. 'I have to apply for a search warrant just to gain access to the fridge, let alone remove anything from it.'

'That's only because you never put things back in the right place,' Christine replied, her eyes smiling in response, even if her mouth seemed reluctant to.

'Anyway,' Tanner continued, keen to avoid another heated discussion about the shared use of the kitchen, 'going back to Henderson.'

'Who...?'

'The new boy? The one who's always late? When I told him to buy himself a louder alarm clock, he said he used his phone, which was fine, up until the point where it became apparent that he didn't seem to know that its volume could be adjusted, leading me to put a call straight through to Oxford University to see if he really did have a degree from them in Criminal Law.'

'You didn't?'

'Sadly, no. I asked Sally to instead.'

Christine sent him the look she often used when unsure if he was joking or not.

'And I'd only just managed to get rid of him when guess who else showed up?'

'Father Christmas, to tell you that you weren't going to get any presents this year?'

'None other than our former DCI, now formally known as Superintendent Forrester. Apparently, he'd been waiting in the queue outside my office along with everyone else.'

'Was he checking up on you to see if you were being nice to your staff?'

'He'd actually come to tell me what an excellent job I'd been doing.'

'Really?'

'Fat chance!' Tanner huffed. 'He was there with news about one of Whitaker's old investigations. I don't suppose you've heard of someone called Samuel Tunk?'

Christine gazed briefly into space. 'Wasn't he the guy who tied up the husband to watch him have sex with his wife?'

'He wasn't a patient of yours, by any chance?' Tanner asked, nodding whilst holding his breath.

Christine shook her head. 'I read about him in one of the trade journals, and in the newspapers, of course. He was one of Whitaker's, was he?'

'Apparently so.'

'I'd no idea.'

'It's one of his many investigations that's now being looked into, the result of which was that he was released this morning.'

Christine stopped what she was doing to stare over at him. 'They released that monster this morning?'

Tanner blinked back at her in surprise. 'Forrester didn't say anything about him being a monster.'

'That's what the papers called him, which was hardly surprising given what he did, that and the fact that he was physically huge. I seem to remember he was a professional wrestler. Why on Earth has he been released?'

'Whitaker was stupid enough to introduce evidence that's since been found to have been manufactured, forcing the original proceedings to be classed as a mistrial.'

'Where was he sent?'

'Broadmoor, on the other side of London.'

'Well, let's just hope he doesn't find himself wandering his way back here.'

'Quite!' agreed Tanner. 'I don't suppose you can remember anything else that was written about him?'

'Only what they said he did, and that he always proclaimed his innocence. I seem to recall him admitting to being there, but said he'd made a run for it as soon as the husband caught him inside the boat.'

'What about the trade journals?'

'From memory, he was diagnosed as being a paranoid schizophrenic. I think they said he'd had a psychotic episode brought on by his wife leaving with his children a few days before, claiming that it wasn't safe for them to be around him. Have they really let him go?' she questioned, turning to stare at Tanner with a look of concerned incredulity.

'So it would appear,' Tanner nodded, just as his mobile phone began to ring. 'For fuck's sake,' he muttered, clawing it out. 'This better not be bloody work.'

Flipping open its leather case, he spent a sullen moment staring down at its illuminated screen. 'It's Vicky,' he eventually said, lifting his eyes to meet Christine's.

'Can't it at least wait until we've eaten?'

'Had I still been just a humble DI, it probably could have, but I'm afraid those days would appear to be long gone.'

- CHAPTER FOUR -

TURNING HIS SLEEK black Jaguar XJS into the car park at the end of Acle Dyke, Tanner stopped for a moment to peer out through his windscreen at the various spinning blue lights, each one being fragmented into a billion shards by the still unrelenting rain. When he saw the person who'd phoned him, huddled underneath a small black umbrella that was barely up to the task, he edged his car forward to leave it parked behind a police forensics van to climb slowly out.

'What've we got?' he called, seeing her running towards him, rain rattling off the top of her umbrella like a tightly bound snare drum.

'Nothing good, I'm afraid,' she replied, dripping to a halt.

'Is it ever?' he muttered, flipping his sailing jacket's fluorescent hood over his head.

'A couple on board their boat. Dr Johnstone's on board now.'

'Do we know who they are?'

'At the moment we're proceeding on the basis that they're an unmarried couple,' she continued, wedging the handle of her umbrella under her arm to pull out her notebook, 'a Mr Jason Blackwell and a Mrs Julia Ward. Their driving licences were found inside an otherwise empty wallet and purse left discarded on the floor in the main cabin, and it looks like someone's been through the fridge, along with all the galley cupboards.'

The crime scene's description had Tanner's mind harking back to the prisoner released the previous day, the one he'd been discussing with Christine only half an hour before. 'You think it was a robbery that got out of hand?'

'Either that or whoever did it found himself strapped for cash shortly afterwards. Hungry, as well.'

As Tanner's mind calculated how long it would take someone to travel from Crowthorne in Berkshire, where he knew Broadmoor Hospital was located, to where they were standing, and why Tunk would choose this particular location to go in search of both food and cash, he cast a steady eye around at the surrounding vehicles. 'Do we know who found them?'

'The guy who owns the dyke. Paul Morris. He said he was doing his rounds, collecting mooring fees.'

'What, at this time?'

'That's what he said.'

'What else did he say?'

'Not much. He was in a right state when I arrived. He's currently in the back of one of the ambulances being treated for shock.'

'Has the area been sealed off?'

'As best we can.'

'What about the neighbouring boats?'

'Cooper and Townsend are going around now, asking if anyone either saw or heard anything.'

'So we know when the incident happened?'

'Johnstone has yet to say.'

'Then why the hell is Cooper going around asking people what they saw when we don't even know when they were supposed to have seen it?'

'Don't ask me! It was his idea!'

Tanner shook his head with irritated incomprehension. 'What about the new guy?'

'He's proving to be of even less use than the person who found the victims.'

'You're saying he isn't here?'

'Oh, he's here alright. He's in the trees somewhere, throwing up all over them, or at least he was the last time I saw him. He turned green the moment he saw the bodies and ran out. We were lucky he wasn't sick all over the crime scene.'

'It's probably the first time he's attended an actual murder,' Tanner mused. 'I still remember mine. I was nearly sick all over the place as well.'

'I wasn't,' Vicky mumbled, under her breath.

'Anyway, you'd better show me where it happened.'

'The murder, or where he was sick?'

Tanner narrowed his eyes.

'How should I know?' she smirked. 'They're both equally as disgusting.'

- CHAPTER FIVE -

FOLLOWING VICKY BETWEEN a squad car and the forensics van, they emerged out onto a grassy bank to see a long line of boats, each one shimmering in the still pouring rain.

'It's the wooden one, straight ahead,' she called behind her, leading him over a series of raised aluminium platforms linking the edge of the car park to the side of the boat like a row of prefabricated stepping-stones.

Reaching the boat's side, Tanner left Vicky where she was to heave himself onboard, up through a rolled-up section of the boat's billowing canopy, to find himself entering a spacious cockpit.

Having donned a pair of white latex gloves and slip-on shoe covers, he proceeded to make his way down the boat's companionway steps into a resplendent wood-panelled interior, where a waiting constable directed him through to a cabin at the back. There, on a large double bed, lay the slim sun-bronzed figure of a middle-aged man, his wrists tied to a curving bronze lamp attached to the bulkhead behind his head, the torso of his fully exposed body marked by a series of crimson puncture wounds.

'Detective Inspector Tanner?' came an upbeat voice calling him from behind.

Turning to see the bespectacled face of Dr Johnstone, shuffling his way down the passageway towards him, he smiled to offer the man a disingenuous aloof expression. 'It's Detective *Chief* Inspector, actually!'

'Sorry, yes, of course. Old habits and all that. How's the new job?'

'At this precise moment in time, very much like the old one.'

'I suppose it must be. You do know that you don't have to be here, don't you?'

'For what would appear to be my first murder investigation since being promoted, I thought I'd better make the effort to take a look for myself.'

'Fair enough,' Johnstone remarked, nudging his way past.

'And thankfully, I did,' Tanner continued. 'From what I can make out, it would appear that we're already missing something rather important.'

Johnstone stopped dead in his tracks to glare back at him. 'Missing something?'

'DI Gilbert said it was a murdered couple. I only count one.'

'Oh right. The girl's on the floor, on the other side of the bed.'

Tanner stepped to the side to see the pale blood spattered body of an attractive young woman, her curvaceous naked body curled up on the carpet.

'The woman's had her throat cut,' Johnson continued. 'As you can see, the male victim's received multiple stab wounds to the chest.'

Tanner looked back at the man, in particular the way his hands had been tied. Remembering what he knew about Samuel Tunk, how he'd tied up the husband, forcing him to watch him have sex with his wife before killing them both, he glanced over at Johnstone to catch his eye. 'Are there any indications that the woman may have been raped?'

Johnston raised an introspective eyebrow. 'You mean by the man lying on the bed, the one with his hands tied above his head?'

'By whoever murdered them, obviously,' Tanner retorted.

Endeavouring to hide a misplaced smile, Johnstone pushed his glasses up the bridge of his nose. 'At this stage, I can't say, but I don't think it's likely, unless it took place afterwards. At the moment, all I know is that they'd been having sex, most likely at the time of their attack.'

'You think she was on top of him?'

'With the amount of blood covering the man's hips and thighs, I'd say that was the most likely scenario. Assuming his hands were tied as part of their carnal pursuit, he'd have been unable to defend either the woman or himself, leaving him open to attack once she'd been dispatched.'

'Time of death?'

'Two, maybe three hours ago?'

'Is it safe to assume that the cause is as it would appear?'

'Most likely, but I'll be able to give you a more definitive answer when I get them back to the lab.'

- CHAPTER SIX -

THE SOUND OF raised voices from somewhere outside had Tanner excusing himself to hurry out the way he'd come.

'What the hell's going on out here?' he demanded, reaching the cockpit to stare out at Vicky and two uniformed police officers, each confronting an agitated young woman holding an umbrella in one hand and a suitcase in the other.

'Are you in charge?' the woman called out, lifting her head to fix her eyes onto his.

'I'm Detective Chief Inspector Tanner,' he replied, the new title still feeling strange on his tongue.

'Does that mean you are, or you aren't?'

Tanner climbed down to make his way over, searching his pockets for his newly printed formal ID. 'I am,' he eventually replied, opening it for her to see.

'Then I demand to know what the hell you're doing? More to the point, why nobody will let me on board my own boat?'

'This is *your* boat?' he queried.

'As good as,' the woman replied.

'May I ask your name?'

'Julia Ward,' she stated, leaning forward to study Tanner's still proffered ID.

'*You're* Julia Ward?'

'Is there some reason why I shouldn't be?'

'No, it's just... I don't suppose you have some

identification on you?'

'I was stupid enough to leave my purse onboard. Now, will you please tell me what's going on? Where's Jason? Why's he not here?'

'Are you a relation?'

'As good as.'

'Is *that* a yes or a no?'

'I'm his girlfriend!' Ward replied, sending Tanner a belligerent glare.

'Then it looks like I have some distressing news for you.'

Tanner watched the woman's jaw stiffen, her eyes darting erratically between his.

'The body of someone who we believe to be Jason Blackwell was found onboard about two hours ago.'

'I'm – I'm sorry – I'm not with you.'

'It would appear that he'd been attacked by an intruder.'

Tanner watched the young woman blink at him before staring off into space.

'You say you left your purse on board,' he eventually continued, digging out his notebook. 'May I ask where you've been?'

'To see my parents – for the weekend. I've just come back by train.'

'When did you leave?'

'After work on Friday.'

'Would you be able to provide us with their address? We'll need their names as well, together with a contact phone number.'

'Sorry, but – why do you want their names and phone number?'

'To ask them to confirm that you were there,' Tanner replied, watching her reaction as he did. 'We'll also need to take a sample of your fingerprints and DNA.'

With the woman now staring at him with apparent confused incomprehension, Tanner glanced down at her soaking wet suitcase. 'Do you have anywhere to stay tonight?'

'I can't stay here?' she asked, her skin becoming increasingly taught.

'I'm afraid that won't be possible.'

'What about Edward? He's alright, isn't he?'

'Er... Edward?' Tanner repeated, sending Vicky an anxious glance.

'Jason's son? His mother asked him to look after him for the weekend. Why? Is he not on board?'

- CHAPTER SEVEN -

HAVING ASKED THE boy's age and for a brief description, Tanner beckoned one of the police constables over to take the woman's formal statement before leading Vicky privately to one side. 'I take it a quiet, shy, twelve-year-old boy with pale skin and short dark hair wasn't found on board anywhere?'

Vicky replied by shaking her head with an anxious frown.

'OK, let's try not to panic. It's possible he could be hiding on board, or maybe he managed to escape into the trees.'

'What do you want us to do?'

'We're going to have to conduct a thorough search of the boat, preferably without disturbing the good work of our forensics department. If he's not there, then we'll need to widen the search. Does anyone know who his mother is?'

'*Mrs* Blackwell, presumably?'

Tanner took a moment to narrow his eyes at her before turning to look back at the boat. 'I don't suppose it's possible that she's the female victim?'

'I doubt it,' Vicky replied. 'She looked far too young.'

'OK, for now, find Townsend and Cooper. Somehow this boat has to be turned inside out.'

'What about Henderson?'

Tanner cast his eyes back at the trees. 'If he's well enough. Just make sure to keep him away from the cabin where the bodies were found.'

'Excuse me?' came the shrill sound of a man's questioning voice, calling over to them from out of the darkness.

As they turned their heads to watch a tall stick-like figure, hurrying along the other side of the flickering line of Police Do Not Cross tape, Vicky leaned her head in towards Tanner's. 'It's the guy who found the bodies. Paul Morris.'

'OK, I'd better have a chat with him whilst you start searching for that missing boy.'

'Sorry to bother you,' Tanner heard the figure continue, waving at him from the other side of the tape. 'I was just wondering if it would be possible for me to go home now?'

'Mr Morris, isn't it?' Tanner responded, stepping lightly over the aluminium platforms to where the man dutifully waited.

'That's correct.'

'Have the paramedics given you the all-clear?'

'They said I should go home and get some rest, which is why I thought I'd better ask if it was OK before doing so.'

'Sure, no problem. Would you mind if I took a quick statement from you first?'

'To be honest, I was kind of hoping to go home now. I told my wife I'd only be a few minutes. That was over an hour ago.'

'Don't worry, it won't take long,' Tanner replied, ducking under the tape to lead him under the nearest tree to escape the still unrelenting rain. 'I understand you own the dyke?'

'I own the gift shop at the end. The dyke just happened to come with it. I'm trying to sell it, if you're interested?'

'Oh, I – er – I doubt I'd have the time to look after it.'

'No, me neither.'

'Anyway, if you could tell me what happened – how you came to find them?'

'As I think I told one of your officers, I was doing the rounds – collecting mooring fees.'

'And it's normal for you to climb on board someone else's boat to do so?'

'I – I must have seen something through the windows.'

Tanner turned to look back at the boat. 'But the curtains are all closed?'

The man's eyes suddenly darted between the line of boats and the car park, as if looking for a means of escape. 'I – I suppose I just knew he was on board.'

'He, as in Mr Blackwell?'

Morris nodded, his eyes returning to rest on Tanner's. 'I think there must have been a light on in the cabin at the back. People tend not to leave lights on in boats as they drain the battery. Besides, there was no way he'd have gone for a walk, not in this weather, so I knew he must have been on board.'

'So, you thought you'd take a look?'

'The guy hasn't paid me for months. Every time I make the effort to see him he always comes up with some lame excuse, and it's not as if he hasn't got money.'

'Sorry, but what makes you say that?'

'I thought you said you knew who he was?

'Well, yes, but only by name.'

'Which is Blackwell – as in the pharmaceutical company?'

Tanner's head jolted back in surprise. 'The man on board the boat own's Blackwell Pharmaceuticals?'

'Well, his family does, which is why I knew he could definitely afford to pay his mooring fees. And I know I shouldn't have gone on board, but something wasn't right. Whenever I knocked before, he'd always come out to offer me yet another excuse for not having any cash. It always seemed like some sort of hilarious game to him. Unfortunately, it isn't for me. Not with the way the cost of living keeps constantly increasing. The last interest rate hike left me barely able to pay the mortgage, let alone my credit card bill. *He* may not need the money, but I certainly do!'

'It's probably of little consolation, Mr Morris, but I suspect you're right,' Tanner responded, offering the man an unsympathetic frown. 'I doubt he does need the money, being that he's dead and everything.'

Morris's chin fell to the ground. 'Of course, yes, sorry. It's just been difficult recently. It's not as if he's the only one who hasn't paid their fees, either.'

'If you're having money troubles, Mr Morris, then I'm sure there are plenty of organisations who'd be able to help, but for now I need to know what happened after you knocked on the side and there was no reply.'

'As I said, I climbed on board; I suppose to see if he was OK. The cockpit door was open. When I saw the mess inside I knew something wasn't right. I called out his name a few times, but I didn't hear anything. Then I went inside, through to the cabin at the back, where – as I said – the light had been left on. That's when I...' Morris swallowed, glancing away. 'That's when I saw them.'

'What did you do then?'

'I – I can't remember. I think I just ran out the same way I came in.'

'You didn't happen to see a young boy on board, about twelve years old with pale skin and short dark hair?'

'You mean Mr Blackwell's son? To be honest, I'd completely forgotten about him. I knew he was on board. He'd been staying with them for the weekend.'

'So, you didn't see him?'

'I'm sorry, I didn't,' Morris replied, shaking his head. 'If he saw what I saw actually happen, then he must have been terrified. Have you checked all the cabins?'

'We've only just found out he's missing.'

'Then he must be on board somewhere, maybe inside one of the lockers, unless – unless whoever did that to his father...'

'Anyway,' Tanner interrupted, before the man had a chance to say out loud what he was already dreading, 'can you tell me anything about the woman he was with?'

'I'm sorry, I was in such a state, I didn't take the time to see which one it was.'

Tanner raised a curious eyebrow. 'Just how many girlfriends did he have, exactly?'

'Three that I know of, but I wouldn't be surprised if there were more.'

'I take it he was a bit of a womaniser?'

'I'd say he was more than a bit! His sole purpose in life seemed to be trying to find out how many he could sleep with without any of the others finding out.'

'Do you recognise that woman over there,' Tanner asked, turning to point through the rain at the lady he'd been speaking to earlier, now talking to one of his uniformed constables.

'That's Julia. She's here most of the time.'

'Can you tell me anything about her?'

'Only that he doesn't deserve her.'

'I don't suppose you could be more specific?'

'She's a nurse at Norwich City Hospital. She's

helped treat my wife a few times. My wife's a diabetic, so we have to make regular trips. Julia is about as kind and compassionate as a person can be. She certainly didn't deserve to be treated so badly by a man who seemed to have such little respect for her.'

'Do you think she knows that Mr Blackwell was seeing other women?'

Morris shrugged with an indifferent air. 'I've no idea.'

'You didn't think to ever mention it to her?'

'It's not my place to poke my nose into other people's lives, let alone their personal relationships.'

'How about your wife? Could *she* have told her?'

'If you're endeavouring to insinuate that Julia was responsible for what happened on board that boat, then you're most definitely barking up the wrong tree. It's difficult to imagine her being able to hurt a fly, let alone brutally murder two innocent people, even if one had been cheating on her with the other. Besides, she wasn't here. She went away for the weekend to see her mother.'

'So she said,' Tanner muttered, pausing for a moment to take notes. 'What about Mr Blackwell's wife. Do you know anything about her?'

'I'm fairly sure they're divorced.'

'OK, ex-wife.'

'Only what I've heard.'

'And what's that?'

'That she's a heartless bitch who only married him for his money.'

'Have you ever met her?'

'No, but I have seen her before.'

'Was she the other victim you saw in the cabin?'

Morris shook his head, as if trying to rid his mind of the images lurking inside. 'She's older.'

'Can you remember when you saw her last?'

'It was Friday night. She was dressed up like she'd just stepped off a catwalk.'

'Do you have any idea what she was doing here?'

'Dropping the boy off.'

'Did she speak to her husband?'

'Yes.'

'Did you hear what they said?'

'I did, but please don't think I was eavesdropping. The way they were screaming at each other, anyone within half a mile would have done.'

'And what was that?'

'They were arguing about how neither of them wanted to look after the boy, right in front of him as well! God knows what that must have been like for him. It certainly can't have been much fun being brought up by either his mother who by all accounts spends her entire life going on holiday, or by his father who spent his life getting drunk whilst trying to sleep with as many women as possible.'

'OK, I think that will do for now,' Tanner said, finishing off his notes. 'We'll naturally be needing a sample of your DNA and fingerprints.'

'Yes, of course. Anything to help.'

Closing his notebook, Tanner glanced up to find the man was still standing in front of him, now wearing a look of fretful expectation. 'Was there something else?'

'Nothing in particular. I suppose I was just expecting you to ask me about the other man I saw.'

'Sorry, what other man was that?' Tanner enquired, his interest most definitely piqued.

'I did tell one of your police constables, when they first arrived. It was when I was doing the rounds, just before I tried Mr Blackwell's boat.'

'Go on.'

'There's not much to tell, really. It's just that I saw

someone running through the rain, away from the boat.'

'Don't you think you could have told me this before?' Tanner questioned, glancing furtively about.

'I'm sorry, but as I said, I thought you already knew.'

'Did you at least see which way he went?'

'That way,' he pointed, 'towards the river.'

'And you didn't see a boy with him?'

'He was on his own. I must admit, I wouldn't have given it a second thought had it not been the sheer physical size of him, and what I was to find when I climbed on board the boat, of course.'

- CHAPTER EIGHT -

TURNING HIS HEAD to see Vicky, Cooper, and Townsend, hurrying along the dyke towards him, Tanner directed Morris over to the nearest overall-clad forensics officer before addressing his rapidly approaching staff.

'The guy who found the bodies...' he began, catching each of their eyes as they came to a breathless halt, '...he said he saw a man running away from the boat, supposedly heading for the river.'

'Was the boy with him?' Vicky demanded.

Tanner shook his head. 'But the witness described him as being physically huge, which can only point to one man.'

'You think it was that guy released from Broadmoor?'

'A young couple murdered; the man tied up to possibly watch the woman being raped in front of him? That, plus the food and money which looks likely to have been stolen? I think it's all too much of a coincidence for it not to be. I don't suppose you found any other witnesses?' he continued, the question directed at Cooper.

'Nobody on board the other boats said they heard anything.'

'If it was raining like this,' Tanner replied, taking a moment to gaze about at all the moored up boats, jostling for position along the grassy water-logged bank, 'I can't say I'm surprised. The noise it makes on your average coach roof makes hearing anything virtually impossible, inside or out. Anyway, we can't let this detract from our primary objective. We have to find that missing boy! Let's just hope he's hiding on board somewhere.'

'I suppose it's possible that his mother came back to pick him up?' proposed Vicky.

'Good point. I'll give her a call. I need to speak to her anyway.'

'And if he isn't hiding on board and his mother didn't pick him up?' Cooper questioned.

'Then he must have run away when he saw what happened.'

'What if he did neither, but was discovered inside the boat by whoever murdered his father?'

'As I said, the witness told me that the man he saw running away was alone.'

'I didn't mean he kidnapped him.'

'OK, but his body isn't on board, at least we haven't found it yet. If the boy was killed as well, it seems unlikely the murderer would decide to hide what was left of him, not when he'd already left the couple lying where he'd found them.'

Emerging out from behind Vicky and Cooper, Tanner saw Townsend step cautiously towards the edge of the dyke.

'There is another possibility,' the young constable commented, directing his torch down at where the water lapped lazily against the boat's varnished wooden hull. 'Has anyone thought to take a look down there?'

- CHAPTER NINE -

IT WASN'T UNTIL over an hour later when Tanner saw Vicky climb slowly down from the side of the boat, black greasy smudges marking the sides of her lightly freckled face.

'Anything?' he asked, watching her tug at the fingers of a pair of blackened latex gloves.

'We've looked everywhere,' she eventually replied. 'Even inside the engine bay. There's no way the boy's on board. I don't suppose you were able to get hold of her mother?'

'Only briefly,' Tanner replied, his gaze drifting out to where the dyke met the river.

'And?'

'She sounded like she was drunk. Either that or she'd just woken up.'

'What about her son?'

'She said she hadn't seen him since she dropped him off on Friday.'

'Did you say anything to her about her husband?'

'Not over the phone. I've arranged to see her first thing tomorrow.'

'What's everyone else been up to whilst I've had my head stuck down an engine bay?'

'Cooper's talking to the boat owners on the other side. Townsend searched the edges of the dyke. He's now having a quick look along the riverbank with some help from uniform.'

'And Henderson?'

'He didn't seem up to doing much of anything, so I sent him home. Speaking of which,' Tanner continued, tugging at the soaking wet sleeve of his sailing jacket to glance down at his watch, 'it's probably time you all did.'

'What about you?'

'I still need to tell Johnstone to cross check any fingerprints and DNA found against the Broadmoor prisoner. I suppose I'm also going to have to give Forrester a call, to let him know what's been going on.'

Vicky cast a pair of concerned eyes into Tanner's. 'And then you're going to go home?'

'I'll probably stay on for a while longer, at least until Dr Johnstone has finished. If you could radio everyone to let them know to call it a day, and to tell them to be in the office for half-eight tomorrow, I'll brief the office when I come in.'

- CHAPTER TEN -

Tuesday, 26th April

HAVING ONLY MANAGED a few fitful hours of sleep the night before, at a quarter past nine the following morning, Tanner forced himself to the front of the station's main office to face his assembled staff.

'If I could have everyone's attention,' he began, his voice falling flat to leave the myriad of mumbled conversations to continue unabated.

Recalling how his predecessor's voice used to resonate into every corner of the room, he paused for a moment to draw in a lungful of air. 'Everyone, can I have your attention, please!'

As conversations ground to a halt, with dozens of eyes latching themselves onto his, Tanner shifted his weight from one foot to the other. 'As I'm sure you're all aware by now, at around nine o'clock yesterday evening the bodies of a man and a woman were found inside a boat moored up along Acle Dyke.'

In a bid to deflect everyone's attention away from himself, he steered their gaze towards the whiteboard on the wall behind him where Henderson had already posted a series of macabre photographs. 'As you can see, the female victim had her throat cut, whilst the man received multiple stab wounds to his chest. Our medical examiner is currently of the opinion that they were in the act of enjoying carnal relations at the time. Who tied the man's hands to the lamp above his head; the woman, or their attacker, as yet we don't know. As for their identities, at the moment we're proceeding on the basis that the man is Mr Jason Blackwell, the grandson of none other than Lord Alfred Blackwell, founder of Blackwell Pharmaceuticals, a global corporation which I'm sure most of you have already heard of.'

Tanner paused to allow a flurry of whispered remarks to circle the room before re-opening his mouth. 'Unfortunately, we still don't know who the woman is. All we do know is that she *isn't* who we originally thought she was, his girlfriend, Miss Julia Ward. She arrived when we were there, saying she'd spent the weekend with her parents and had accidently left her purse on board the boat. We've taken her prints and DNA, but someone will need to check her alibi.'

Tanner quickly scanned the room looking for Sally Beach, Superintendent Forrester's attractive young niece. Finding her perched on the edge of a desk, her curvaceous body nudged up against Townsend's, he lifted his chin to single her out. 'Sally, if I can leave that with you?'

Blushing slightly as everyone turned to look at her, he saw her nod before her eyes dropped swiftly to the floor.

'The couple were found by the man who owns the dyke,' Tanner continued, 'and the corner shop at the end. A Mr Paul Morris. According to him, he was doing the rounds, endeavouring to collect mooring fees from those staying on board the boats. I must admit, I neglected to ask him why he'd chosen such a peculiar hour to do so, slap-bang in the middle of a rainstorm as well. Maybe if someone could do that for me at some point?' he asked, catching Vicky's eye. 'Fortunately,' he continued, seeing her nod briefly back, 'I did at least think to ask what made him climb onboard someone else's boat without having gained the owner's permission first. His initial response was that he thought he'd seen something through the windows; that was until I pointed out that all the curtains were closed. He then changed his mind to say that a light had been left on instead, which he said was odd. He also told me that the man he found on board owed him several months of mooring fees, something he appeared to be in desperate need of. All that aside, for now at least, what he said that was of most interest was that he saw a larger-than-average man running through the rain away from the boat, which brings me to the person who I believe needs to be considered our prime suspect.'

Tanner stepped over to the whiteboard to point at the photograph of a man glaring belligerently back, his neck far wider than the shaved anvil-shaped head that rested awkwardly on top of it.

'This is the picture taken of Samuel Tunk when he was first arrested. Some of you here may remember that he was the man convicted of murdering an entire family on board their boat about ten years ago. Thanks to the unlawful actions of the late Superintendent Whitaker, he was released from Broadmoor Hospital on Monday morning, having had his multiple-life sentence overturned. Unfortunately, for us at least, I've been informed by HQ that he was seen getting off a train at Norwich Station yesterday afternoon. At the moment, exactly where he went afterwards is unknown, but with what the dyke's owner told me about the size of a man he saw running away, what we found inside the boat, and that it appeared to have been searched for food and money, I don't think we'd be doing our jobs if we didn't have him at the top of our list of suspects.'

Gratified to hear everyone making noises of approval, Tanner drew in a breath to continue. 'However, as disturbing as the idea is that there's a convicted psychopathic murderer roaming the Norfolk Broads in search of food, money, and frolicking couples to take pleasure in stabbing to death, our priority has to be to find Jason Blackwell's twelve-year-old son. According to Julia Ward, he should have been on board, but despite DI Gilbert's very best efforts, it soon became clear that he wasn't. I spoke briefly to his mother last night, but he's not with her either. Neither was he with the man seen running away from the scene. With any luck, the boy simply ran off to find somewhere to hide. If that is the case, we need to get the word out that he's missing. If it isn't, then unfortunately the first place that needs to be searched is the bottom of the dyke. Cooper, if you can get a dive team over there this morning, that would be appreciated. Meanwhile, Vicky, if you can organise a press conference for this afternoon, we should know by then if he's missing or not.'

'Do we have a picture of the boy?' she called out in response.

'Not yet, but I've already asked his mother if she'll be able to provide us with one. I've arranged to meet her this morning, so hopefully I'll be able to pick it up then, which reminds me,' he continued, casting his eyes around the office again, 'is DC Henderson here?'

Seeing a long lanky arm rise slowly from the back of the room, Tanner shifted himself to the side to see Henderson's donkey-like face. 'Could you email me her address? Whilst you're at it, if you could do a little digging for me about her before I go, that would be useful?'

Seeing him tug a notebook awkwardly out from inside his crumpled ill-fitting suit, Tanner returned his attention to the room. 'We also need to locate the other members of the Blackwell Family. If Tunk isn't responsible, then it's most likely to have been one of them, especially if we discover any who are likely to benefit directly from Jason Blackwell's death. Townsend, if I can leave that with you?'

Finding the young detective constable staring longingly down at Sally's thighs, and the miniskirt riding up to the top of them, Tanner cleared his throat.

'Sorry, what was that?' Townsend replied, looking up with a start.

'If you can identify who the other members of the Blackwell Family are, that would be useful,' Tanner repeated, sending Townsend a disapproving scowl.

'Right, yes, of course.'

'If you could also dig up a copy of his will. Then maybe Cooper can help you to start interviewing them all?'

'I thought I was overseeing the dive team?' Tanner heard Cooper moan from the other side of the room.

'I'm fairly sure you'll have finished by then.'

'Not if they find something.'

'Then let's just hope they don't! Now, if there's nothing else, I suggest we push on.'

As the crowd began to disperse in a cacophony of noise, Tanner held up his hands in a bid to regain their attention. 'Before you all go, please remember – no talking to the press. In particular, I don't want any mention of the Blackwell name. If word gets out about who they are, they'll be descending down upon us like a plague of half-starved locusts.'

- CHAPTER ELEVEN -

TANNER HAD BARELY reached his desk when he heard a knock at the door, the sound immediately followed by Townsend's apologetic voice.

'Sorry to bother you, boss.'

'You will be if you keep calling me boss all the bloody time,' Tanner muttered, sinking slowly down into his chair.

'I just thought I'd let you know that forensics' interim report came through during the briefing. Dr Johnstone's as well.'

'OK, good,' Tanner replied, shunting his chair forward to reach for his mouse. 'Let's take a look.'

'I also wanted to ask if you'd had a chance to think about what we were talking about yesterday?'

'Sorry, you're going to have to remind me.'

'About the possibility of me working with someone other than Cooper?'

Tanner shook his head whilst navigating his way to his email account. 'Surely there are slightly more pressing matters?'

'I was just wondering if you'd been able to give it some more thought.'

'I suppose you'd like to be working alongside Sally?'

'Well, yes!' the young DC replied, his face instantly brightening. 'That would be great!'

'I've no doubt it would, Townsend, but I suspect she'd be a little too much of a distraction for you.'

'I can assure you that she wouldn't.'

'And I can assure you that she would!'

'Honestly, boss, I'd be fine.'

'Oh, c'mon, Townsend,' Tanner continued, opening up the first of the reports, 'I saw the way you were ogling the poor girl's legs during the briefing. If I let you two work together, I can't imagine how either of you would get anything done, at least nothing that didn't involve a darkened room and a family-sized packet of industrial strength condoms.'

Seeing Townsend's face redden around the edges, he was about to apologise for his flippant if not rather amusing remark when none other than Sally's head appeared around the door to stare first at Townsend, then over at Tanner.

'Yes, Sally, can I help you?'

'Sorry, boss. A couple's just come in about their daughter. Apparently, they haven't heard from her since Sunday.'

'Right,' he replied, his head rolling forward as he realised what that was likely to mean: that he was about to have to tell two distraught parents that their daughter was dead. 'If you could show them into one of the interview rooms, maybe offer to make them a coffee as well, I'll be with them in a moment.'

Seeing her nod, he waited for her to leave before returning his attention to the report.

'Anything of interest?' queried Townsend.

'Are you still here?'

'I'm recovering from the shock of being told that I should be using industrial strength condoms,' the young DC replied. 'I'd never thought of it before, but you're probably right. I don't suppose you know where I can get them from?'

'Try B&Q,' came Tanner's dismissive response.

'B – and – Q,' Townsend replied, reaching for his notebook.

Tanner turned his head to watch Townsend making a note of the DIY store's name. 'You do know that I was joking?'

'You do know that I wasn't,' Townsend retorted. 'That girl can go all night!'

'Thank you, Townsend. I really wanted to know that.'

'No problem, boss. Anyway, what does it say?'

'What does what say?'

'The forensics report.'

Tanner took a quiet moment to continue reading through its contents. 'From what I can see,' he eventually continued, 'it's what it doesn't say that's most annoying.'

'And what's that?

'That neither Samuel Tunk's fingerprints, nor his DNA, have so far been found.'

'You mean it wasn't him?'

'Er, no, Townsend. It just means that they've yet to find any physical evidence to prove it was, and all that means is that the man isn't stupid. Having narrowly escaped being locked away for life, he's clearly being careful.'

'But it still doesn't explain why he would pick that particular boat in that particular place. I mean, an old wooden boat moored up down a small narrow dyke, side-by-side with dozens of others? It's not exactly an obvious target.'

'Maybe that was why he chose it – because it wasn't? Maybe he just happened to hear what they were doing and couldn't help himself from taking a closer look.'

Townsend sat on the edge of Tanner's desk to lean

his head in towards the monitor. 'Does it say anything else?'

'Just about the normal series of unmatched fingerprints and DNA samples.'

'How about Johnstone's report?'

Swivelling the monitor around for Townsend to see, Tanner closed one file to open another.

The room fell silent as they both read quickly through it.

'It would appear to simply reiterate what he said last night,' Tanner eventually said, 'that the woman died from having had her throat cut, the man from multiple stab wounds, and that they were likely to have been having sexual intercourse when the attack began.'

'It also says that it's likely that the man's hands were tied *before* the attack started,' interjected Townsend, drawing Tanner's attention to one of the shorter paragraphs.

'Likely, but not definitely.'

'What's that about the possibility that the attacker was a woman?'

Tanner leant forward to blink at the screen. 'Where does it say that?'

'Where it mentions about the majority of stab wounds being shallow in depth,' Townsend replied, lifting a hand to highlight one of the paragraphs, 'indicating the possibility that the assailant was a woman.'

'Or a man weakened by having spent the last ten years in solitary confinement.'

'Perhaps, but he looks far from being weak and feeble in that photograph of him pinned up outside.'

'As I said at the briefing, that was taken when he was first arrested. There's every chance that he's changed beyond all recognition since then.'

'Unless, of course, the attacker *was* a woman?'

Another knock at the door had them both glancing up to see Vicky's head peering around at them from the other side.

'Henderson's just found out something about Lee Blackwell's wife, which I thought you might find interesting.'

'You mean his *ex*-wife,' corrected Tanner.

'That's what he discovered. She's *not* his ex-wife. They're only separated, not divorced.'

'Which means she'll be the first to inherit everything he owns,' Tanner muttered, his eyes drifting over to Townsend.

'Unless he made her sign some sort of prenuptial agreement before they got married?'

Tanner pushed his chair away from his desk to climb to his feet. 'OK, I think it's time I had a little chat with her.'

'What about Mr and Mrs Betton?' questioned Vicky.

'Who?'

'The couple outside, saying their daughter has gone missing. Sally *did* tell you they were here, didn't she?'

'Sorry, yes, she did.'

'I can interview them, if you like?'

'No, it's OK. It shouldn't take long. Has anyone made them a coffee?'

'I was about to when Henderson found me.'

'OK, you'd better get back to organising that press conference. Townsend, if you could do the coffee round, then you may as well join me in the interview room.'

- CHAPTER TWELVE -

'SORRY TO HAVE kept you waiting,' Tanner apologised, opening the door to one of the station's interview rooms to find a frail grey-haired couple peering up at him from behind its small wooden table.

Having expected them to be far younger, he looked at them twice before opening his mouth. 'Detective Inspector – I – I mean Detective Chief Inspector Tanner. I understand that you think your daughter might be missing?'

The couple glanced anxiously around at each other as the woman clutched at a handkerchief.

'We haven't heard from her since Sunday,' came the man's eventual response, clasping his hands together on top of the table.

'Perhaps we could start with her name?' Tanner began, reaching for his notebook as Townsend stepped quietly inside, a mug of coffee held at the end of each arm.

'Deborah, Deborah Betton, but she likes to be called Debbie.'

'And you are?' Tanner continued, waiting for Townsend to set the mugs down in front of them before taking a seat.

'Harold and Carole Betton. We're actually her grandparents.'

Glancing over at Townsend to find him clawing out

his notebook, Tanner returned a curious frown to the elderly man. 'May I ask where her parents are?'

'Our daughter passed away in a car accident along with her husband, shortly after Debbie was born.'

'I'm very sorry to hear that.'

'It was a long time ago, but thank you.'

'May I ask how old your granddaughter is?'

'She'll be twenty-one tomorrow.'

Tanner clasped his own hands together, his mind now earnestly praying that the woman they'd found on board the boat *wasn't* their missing granddaughter. The idea of having to tell them that they'd lost her the day before her twenty-first birthday, having already lost their own daughter some twenty years before, wasn't going to be easy. 'Would it be possible to describe her for us?'

'We've actually brought in a photograph,' the man replied, a skeletal hand reaching inside his raincoat. 'It's not very good, I'm afraid. It was taken at her nineteenth birthday party.'

As Tanner's eyes fell to the photograph being laid down in front of him he felt his stomach immediately tighten. He knew it was her. The hair was identical in both colour and length, and her small pretty nose had the same distinct smattering of freckles.

Tanner offered Townsend an uneasy glance before returning his attention to the elderly couple, now staring at him with eyes filled with angst ridden trepidation. 'Is it alright if we keep this?' he asked, placing a respectful finger onto one of its corners.

'Of course. We have plenty more.'

Drawing it slowly towards him, Tanner took a procrastinating moment to stare down at it. 'May I start by asking if she'd been seeing anyone recently?' he eventually asked, glancing up.

Tanner saw the woman's eyes fix firmly onto his.

'If you mean a *man*,' she replied, her nostrils flaring with revulsion, 'then I can assure you that she's not that sort of a girl!'

'No, of course. Maybe she has a special male friend?' Tanner continued, doubting if either of them knew the half of what she got up to when they weren't around.

'Not that we know of.'

'The name Jason Blackwell doesn't ring a bell?'

'Never heard of him!' she stated, her eyes remaining focussed on Tanner's.

'You said the last time you heard from her was on Sunday?'

'That's correct.'

'Did she phone you from somewhere?'

'She said she was staying on board one of her friend's boats.'

'She didn't say who that friend was?'

'One of her girlfriends. I can't remember her name, but she's stayed with her before.'

'Did she say where the boat was moored?'

'Only that it was kept down a dyke somewhere. She did promise that she wouldn't be going out in it, so she couldn't have gone to sea or anything.'

Sliding the photograph over the table to Townsend, Tanner drew in a fortifying breath. Asking any more questions would only be delaying the inevitable. 'Mr and Mrs Betton,' he began, his eyes resting gently on theirs, 'It is with a heavy heart that I have to tell you that the body of a young woman was found on board a boat yesterday evening.'

He watched with anxious dread as their eyes began dancing erratically between his.

'At the moment, we don't know who she is,' he continued, 'but with the information you've just provided, I think there's a strong possibility that it could be your granddaughter.'

Tanner found himself holding his breath, waiting for the inevitable bout of vehement denial, but nothing came. Both of them just kept staring at him with an expectant look, as if waiting for him to complete an unfinished sentence.

'Naturally,' he continued, shifting uncomfortably in his seat, 'we're all praying that it isn't her, but I do think it may be wise to prepare yourselves for the worst.'

Still there was no response.

Tanner cast an uncertain eye over at Townsend before clearing his throat. 'At this stage, what we really need is to find out if it's her or not. Is there anything you could tell us that would help to identify her; distinguishing marks, tattoos – that sort of thing?'

The couple both blinked rapidly, as if being awoken from a hypnotic trance. 'I – I don't think so,' Mrs Betton eventually replied, her eyes turning to her husband.

'She does have that scar on her wrist,' he responded, his voice rasping like a rusty saw as he turned to look back at Tanner. 'She burned herself on the edge of a saucepan, but it's very faint.'

'Can either of you remember what she was wearing when you last saw her?'

Mrs Betton sat up in her chair. 'She didn't dress provocatively, if that's what you're implying!'

'Not at all,' Tanner replied, taking an apologetic tone. 'It would just be useful to know what sort of clothes she was wearing: jeans, jumper, jacket?'

The woman took a moment to exchange an unknowing glance with her husband. 'I'm – I'm not sure we can remember. She had quite a few clothes, but nothing fancy.'

Tanner drew in a breath. 'I don't suppose either of you would be prepared to see if you can identify the person we found? It would certainly help us to know if it is her or not.'

'I'm not sure there would be much point,' Mrs Betton continued. 'Whoever you've found, Inspector, it isn't our Deborah. She's most likely still on board the boat and can't get any reception, or her phone's died and she can't find anywhere to charge it. If we knew where the boat was moored, we'd drive over there ourselves.'

'Yes, of course, and hopefully that will be the case. However, the person we've found is of similar age, her hair is the same length and colour, and she was found on board a boat moored down a small narrow dyke.'

Stuffing her handkerchief back inside her handbag, Mrs Betton snapped the lid closed to stand abruptly up. 'Thank you for your time, Chief Inspector, but I'm afraid we have to go. We have things we need to be getting on with at home.'

Tanner sat back in surprise. 'I'm sorry, I didn't realise.'

'Besides,' the woman continued, 'it's fairly clear that you have no real intention of finding our granddaughter. We'll just have to do it ourselves. C'mon, Harold, we're leaving!'

- CHAPTER THIRTEEN -

'WAS THE COFFEE really that bad?' queried Tanner, watching the door close to leave Townsend and himself sitting on their own inside the otherwise empty interview room.

'They probably left the oven on,' Townsend replied, retrieving his still open notebook from off the desk. 'Still, at least we know who the female victim is.'

'But not formally.'

'Then we'll have to ask Dr Johnstone to dig up her dental records.'

'Something which will take time. No matter, I suppose, but we will need to get hold of their DNA and fingerprints, at some point at least.'

'You don't seriously think they did it?'

Tanner cast a sagacious eye at him as they both climbed to their feet. 'One thing you'll learn, young Townsend, is to never un-suspect anyone.'

'And that's a word, is it?'

'Probably not, but you know what I mean. Anyway, I suppose I'd better head over to have a chat with Jason Blackwell's estranged wife, else I'm not going to make it back in time for my own press conference, which would be a shame.'

Glancing up to find Townsend staring at him like a puppy in need of a good home, Tanner let out an irritated sigh. 'I need you here, Townsend, helping Cooper. I can't take you with me.'

'I'm fairly sure he can cope on his own. Besides, won't you need someone to take samples of the mother's DNA and fingerprints?'

'And you can do that, can you?'

'Well, admittedly, I haven't done it before, but I have been trained to.'

Tanner took another look at the earnest desperation in Townsend's eyes before letting out a sigh of reluctant capitulation. 'Very well. Just this once, mind.'

'Yes, boss!' Townsend replied, standing to attention with a victorious smile.

- CHAPTER FOURTEEN -

AS TANNER'S SOMEWHAT dated jet-black Jaguar XJS swept around a large circular brick-paved driveway, Townsend had his face pressed up against the window as he stared out at the entrance to the impressive Tudor-style mansion they were gradually making their way towards.

'Now that's what I call a house!' Tanner heard him remark, bringing his car to a steady halt besides a sleek bullet-grey Aston Martin. 'Something that big *must* have a butler. What d'ya reckon?'

'I'm not sure,' Tanner mused, casting an admiring if not envious eye over at the car, 'but if one doesn't answer the door, then I suggest we make a point of asking her. If she does have one, then he's bound to have done it.'

Heaving himself out, he stepped quickly over to the arched wooden front door, leaving Townsend dawdling slowly behind, his eyes gazing up to the building's overhanging eaves.

'Are you coming or not,' Tanner barked, tugging down on a somewhat ostentatious cast-iron bell pull.

With a heavy chime ringing out from inside the house, Townsend picked up his feet to hurry over.

'You've got the forensics bag?' Tanner enquired, glancing around.

Townsend lifted it up for him to see.

'Did you check inside, before we left?'

'Er...I assumed it would be packed and ready to go.'

Hearing the shuffle of approaching footsteps, Tanner rolled his eyes to dig out his ID. 'Then I suppose we'd better just hope it isn't empty.'

'Don't worry, boss, there's definitely something inside. It's certainly heavy enough.'

'I hope so, for your sake,' Tanner muttered, straightening his tie to look back at the door. 'Anyway, you'd better let me do all the talking.'

'Can't I at least do *some* of the talking?'

Tanner swivelled his head to see the detective constable's handsome young face smirking back at him. 'You know, it might be better if you waited in the car.'

'Too late now,' Townsend muttered, his eyes bringing Tanner's attention to the arched wooden door being slowly opened in front of them.

Taking a half-step back, both men found themselves staring wide-eyed and opened-mouthed at the curvaceous half-naked body of the woman stepping out from behind it.

'Mrs Abigail B-Blackwell?' Tanner heard himself stutter, doing his best to keep his eyes firmly focussed on the woman's heavily made-up face, and not the tops of her voluminous heaving breasts, both of which looked as if they were about to burst over the edge of the skimpy black lace bra she was wearing like the lolloping water of an over-filled dam.

'I am, yes. May I help you?'

'It's Detective Inspector – I – I mean Detective Chief Inspector Tanner, and my colleague...'

'Detective Constable Townsend,' Townsend blurted out, fumbling inside his coat for his ID.

With her doing nothing in response but to stare vacantly out at them, Tanner engaged her eyes to open his mouth. 'I spoke to you last night – about your son?'

'Right – yes – of course.'

'We were hoping you'd be able to provide us with a picture?'

'I emailed one over to you this morning.'

'Oh, right. Sorry, I didn't know.'

'I assume that means you still haven't found him?'

'Not yet, but I can assure you that we have every available officer out looking for him.'

'You mean, apart from you two?'

'Er...' Tanner began, wracking his brain for a suitable reply.

'Don't worry. I'm sure he's fine. It's not exactly the first time he's run off.'

'Either way, we'll leave no stone unturned until he's been found.'

'That's admirable, thank you, but it doesn't explain what you're doing here. I've already told you that I haven't seen him.'

'We've actually come to talk to you about your husband.'

'Why? What's he done now?'

'Is it alright if we come in?'

'Can't you tell me here?'

'We'd prefer it if we could step inside for a moment.'

'If you must!' she replied, with an indignant huff, before glancing briefly down at herself, 'but you're going to have to wait there for a moment whilst I put some more clothes on.'

Watching her disappear back inside, Townsend leaned his head forward to try and peer through the gap left in the half-closed door. 'No need to on our account,' he whispered, under his breath.

Tanner pulled him back to offer him a reproachful

scowl.

'What?'

'She's a suspect in a murder investigation, Townsend, not some tart you just met down the pub.'

'That's as maybe, boss, but considering her age, and the fact that she's the mother of a twelve-year-old child, she is *seriously* fit! You did see her, didn't you?'

'Indeed I did, thank you. Far more than I probably should have.'

'OK, well, make sure to let me know when you want me to take a sample of her DNA,' Townsend continued. 'I'm totally up for it!'

'I've no doubt you are.'

'I might even ask if we could do it in the bedroom, preferably on her bed, with me lying on top of her.'

'If she's amenable to your carnal advances, Townsend, then be my guest. But before you do, you better know that whatever you did with her would have to be included in my report, which no doubt everyone in the office would read, at some point at least, Sally included.'

Townsend gave him an indignant glare. 'What happened to, "What happens in the field stays in the field"?'

'You're thinking of cricket.'

'I don't think I am.'

With the sound of her returning, Tanner and Townsend fell immediately silent.

'Sorry about that,' came Mrs Blackwell's breathless voice, pulling the door open again to reveal that all she'd done was to drape a black transparent nightgown over her elegant square shoulders, something that did nothing at all to cover up the skimpy lingerie she was wearing underneath. 'Now, where would you like me?'

Hearing Townsend gulp beside him, Tanner

cleared his throat. 'Anywhere is fine, thank you, Mrs Blackwell.'

'Please, call me Abigail,' she replied, offering Tanner a vivacious smile, 'or even Abi, if you prefer?'

'As I said before, Mrs Blackwell,' Tanner continued, deliberately ignoring her request, 'we need to talk to you about your husband.'

'Yes, but you never said what it was about?'

'If we could come in?'

'Then I suppose you'd better follow me through to the kitchen. Tea or coffee?' she enquired, spinning gracefully around to begin leading the way down a wide bright hallway, her transparent nightgown billowing seductively behind her.

'Er, coffee, thanks,' Tanner replied, glancing around at Townsend to find him grinning from ear to ear. 'Milk, no sugar, for both of us,' he added, giving the young detective constable a look of stern condemnation before stepping inside to follow on after.

- CHAPTER FIFTEEN -

ENTERING A LAVISH Georgian-style kitchen with cream-coloured wooden cabinets surrounding a large central island, Tanner stopped for a moment to stare about.

'So anyway,' he heard Mrs Blackwell say, her voice lifting above the noise of her filling the kettle, 'you'd better get on with it. I have a hair appointment at twelve.'

Tanner cleared his throat to flatten his tie. 'A man was found on board his boat last night. At this moment in time, it is our belief that that man is your husband.'

'What do you mean, it is your belief? Hold on. Let me guess. He was so drunk he couldn't even remember his own name?' she laughed.

'With regret, Mrs Blackwell, it was his body we found.'

Turning the kettle on, she turned to face them with a confused frown. 'Sorry, I'm not with you.'

'We believe he was attacked by an intruder.'

The woman's eyes flickered between Tanner's and Townsend's with anxious uncertainty. 'You're not seriously telling me that Jason is...that he's...dead?'

Remaining silent, Tanner answered with a solemn nod.

'I'm – I'm sorry – but – but that can't be,' she continued. 'Someone would have told me if he was.'

'Which is why we're here.'

'Then why didn't you tell me last night?'

'We find it best to inform relatives of such matters face-to-face. We were also more concerned with locating your son at the time. Besides, you didn't sound exactly compos mentis.'

'Compass what...?'

'Clear-headed,' Tanner clarified.

'No, well, I'd probably drunk more than I should have,' she replied, her gaze drifting slowly away.

'May I ask where you were?'

'Sorry...?'

'I was asking where you were last night?'

'Oh – right. I was at a party.'

'Which was where?'

'At a friend's house.'

'Nearby?'

'The other side of Norwich.'

'I assume there'll be someone there who'll be able to verify that?'

The woman's head jolted back in surprise. 'You're not seriously suggesting it was me who killed him?'

'We're not suggesting anything at all, but we do need to know the location of everyone who knew him, especially members of his immediate family.'

'Right. Yes. It's just – it's just been a bit of a shock, that's all.'

'We'll need a formal statement from you as well, together with a sample of your fingerprints and DNA.'

Tanner watched her gaze drift away again.

'Would that be OK?' he prompted, endeavouring to recapture her attention.

'Sorry,' she eventually responded, her eyes flickering back to his, 'you'll need what?'

'To take a statement, together with a sample of your fingerprints and DNA. Not necessarily because you're a suspect, mind.'

'Not *necessarily?*'

'They'd be to help us eliminate you from our enquiries.'

'And just exactly how will having my fingerprints and DNA on your police database help to eliminate me from your enquiries? Surely it would only serve to do the opposite.'

'Only if you're guilty.'

'Well, I can tell you now that you're definitely going to find my prints and DNA all over that stupid boat of his. He used to drag me out on it every bloody weekend.'

'When was the last time you were on board?'

'What?'

'The last time you were on board. When was it?'

'Probably when I was last forced to go over there to try and persuade him to agree to a divorce, a subject he's recently become rather keen to avoid.'

'Which was?'

'Shouldn't you be out there trying to find my son instead of standing there asking me a series of ultimately pointless questions, given that it wasn't me who killed him?'

'OK, then may I ask when you saw *him* last?'

'Who – my husband?'

'No, Mrs Blackwell, your son.'

'When I dropped him off on Friday.'

'I assume you saw your husband then as well?'

'Unfortunately.'

'Was that the last time?'

'Milk, no sugar, wasn't it?'

'Mrs Blackwell, you need to tell us when you saw your husband last.'

Tanner waited patiently for her to turn back, two gently steaming mugs held at the end of each arm.

'Did you hear me?'

'OK, look,' she began, setting them down on the kitchen island, 'I admit, I did go round to see him last night, but only to ask for the divorce he's been promising me for years now.'

'Did you step on board?'

'Only into the cockpit.'

'Was anyone else inside?'

'He wouldn't let me into the saloon.'

'Did you hear anyone?'

'If you're trying to work out if I knew he was with another woman, then yes, I did. I could hear her cackling laugh from about two miles away, but don't worry, I'm hardly the jealous type. Neither of us have been exactly faithful.'

'Is that why you decided to separate?'

'In part.'

'What were the other parts, if you don't mind me asking?'

'If you must know, it was because of our son. I married him on the sole condition that we wouldn't have children. I'm a model, or at least I used to be. I knew it would end my career if we did. Then I fell pregnant, and he refused to let me have an abortion. He said that if I did, he'd file for divorce, making sure I'd be left with nothing. So I did what he wanted, only for him to start sleeping with just about every woman he met the second I started gaining weight. And what was I left with? A child who hates me, a husband who now seems to have more girlfriends than there are days of the week, and my modelling career in tatters after my agency failed to renew my contract the moment they discovered that I was unable to fit into a size six dress, no matter how much I breathed in.'

'And yet, here you are,' Tanner continued, his eyes roaming the kitchen, 'living in this rather resplendent

Tudor mansion, with what would appear to be a brand new Aston Martin parked outside.'

'The house is in Jason's name. He only allows me to stay here because he prefers to live on board that stupid boat of his.'

'And the car?'

'Well, yes, that does belong to me, but probably not for long. I'm struggling with the repayments. If I can't find work soon, I'll be left with no choice but to sell it.'

Tanner paused for thought, picking up one of the coffee mugs to take a tentative sip. 'Can you tell me anything about his family?'

'Good God! I wouldn't know where to start!'

'Does he have any siblings?'

'A brother, Jeremy. Apparently, he used to have an older sister as well, but she died.'

'Do you know how?' Tanner enquired, glancing around at Townsend to make sure he hadn't allowed himself to be so distracted by the woman's lack of clothing that he'd forgotten to take notes.

'He never said. Whenever it came up in conversation he'd always change the subject.'

'What about his brother? Older or younger?'

'Younger, although you wouldn't know it. More mature in every way. He runs Blackwell Pharmaceuticals with his father.'

'So, what did Jason do?'

'I've already told you. He spends his life endeavouring to sleep with just about as many women as is humanly possible. I'm not sure he has time for anything else.'

'He doesn't work?'

'He doesn't need to. He has shares in the family business. He also owns around fifty flats around the country, all of which are rented. No mortgages on any of them, either.'

'By the sounds of it, I'm surprised his father didn't disinherit him.'

'Oh, he'd never have done that. He honestly thinks the sun shines permanently out of his arse. I'm fairly sure that's why his will says Jason is first in line to inherit the Blackwell estate.'

Tanner blinked in surprise. 'Despite his younger son running the business?'

'That's what he told me.'

'When was that?'

'Last Christmas. We went under the pretence that we were still a family.'

Mrs Blackwell stared briefly off into space before returning her eyes to Tanner's. 'Does he know yet – about Jason?'

Tanner shook his head. 'You were my first port of call. It also remains our priority to locate your son.'

'Yes, of course.'

'Do you have *any* idea where he might be?'

'Not a clue, sorry.'

'He's definitely not here?'

'Not unless he's hiding in a wardrobe.'

'What about his uncle, or maybe his grandfather?'

'Well, it's possible, I suppose. They both live in the same place.'

'Which is?'

'Blackwell House. It's on a one-hundred acre estate up near Aylsham, so I doubt you'll be able to miss it.'

'Do you think Edward knows how to get there?'

'Well, he's been there before, obviously. Whether he knows its location is another matter. You know what children are like. They spend half their lives living in a world of their own, and that goes double for Edward.'

'OK, Mrs Blackwell, thank you for your time,' said Tanner, setting the coffee mug down to glance around at Townsend. 'I assume it's OK for my colleague to take a fingerprint and DNA sample?'

'What, now?'

'It won't take long,' Tanner continued, turning to see Townsend begin fumbling with the zip on the forensics bag. 'Whilst he does, perhaps you can tell me how much you expect to get, now that your husband has passed away in such tragic circumstances?'

Mrs Blackwell opened and closed her mouth with a look of horrified disgust. 'Now you're insinuating that I killed him for his money?'

'Well, yes, I suppose I am, but only because it seems a little too much of a coincidence that you went round to see him the night he was killed, that you admitted to hearing he was with another woman, that you're having money troubles which you've made abundantly clear is his fault, that the child you never wanted has gone missing, and that your husband is the oldest son of Lord Alfred Blackwell, founder and owner of one of the largest pharmaceutical companies in the world.'

'But I won't get any of that. His shares will be distributed to the other shareholders.'

'You've given it some thought, then?'

'I just know that's what will happen, that's all.'

'What about the house you're currently living in? It must be worth a small fortune in itself. Then there's all the properties you've just told us he owns, all of which I assume will automatically transfer into your name, being that they'd be part of his estate.'

'I can assure you, Chief Inspector, that if I *had* decided to murder my husband, for no other reason than to get my hands on his money, I would have had the good sense to wait until his father was dead, at which point Jason would have inherited his entire fortune, which by all accounts shouldn't be too long now, given that the poor man's heart is about to pack-up and he's been given only a few more years to live.'

'Or maybe you were so upset to have found him in bed with another woman, you decided to move your plans forward a little.'

'If it was the first time I'd caught him in bed with another woman then you could well have been right.'

'Anyway, we're not accusing you of doing anything, at least not officially, but if you could make sure to let us know if you decide to jump on a plane to some remote Caribbean island, now that you can afford it, we'd be very grateful. Oh, and if you do happen to see your son, the one you wish you'd never had, please let us know. You may not want him to be found, but I can assure you that we most definitely do.'

- CHAPTER SIXTEEN -

'WELL, THAT WAS all rather interesting,' commented Tanner, hearing Mrs Blackwell close the front door behind them.

'It certainly was,' agreed Townsend, grinning like a recently fed Cheshire cat.

'I meant about what she had to say for herself, not what she'd chosen to wear, or should I say *not* to wear.'

'To be perfectly honest, I hardly noticed what she was wearing.'

'Oh, really!'

'Not at all. I was far more interested in what lay hidden underneath.'

'I wasn't aware of anything lying hidden underneath. As far as I could make out, it was all very much in public view. I take it you managed to get her fingerprints without shaking too much?'

'Just about. Some of them may be a little smudged, but I blame her reluctance for having them taken more than my inability to stop staring down her cleavage whilst doing so.'

'For God's sake, Townsend. Do you really have to be quite such a pervert all the time?'

'I'm not sure there's anything perverted about a man being attracted to a woman.'

'Maybe not, but most of us seem to get by with a

little more discretion,' Tanner replied, reaching the driver's side door to cast his eyes back at the house. 'Putting her physical appearance to one side, if that's possible of course, do you have any thoughts as to what she said?'

'Sorry, boss. Was I supposed to be listening?'

'I take it you did at least take notes?'

'Only of her physical measurements,' Townsend continued, retrieving his notebook with a nonchalant air, 'estimated, at least.'

'If you're incapable of answering me seriously, I'll put you back with Cooper.'

'I thought you were going to anyway.'

'Then I'll just have to fire you instead.'

'Did I ever tell you how much I like your car?'

Tanner folded his arms to glare impatiently at him over the Jag's polished black roof.

'OK, yes, I was listening,' Townsend eventually replied.

'And...?'

'If you want to know if I thought she did it or not, then no, I don't think she did.'

'And you reached that conclusion having considered all the available evidence at hand with a clear head and an open mind, and not because you couldn't imagine how a woman with such a perfectly formed pair of breasts could have ever stabbed her husband to death, despite the fact that he's stinking rich and she's completely broke and that she'd already admitted to having visited him the night he was murdered?'

'Call it a gut feeling,' Townsend replied, with a nonchalant shrug.

Tanner smiled sarcastically back. 'There's something else we need to consider as well.'

'You mean...her perfectly formed bum?'

'I was thinking more about what Dr Johnstone's report said; about the shallow depth of the stab wounds, and how he thought they may have been caused by a woman.'

'You're basically saying that you think it was her.'

'Unfortunately, despite my better judgement, I find myself agreeing with you.'

'Oh – right.'

'Which leaves me questioning whether that's because she's telling the truth, in that she didn't kill him, or I'm suffering from the same problem you are.'

'And what's that?'

'That I'm just a sad heterosexual man who, despite my very best efforts, was unable to keep my eyes off all the parts of her she seemed so determined to have out on permanent display.'

'Does that mean you don't think I'm some sort of pervert?' Townsend queried, sounding a little disappointed.

'Oh, I'm sure you are. But don't worry, I doubt if you're the only one. I suspect it's a common trait amongst us men, something I'm sure she's very much aware of, which makes me wonder if her choice of attire was a deliberate attempt to try and distract us. Anyway, next time I'll make sure to bring someone who shouldn't be quite so easily side-tracked. Vicky, for example, which reminds me,' Tanner continued, digging out his phone. 'I'd better give her a call to see how they've been getting on without us.'

Dialling her number, Tanner tugged open the car door to rest a foot on its stainless steel footplate. 'Vicky, it's Tanner. Any news on the boy?'

'Nothing yet, I'm afraid.'

'Is Cooper still out with the dive team?'

'He phoned in earlier.'

'And...?'

'He's been warned that it's probably going to take the best part of the day.'

'OK, well, fair enough.'

'The divers have said that if the boy did go in, then it's unlikely he'd have been carried out into the river, which is something, I suppose.'

'Unless he swam out,' Tanner mused. 'What about Samuel Tunk? Any news?'

'Again, nothing, I'm afraid. How's it going from your end?'

Tanner glanced over the car's roof to see Townsend wandering away, his thumbs tapping out a message on his phone. 'To be honest, not great. With hindsight, I should have brought you with me instead of Townsend, someone who'd have been a little less distracted by the disarming charms of a half-naked woman.'

'You took him to a strip club?' questioned Vicky, in a tone of reprimanding incredulity.

'Sadly, no. We went to see the male victim's wife, Mrs Blackwell.'

'Sorry, I'm confused.'

'To be honest, so am I. Despite listening to her eventually admit to having seen her husband the night he was killed, and that she seemed to have a long list of motives for wanting him dead, I came away doubting she had anything to do with it.'

'Any reason why?'

'Just a gut feeling, I suppose,' Tanner replied, happy enough to quote Townsend. 'She did tell us that Jason had a younger brother. He runs Blackwell Pharmaceuticals with his father. Apparently, they live at the same place – well, on the same estate at least, so I thought I'd head over there now to see if we can have a chat.'

'But what about the press conference I've spent the

last two hours arranging?'

'Shit! Of course. I don't suppose there's any chance you'd like to do it for me?'

'I do hope you're joking?'

'Was that a no?'

'It wasn't a yes.'

'Fair enough. What time did you arrange it for?'

'One o'clock.'

Tanner glanced down at his watch. 'OK, we should be back in time.'

'And if you're not?'

'Then they'll just have to twiddle their thumbs for a while, but don't worry. Apparently, that's what journalists do best. Anyway,' Tanner continued, raising a hand to garner Townsend's attention, 'we'd better be off. If you hear anything regarding either the boy or Samuel Tunk, call me!'

- CHAPTER SEVENTEEN -

'JESUS CHRIST!' EXCLAIMED Townsend, staring out of Tanner's car window as it swept sedately down a long tree-lined road towards a lavish stately mansion. 'And I thought the last place we went to was impressive.'

'I suppose that's what you get when you own a global pharmaceutical business and you're one of the richest people in the UK.'

'Even so, this looks more like somewhere the Royal Family goes to on holiday. I mean, they've even got herds of wandering deer.' Townsend continued, gesturing ahead as a rangale of young bucks leaped effortlessly over the road ahead. 'The driveway alone must be a mile long! Are you sure we shouldn't have stopped somewhere to buy a ticket?'

As a number of gleaming vintage motorcycles came into view, just to the side of a series of elegant stone steps leading up to a vast Romanesque pillared vestibule, even Tanner was struggling not to be impressed.

'OK, now listen. Just because they've got a bit of money...'

'I think they've got a little more than a bit.'

'...it doesn't make them any different from the rest of us.'

'You're saying that I shouldn't allow myself to be intimidated by them.'

'That's exactly what I'm saying.'

'OK, well, I'll try not to be.' Townsend replied, his attention drifting towards where a herd of horses could be seen grazing in a distant field. 'You know the guy who owns all this,' he soon continued.

'The "guy" as in Lord Blackwell?' Tanner sought to clarify.

'That's the one.'

'What about him?'

'I was just wondering how we were supposed to address him? Should we call him Your Lordship whilst bowing deeply, or does he go by the name of His Royal Majesticness?'

'The former, probably.'

'With or without the bow?'

'I think that's up to you.'

Tanner watched with wry amusement as Townsend mouthed the words "Your Lordship" whilst endeavouring to tilt the top half of his body forward, only for the seatbelt's automatic locking mechanism to prevent him from doing so.

'Bloody seatbelt,' Townsend eventually cursed. 'Can I take it off to practice?'

'Not with my driving, you can't. Anyway, placing royal etiquette to one side, my remark about not allowing the wealthy elite to intimidate you was serious. As you'll no doubt discover, at least at some point during what I hope won't be a completely pointless career, more often than not it's the class of people we're about to meet who end up being responsible for whatever crime it is that you find yourself having to investigate. I'm sure it's not because they're bad people, at least no more than anyone else, nor because they think they're better than the rest of us, which they're most definitely not. I suspect it's because they spend their entire lives living in a world beyond the realms of normal society, which ends up giving them a warped misguided belief that the rules that govern the humble masses simply don't apply to them.'

'That's probably because they don't.'

'Perhaps not when it comes to paying their taxes, or should I say not paying them, but when it comes to murder, the same rules most definitely *do* apply, they just don't realise it until they're standing in the dock being told that they'll be spending the remainder of their days locked inside a maximum security prison.'

As they finally reached the end of the drive, Townsend turned to face Tanner with a quizzical expression. 'Does all that mean I should or shouldn't bow?'

'Perhaps it's best if you let me do all the talking,' proposed Tanner, steering his car towards where a grubby-looking man could be seen stooped beside one of the dozen or so motorcycles, dressed in a pair of what had probably been white mechanics' overalls but were now more of a dull grey colour.

'What, again?' Townsend complained.

Ignoring him, Tanner stepped quickly out to begin crunching his way towards the overall-clad man. 'Good morning!' he called out. 'Sorry to bother you. I was just wondering if Lord Blackwell was in?'

'May I enquire who's asking?' the man replied, with a distinctly clipped British accent.

'Detective Chief Inspector Tanner,' Tanner replied, digging out his formal ID.

'Then it looks like you're in luck!' the man exclaimed, standing up to straighten his back.

'You're Lord Blackwell?' Tanner replied, jolting his head back in surprise.

The old man offered Tanner a benevolent smile. 'The one and only.'

'Sorry, I was just expecting someone a little...'

'...better looking?'

'Better dressed,' Tanner corrected.

'Don't worry. You're hardly the first to have made that mistake. I have a rather peculiar passion for motorcycles, you see, in particular old British ones that leak oil and rarely start. Fortunately for me, I enjoy fixing them as much as I enjoy riding them, that's when I can get them started of course, but that does tend to leave me spending half my life looking like a garage mechanic.'

'Well, they certainly are stunning machines!' Tanner exclaimed, as Townsend came to a halt beside him.

'I see you're something of a collector yourself,' Lord Blackwell continued, casting an admiring eye at Tanner's recently polished jet-black Jaguar XJS.

'It gets me from A to B,' came his modest reply. 'At least it does when it isn't being towed behind an AA van.'

'I must admit, I've always liked the look of them. Never had the chance to own one, though. I don't suppose you've considered parting with it?'

'Normally about thirty seconds after I get a call from the garage telling me how much it's going to cost to fix.'

'Then maybe you'd be willing to accept an offer?'

Realising he was being serious, Tanner's eyes lifted briefly to the stately home before remembering why he was there; that the man's grandson was missing, there was a convicted psychotic murderer roaming the Broads, and that he'd yet to tell him that his oldest son had been found stabbed to death. 'I probably would, but unfortunately, this isn't the time.'

'No, of course it isn't. Now, how can I help?'

Tanner pulled his shoulders back in preparation for what he had to tell this seemingly kind and gentle old man. 'I'm here about your son, Jason.'

'Christ! Not again! Let me guess, he's been arrested for being drunk and disorderly?'

'The body of a man meeting his description was found on board a boat moored up along Acle Dyke last night. We've yet to make a formal identification, but having just spoken to his wife, at the moment we're proceeding on the basis that it's him.'

Lord Blackwell remained where he was, a spanner held loosely in his hand as his soft grey eyes stared unblinking into Tanner's. 'You're mistaken, surely?'

'It's *possible,*' Tanner replied, in a tone that suggested it wasn't.

'May I ask how he...how he...?'

'It is our current belief that he was attacked by an intruder.'

'What about Abigail – and my grandson, Edward?'

'Fortunately, Mrs Blackwell wasn't with him at the time.'

'And Edward?' he repeated, his voice lifting with concern.

Tanner glanced fitfully at Townsend before returning to the missing boy's grandfather. 'We're still looking for him.'

'Do you at least know if he's OK?'

'We hope so.'

'But – you don't know?'

'There's no reason for us to believe he isn't. We think the most likely scenario is that he escaped after seeing what happened to his father and is now hiding somewhere.'

'My God! The poor boy!'

'Which was one of the reasons for our visit.'

'He's not here, if that's what you mean.'

'Are you sure?' Tanner questioned, his eye's drifting towards the house.

'OK, well, I suppose he could be, but I've no idea how he could have travelled all the way here? The nearest train station is miles away.'

'What about a bus stop?'

'There isn't one. The only way he could have made his way here would have been if he'd called a cab, but if that was the case he'd have found me, and it's not as if *I've* been hiding.'

'What about your other son? Jeremy, isn't it? Could he have gone to see him?'

'Well, again, he could have, but Jeremy lives on the estate with me. If he'd seen him, I'm fairly sure he'd have mentioned it.'

'Is Jeremy here? Can we talk to him?'

Lord Blackwell shook his head. 'He works out of our Norwich office. Although, saying that,' he continued, casting his eyes over Tanner's shoulder where the sleek muscular lines of a midnight blue Bentley Continental could be seen flickering past the trees alongside the driveway, its engine rumbling over the estate like rolling thunder, 'this looks like him now.'

- CHAPTER EIGHTEEN -

THE THREE MEN waited in silence as the car grew closer, eventually skidding to a halt on the gravel besides Tanner's XJS.

'You're back early,' Lord Blackwell called, as a slender middle-aged man stepped quickly out, concern etched out over his long bony face.

'Have you heard the news – about Jason?' came the man's breathless response.

Lord Blackwell's lower lip quivered for just a fraction of a second. 'These gentlemen are from the police.'

'So, you *have* heard?'

'Only that they think it's him.'

'And Edward?'

Lord Blackwell offered his son a regretful nod. 'This is Detective Chief Inspector...Inspector...?'

'...Tanner,' Tanner responded, retrieving his formal ID, 'and my colleague, Detective Constable Townsend. I take it you're Jason's brother, Jeremy?'

'That's correct.'

'I also understand that you help your father with the day-to-day management of Blackwell Pharmaceuticals?'

'Actually, I made Jeremy the CEO last month,' Lord Blackwell replied, 'which effectively means he now runs the company.'

'And you?'

'Retired, as you can see. Fortunately, the business is in excellent hands. Jeremy's always been a dab-hand at that sort of thing.'

'Am I correct in thinking that Jason was never involved?'

'He was always welcome. He just never had much of an interest.'

'Didn't that bother you?' Tanner continued, his attention reverting back to Jeremy. 'That *you* did all the work whilst your brother did nothing more productive than drink and chase women?'

Tanner watched the man glance briefly at his father before taking a defensive stance.

'I've always preferred to keep myself busy.'

'You're honestly trying to tell me that you didn't envy your brother's easy-going hedonistic lifestyle?'

'Look, sorry, I know you're the police and everything, and I don't mean to be rude, but what the hell's this got to do with you?'

'Someone killed your brother, Mr Blackwell.'

'And you think that someone was me?'

'In my profession, it's often best to start with those closest to home, especially when there's so much money involved.'

'Look, of course there were times I resented him. I doubt I'd have been human if I hadn't – at least a little. But at the end of the day, the vacuous life my brother seemed to enjoy was of little interest to me. There's a reason why I haven't taken a holiday in over ten years, and it's not because I'm paid by the hour.'

'As I mentioned before,' Lord Blackwell interjected, offering Tanner a placating smile, 'Jeremy has always been extremely industrious. Even at school he'd come home actually wanting to do his homework, whereas Jason was – well, he was more normal.'

'You're trying to tell me that you didn't care that he seemed happy enough to live off you like a proverbial sponge?'

'Jason was my son! I loved him dearly! Why on Earth should I have minded?' As the words began tumbling out, so did the emotion. 'And now you're telling me he's gone,' the old man continued, his eyes filling with tears, 'and I'm never going to see him again? Why should I have minded?'

As his body began to shake, Jeremy shoved his way unceremoniously between Tanner and Townsend to place a consoling hand on the old man's shoulder. 'Honestly, father, I really don't think it's him. I'm sure Jason is more than capable of defending himself against some drugged-up intruder.'

Tanner watched Lord Blackwell fight with his emotions.

'I'm – I'm not so sure. You know what he was like – drunk half the time – his mind constantly pre-occupied by women. If someone had attacked him after he'd been drinking, I doubt he'd have been able to put up much of a fight. I also doubt if a police Chief Inspector would come all the way out here if they weren't fairly convinced that it was him, not when Edward is missing as well.'

'If one of you would be willing to take a look at the person we found,' Tanner asked, 'it would at least help us to clarify the matter, once and for all.'

A moment of silence followed as Lord Blackwell laid a frail hand on this son's forearm. 'Could you do it for me, Jeremy? I really don't think I could cope – not if it is Jason.'

'Of course, father. Don't worry. I'll take care of it.'

'It wouldn't be so hard had it not been for Sarah,' the old man continued, his tear-filled eyes drifting into the distance.

'Sarah?' Tanner enquired, raising a curious eyebrow at the man's youngest son.

'My sister. She passed away.'

'I'm sorry to hear that,' Tanner replied, electing not to mention that he already knew.

'Don't worry. It does sometimes feel like it was only yesterday, but in reality it all happened a very long time ago.'

'May I ask how she died?'

Jeremy's forehead rippled as his eyes flickered briefly at his father. 'Another time, perhaps?'

'Of course. Sorry. Another time.'

'Do you have any idea where Edward might be?' Jeremy enquired.

'To be honest, I was hoping to ask you the same question.'

'He's not with his mother?'

'We've just come from there. You can't think of anywhere else he might have gone, another family member, perhaps?'

'I'm afraid we're all the family he has.'

Tanner took a moment to glance down at his watch. 'OK, well, I'm due to give a press conference this afternoon to help spread the word that he's missing. Hopefully, he's simply hiding out on the Broads somewhere. If that's the case, then someone is bound to have seen him.'

'And if he isn't?'

'There's no reason for us to believe that the person who broke into your brother's boat even so much as saw him, let alone hurt him in any way.'

'I don't suppose you have any idea who that person was, apart from me, of course.'

'It's too early to say, but we will need to take samples of your fingerprints and DNA,' Tanner replied, his gaze resting on Lord Blackwell.

'You don't mean my father as well?'

'It's a formality everyone has to go through, I'm afraid.'

'For Christ's sake! What possible reason would he have for murdering his own son?'

'We're not charging either of you, Mr Blackwell, nor are we taking you in for questioning. We're simply endeavouring to eliminate you from our enquiries which, in turn, will help us identify the person who's really responsible.'

'OK, but apart from my father and I, there must be some more likely candidates?'

Tanner took a moment to collect his thoughts. 'There is someone we are looking to speak with, a man by the name of Samuel Tunk.'

The moment he'd spoken his name, Lord Blackwell's head whipped around to fix Tanner's eyes with a demented glare. 'What did you say?'

'That we're looking to speak with a man by the name of Samuel Tunk. Why? Do you know him?'

'How could I not know him!' the old man spat with venomous rage. 'He's the psychotic bastard who butchered my daughter!'

'I'm s-sorry,' Tanner stuttered, unable to hide his surprise. 'I honestly had no idea.'

'He raped her in front of her entire family, then proceeded to murder the lot of them.'

Jeremy turned to glare back at Tanner. 'Is he not locked up behind bars?'

'He was,' Tanner replied, looking away.

'What do you mean, he was?'

'He was released on Monday. His original conviction was overturned after it was discovered that manufactured evidence had been introduced by the man leading the investigation.'

'Well, I hope at least *he's* doing time at His

Majesty's pleasure.'

'He killed himself two months ago.'

Tanner's reply had Jeremy blinking silently back.

'Sounds like he made the right decision,' Jeremy eventually muttered. 'So, anyway, what are you doing to track down your missing prisoner?'

'At the moment, our priority is to locate your nephew.'

'If it was this Samuel Tunk character who murdered my brother, then the chances of finding young Edward alive seem to have diminished somewhat, don't you think?'

'For a start, we don't know that Samuel Tunk *was* responsible for what happened to your brother.'

'You mean...apart from the fact that he murdered my sister and was released from prison the morning before my brother was killed?'

'He would still need to have some sort of motive for doing so,' Tanner replied, casting a questioning eye at Jeremy's father. 'I don't suppose either of you are aware of one?'

'Only that Jason hated him even more than I did,' Lord Blackwell hissed.

'Did he do anything that might have made him a target?'

Lord Blackwell glanced away, a guilty shadow appearing beneath his watery eyes. 'I – I don't know.'

'Are you sure?'

A sullen silence followed, eventually broken by Jeremy's imploring voice. 'Father, if you know something, you have to tell them.'

They watched impatiently as the old man drew in a shallow breath. 'He used to visit him in prison,' he eventually replied, his eyes staring at the ground.

Tanner baulked in response. 'But – that's not possible! He'd have needed to have been on Tunk's visitor's list.'

'Apparently, he was. Jason wrote to him when he was first locked up, asking permission to see him.'

'And Tunk agreed?'

'That's what Jason told me.'

'Jesus Christ! Do you know how often he went?'

'Every week for the first six months. After that, I'm not sure.'

'And did he tell you *why* he went?'

'He said it helped him to deal with the loss of his sister – being able to talk face-to-face with the man responsible for her death.'

'My God! I'd have thought it would have done the opposite. Do you have any idea what they spent all that time talking about?'

'He never said, and I never asked. I implored him not to go, but that was one of Jason's many traits. Whatever you told him to do, he'd always end up doing the opposite.'

- CHAPTER NINETEEN -

'LOOKS LIKE MR Samuel Tunk is back to being our prime suspect again,' commented Tanner, leading Townsend quietly back to his car.

'Because Jason used to visit him in prison?'

'It's not so much that he used to visit him,' Tanner replied, cupping a hand under the Jag's chrome door handle, 'but more likely what he said to him when he did.'

'Like what? "I'm jolly cross with you for killing my sister"?'

'What if he went there to tell him, over-and-over again, that he was a sad fucked-up psycho, and that he was going to use all his power and influence to make his life inside prison a living hell. For all we know, he could have gone on to say that if he ever did get out he'd first torture, then kill him for what he did to his sister. If I'd just been locked up for life to find myself having some stuck-up Etonian-type popping over to see me once a week to both insult and threaten me, I'd have probably been rather keen to stab him to death myself.'

'But if that was the case, why would Tunk have allowed Jason to visit him? As you said, it's the prisoner's choice.'

'I've no idea,' Tanner replied, tugging open the door. 'Anyway, knowing Jason *did* visit him gives us the one thing we've been lacking: a motive for Tunk deciding to make a special trip to see him.'

As they both opened the car's doors to climb inside, Townsend glanced over at where Jeremy could be seen comforting his father, leaning against his son with a hand pressed to his chest. 'Does that mean Jason's brother is off the list?'

Tanner started the engine to follow his gaze. 'I assume you think he shouldn't be.'

'Well, with his brother out of the picture, and us chasing the guy who murdered his sister, he's now set to inherit his father's estate in its entirety.'

'I suppose he remains a possibility,' Tanner eventually replied, reversing around.

'Looking at the state of Lord Blackwell,' Townsend continued, his eyes remaining focussed on the father and son, 'he may not have all that long to wait before he does.'

'But is that really a strong enough motive for him to have murdered his own brother?'

'I suppose it depends on their relationship,' Townsend shrugged, as the car began gliding effortlessly back along the estate's seemingly endless drive, 'and just how much money is at stake. You've said before about the stupid things people do when large amounts of money are involved, and I doubt if you'll find a much larger amount than the one we're talking about here. I was also curious to know how Jeremy could have found out about what had happened so quickly,' he continued, reaching inside his coat for his notebook. 'Apart from the guy who found the bodies, the only other person who knows is the woman we left back in the kitchen of her deceased husband's luxury mansion, the one who looked like a retired porn star.'

'You're suggesting Mrs Blackwell told him?'

'That there could be something going on between them as well,' Townsend nodded. 'She must have had him on speed-dial for him to have come over so quickly. I mean, she *was* married to his brother. I'm sure nobody would be too surprised to hear that she'd crept her way out of the bed of one only to worm her way into the bed of the other. If you add the family fortune into the equation; the fact that she's flat-broke, whilst Jeremy is now set to become one of the richest men in the country about two minutes after his father dies, then I think the idea of Mrs Blackwell whispering the idea into Jeremy's ear that he murders his brother, so enabling them to finally be together, is hardly beyond the realms of possibility.'

With Tanner not responding, Townsend leaned forward to try and catch his eye. 'What do you think?'

'To be honest, you had me at "speed dial."'

Townsend sat back in his seat with a self-congratulatory smile.

'However,' Tanner continued, 'as good as your theory is, I still think Samuel Tunk is a more likely suspect. It takes a lot to kill someone, especially in cold blood. Far more so if that person is a close relative.'

'Maybe they'd been planning on murdering him in a more pre-meditated way when Abigail caught him in bed with another woman, giving her a reason to bring proceedings forward a little?'

Tanner fell silent again, his attention focussed on turning out of the estate onto the busy road beyond. 'Tell you what,' he eventually said, 'when we get back, take a look at their phone records to see just how often they have been in contact.'

'And their social media accounts?'

'If you're right, and they've been planning this for a while, I doubt they'd have been stupid enough to do it online.'

'Are you sure about that?'

'Not really, but I think you should at least start with their phone records. If you do find they have been chatting to each other on a regular basis, then we can cast our net a little further. Meanwhile,' he continued, glancing at the clock mounted into the Jag's veneered wooden dashboard, 'I need to get back for the bloody press conference I'm supposed to be holding, and if that really is the time, then I'm already late!'

- CHAPTER TWENTY -

TANNER'S STOMACH TIGHTENED when he saw the crowd of reporters gathered in the car park outside Wroxham Police Station. The feeling grew worse when he caught sight of Vicky, standing in the doorway with her arms locked over her chest, her eyes tracking his car like the turret of a Challenger tank.

Resisting the temptation to drive straight past, he turned carefully into the entrance to leave his car parked discreetly around the back.

'Where the hell have you been?' he heard Vicky demand, the moment he'd stepped into the station's otherwise deserted reception.

'Yes, er...sorry I'm a little late.'

'By over an hour!' she continued, making a point of staring down at her watch. 'I've spent the last twenty minutes trying to decide what to do.'

'To either sing them a song, or do a little dance?'

'To hold the thing myself or cancel it.'

'Well look, I'm here now, and the press don't mind waiting. Any news of the boy?'

'Cooper's still down at the dyke,' she replied. 'I'm fairly sure he'd have called if they'd found him.'

'Nothing from anyone else?'

'Not a word.'

'And Samuel Tunk?'

'Again, no news. How'd it go with Lord Blackwell?'

'He offered to buy my car.'

'Anything relating to the current investigation?'

'I'll tell you later. Anyway, where do you want me?'

'Out the front, giving the bloody press conference! Where do you think?'

'The press conference, yes, of course. I don't know why, but for some reason I seem to keep forgetting about it. I don't suppose I've got time for a coffee first?' he asked, his eyes staring longingly towards his office and the espresso machine he could picture sitting idly in the corner.

'No you bloody don't! Now get out there before they ransack the place.'

'Right, yes.' Tanner took a moment to straighten his tie. 'How do I look?'

'Like the Detective Chief Inspector of Wroxham Police Station.'

'Really?'

Vicky offered him a reproachful scowl. 'Would it help if I brought a coffee out for you?'

'Tell you what. How about if I get the coffee and you do the press conference?'

'Nice try,' she replied, spinning away.

'What about a picture of the missing boy?' Tanner called after. 'I can't do it without that.'

As Vicky reached the doors leading through to the main office, she turned to offer him a smile of smug satisfaction. 'I know, which is why I left a pile of them out on the table for you outside. There are some there of Tunk as well. I also labelled them, just in case you couldn't work out which was which.'

'Sounds like you've thought of everything.'

'Apparently, everything apart from a way to stop you from being late. Now, off you pop. You'll enjoy it once you start.'

'I really don't think I will,' Tanner muttered, only

to find Vicky had already gone.

Shrugging his shoulders, he turned to gaze out through the glass entrance door at the gaggle of reporters he could see waiting for him beyond. 'Once more unto the breach,' he said to nobody in particular, fastening the top button of his suit's jacket to begin marching his way steadily out.

- CHAPTER TWENTY ONE -

AN EXPLOSION OF flash photography erupting from the awaiting journalists had Tanner instinctively raising a hand to help protect his squinting half-blinded eyes.

Stumbling forward, he found the table Vicky had mentioned, behind which he waited somewhat impatiently for the barrage of photography to come splattering to an eventual halt.

'Thank you all for coming,' he was finally able to say, casting his eyes about to see if he could recognise any of them, 'and sorry to have kept you waiting.'

'No problem at all,' replied one of the tallest, a skinny young man with long black greasy hair tied loosely at the back, 'although, if it's to tell us that some high ranking police official has lost his dog, we probably won't be quite so forgiving.'

Offering the man an unamused smile, Tanner waited for the unsurprising ripple of laughter to work its way through the pack before re-opening his mouth, only to hear the same man call out again.

'How's the new job?'

'If we could keep questions to the end, please.'

'That well, eh!'

More laughter followed.

'Sid Fletcher, Norfolk Herald,' the same journalist announced.

Tanner rolled his eyes theatrically into the back of

his head.

'Good to see you're a fan,' Fletcher responded, giving rise to another round of snickered amusement. 'I don't suppose you're here to tell us that you've unearthed yet another member of CID who's been bending the law to help himself become unjustly promoted?'

The image of Cooper's chubby face flashed into Tanner's mind.

'Do you have any idea just how many of your former superintendent's investigations are currently back under review?' Fletcher continued, 'and if any more convicted criminals are going to be released as a result?'

'As I said, if you could keep questions...'

'Samuel Tunk, for example?'

Tanner cursed under his breath. The fact that the reporter knew Tunk had been released was perhaps unsurprising, but it was going to make both him and the rest of the British Police seem grossly incompetent when it came time to start handing out the leaflets Vicky had left on the table.

Before the reporter had a chance to ask anything else, Tanner brought himself to attention. 'At nine o'clock on Monday night, the body of a man and a woman were found on board their boat moored up along Acle Dyke.'

Tanner's opening statement was met by subdued silence.

'From the evidence gathered so far, it would appear that they were attacked by an intruder in search of either money or food. Subsequently, we're treating this as a murder investigation, and we're keen to hear from anyone who was in the vicinity at the time.'

'Have you identified the victims?' someone else

called out, as the press pack cranked themselves back into life.

'How were they killed?'

'Do you have any suspects?'

'Was it Samuel Tunk, by any chance?' came Fletcher's overbearing voice.

'It's far too soon for us to have identified any suspects, but naturally we are of course looking to speak to Mr Tunk.'

'Jesus Christ!' the reporter hackled back, staring around at his colleagues with his mouth hanging open. 'They've only gone and released a psychotic lunatic for him to immediately start carving up yet more innocent people.'

'As I just said,' Tanner responded, forced to raise his voice above the growing cacophony of noise, 'there's no evidence to suggest it was him.'

'But you still want to speak to him?'

'Of course! But only because of the coincidental timing of his release. We have no physical evidence that he was involved in any way, shape, or form.'

With the journalists beginning to resettle themselves, Tanner drew in a fortifying breath. 'As much as we'd like to talk to any witnesses relating to the murder inquiry, our current priority is to locate the boy who we believe should have been on board at the time.'

The jostling press pack immediately erupted once again.

'You must be joking!' came Fletcher's accusatory voice. 'A second ago you said that it was a couple who'd been killed, now you're telling us that it was an entire family?'

'We don't know that the child's been harmed.'

'I'm sorry, but all that means is that you haven't found his body yet.'

'It means what I said!' Tanner stated, leaning forward to pick up the first pile of discreetly labelled leaflets. 'The most likely explanation for his disappearance is that he saw what happened and was able to escape. So we're asking anyone who thinks they may have seen him to immediately call the number on the bottom of this leaflet,' he continued, turning them over in his hands to reveal a portrait photograph of a schoolboy smiling awkwardly at the camera. 'His name's Edward,' Tanner continued, handing them to the nearest journalist, 'he's twelve years old, is about five-foot two and has pale skin with short dark hair.'

'Excuse me?' began the same egotistical journalist, staring down at the leaflet he'd just taken, 'but it doesn't say what his surname is.'

'To protect his family's privacy, we're keeping that confidential, for now at least.'

'It's just that he does seem to bear a striking resemblance to Jason Blackwell's son, the guy who's a direct heir to Blackwell Pharmaceuticals. I seem to remember he has a boat moored down Acle Dyke, and that his son's name is Edward as well.'

'As I said,' Tanner continued, sending daggers into the eyes of the reporter, 'to protect his family's privacy at this difficult time, we've elected to keep their surname out of the media.'

'You mean it is?' the reporter queried, as the crowd of reporters fell into an expectant silence.

Knowing his every word was being recorded, Tanner shifted his weight from one foot to the other as his mind searched for the most suitable, preferably honest response. As the silence grew ever longer, he eventually forced his mouth open to say the only thing his exhausted mind seemed able to think of. 'I can neither confirm nor deny...'

Once again the gaggle of reporters erupted into a chaotic pandemonium of yelling and shouting.

'Does that mean the murder victim is Lord Blackwell's son?' came Fletcher's voice, rising above the cacophony of noise.

Tanner shook his head in furious consternation.

'Does he know Jason's been killed?'

'Can I *PLEASE* bring your attention back to the missing boy?' Tanner demanded, his hands clenching into ever-tightening fists.

'And by the same psychotic lunatic who murdered his daughter. Sarah Jackson, wasn't it?' the reporter questioned, searching his colleagues' faces in the crowd.

'What about Jason's wife?' someone else shouted. 'The model whose career ended after she fell pregnant with the now missing boy. Does she know what's happened?'

'Is she a suspect?'

'Is Lord Blackwell?'

'What about his brother, Jeremy?'

Finally being given a chance to speak, Tanner unclenched his hands to open his mouth. 'Naturally, we're talking to a number of people about what happened, but as I've said twice now, our priority is to find the missing boy. So if anyone has seen him, or thinks they might have, can you please call the...'

'Doesn't it bother you that there's a previously convicted ex-pro-wrestling psychotic murderer wondering the Broads?' came Fletcher's irritating voice.

'Of course it bothers me!' Tanner spat, struggling to maintain control of his temper. 'Which is why,' he continued, grabbing hold of the second pile of leaflets to begin handing them out, 'we've had this photograph printed of him.'

'So, you *do* think he did it?' Fletcher demanded, reaching forward to grab one off the top.

'I didn't say that!'

'But you're out there looking for him?'

'Our priority is to find the missing boy.'

'With a psychotic murderer on the loose, one you've allowed to carve-up yet another innocent family, shouldn't you be warning people to stay indoors or something?'

'*Jesus Christ*,' Tanner muttered under his breath, as his entire body began trembling with a consternated mix of embarrassed humiliation and unbridled rage.

Closing his eyes, he forced himself to take a calming breath, his mind desperate to block out the baying pack of reporters. It was only when he heard another altogether different noise; a deep mechanical growl like the sound of a Spitfire taking off, that he opened them to stare past them all. There, on the road running parallel to the station, was the sleek ostentatious lines of a midnight blue Bentley Continental, rolling off the kerb to roar quickly away.

With his mind becoming pre-occupied as to what Jeremy Blackwell had been doing there, he slowly returned his attention back to the swaying mass of baying reporters.

'Thank you for your time, ladies and gentlemen,' he said, raising his voice above their on-going barrage of demanding questions. 'It's always *such* a pleasure. Before you go, just a reminder that if anyone does have any information regarding the whereabouts of either Edward Blackwell or Samuel Tunk, please call the number given. In the case of the missing prisoner, if anyone does happen to see him, I'd like to suggest that you give him an extremely wide berth. As one of you so accurately mentioned, he is a convicted ex-pro-wrestling psychotic murderer, one who probably wouldn't bat an eyelid whilst cutting off your arms and legs with an axe.'

With his audience falling into a stunned muted silence, Tanner smiled gleefully around at them all. 'Anyway, great press conference. I don't know about you, but I'm already looking forward to the next one.'

- CHAPTER TWENTY TWO -

LEAVING THE JOURNALISTS staring after him in a state of flabbergasted shock, Tanner turned on his heel to head back into the station, only to find Vicky gawping at him from inside the doorway, one hand on the open door, the other holding out his favourite coffee mug.

'You can't say things like that,' she whispered, a look of astonished bewilderment stamped over her incredulous face.

'Fuck-em,' Tanner replied, taking the mug to barge his way unceremoniously past.

'Who, the journalists or the million or so Norfolk residents?'

'There can't be *that* many, can there?'

'Seriously, John,' Vicky continued, allowing the door to swing closed, 'if you go around telling everyone that there's an ex-pro-wrestling psychotic convict wandering the Broads murdering whole families inside their boats you'll have a mass panic on your hands.'

'I only told them what they were going to write anyway. Didn't you hear what they were saying?'

'That's completely different. Nobody believes what reporters write, but they certainly do when being told by their local Chief Inspector.'

'Yes, you're probably right,' Tanner lamented, stopping to take a sip from the mug. 'Oh well. Too late now. Nice coffee, by the way.'

'You're not taking this seriously.'

'I think you're taking this quite seriously enough for both of us. Anyway, what's the worst that can happen? Everyone will remain locked inside their homes, forcing coffee shops to start offering door-to-door delivery?'

'What about Forrester? He's going to come down on you like a tonne of bricks when he hears what you said.'

'It's a good job he's not here then, isn't it?' Tanner replied, with growing irritation.

'Not yet, but you do know that he only lives down the road, don't you?'

Hearing the sound of the entrance door suddenly open, they both jumped around to see a uniformed officer coming in from outside, his hands clawing at a rather sad looking sandwich.

'Anyway,' Tanner continued, shaking his head with relief, 'putting what I said to one side, I was surprised to see Jason Blackwell's younger brother, Jeremy, parked outside the station. Did he come inside for some reason?'

'Not that I know of. He must have been here for the press conference.'

'Fair enough, but he didn't have to drive all the way over here for that, not when he could have watched it on the evening news.'

'You mean, along with the rest of the Norfolk population, before turning it off to start boarding up their windows?'

'Huh?' Tanner responded, deep in thought.

Vicky turned her head away with a flicker of a smile. 'Nothing.'

'Any news from Cooper?'

'He's on his way back now.'

'I take it there's been no sign of the boy.'

Vicky shook her head. 'The dive team called it a day.'

'Hopefully, that means he's still alive, and with word out that he's missing, with any luck, someone will call in to say they've seen him.'

Pushing his way through the doors leading through to the main office, Tanner clapped his hands together. 'OK, listen up everyone!' he called, casting his eyes around the room. 'I'm sure you'll all be delighted to hear that the press conference went exceptionally well. For those of you fortunate enough to hear it, no doubt you'll agree that it was quite possibly the best one ever given. Even if it wasn't, it should at least encourage people to stay indoors and out of trouble, making our jobs slightly easier going forward. Unfortunately, it does mean that we're about to be inundated with what will probably be a larger-than-average number of crank calls.'

Hearing someone's desk phone ring quietly in a corner, he lifted his chin towards it. 'That's probably the first. Anyway, as I was attempting to explain to the vultures – I mean reporters outside, our focus *has* to remain on the missing boy. His body hasn't been found in the dyke, so hopefully that means he's alive and well, probably hiding somewhere scared out of his wits. If that is the case, he'll be hungry, which will have him out looking for food. He may also be in need of some warmer clothes. So when the calls start coming in and you're endeavouring to separate the wheat from the chaff, I suggest you keep your ears open for anyone reporting something we'd probably normally ignore, like items being stolen from the front of a shop, for example. You never know, such a call could also lead us straight to Samuel Tunk, who could well be in a similar predicament, even more so if the child does happen to be with him.'

Seeing a long lanky arm rise slowly into the air at the back of the room, Tanner shifted his head to the side to see it belonged to the new detective constable. 'DC Henderson, you have a question?'

'I was – er – wondering if that would include something like items of clothing being taken from someone's residential property?'

'Yes, that's exactly the sort of thing I was referring to,' Tanner replied. 'Well done!' he added, by way of encouragement.

'It's just that I...er...' Henderson continued, as everyone turned to stare at him, '...I took a call from a woman a while back saying just that, that clothes had been taken from her back garden.'

'I think for it to be relevant it would need to have happened sometime between the time the boy went missing to – well – now, really.'

'When I said a while b-back,' Henderson continued, his voice beginning to stutter, 'I actually meant this morning.'

Tanner glared over the office at him, any pretence of congeniality fast disappearing. 'You took a call from someone this morning saying that her clothes had been stolen from her back garden?' he repeated, far more slowly than was necessary.

Henderson gulped. 'From off her washing line, to be exact.'

Tanner continued staring at him in muted silence together with everyone else in the room.

'Cooper was with me when I took the call,' Henderson continued, his eyes glancing furtively about. 'He told me to ignore it.'

Tanner couldn't help but shake his head in frustration. 'Did you at least make a note of the caller's name and address?'

'I did!' he exclaimed, with an emphatic nod. 'I wrote it down in my notebook.'

'Well, that's something I suppose,' Tanner replied, as another phone burbled into life. 'Right, that's it for now. Man the phones everyone and remember what I said.'

Spinning away, he briefly caught Vicky's eye as he continued searching the room. 'I don't suppose you've seen Townsend anywhere?'

'He's already "manning the phones",' she replied, pointing to his desk.

'Fair enough. When he's done, tell him to grab that address off Henderson and meet me at my car.'

'Where are you going?'

'To see a woman about a washing line.'

'Can't someone else do that, like me, for example?'

'I think I'd better do it myself. Besides, I don't particularly wish to be around when Forrester shows up asking why Norfolk's streets have become strangely deserted as the four hundred and forty-two local coffee shops are suddenly forced to go out of business.'

- CHAPTER TWENTY THREE -

'HELLO, MRS APPLEBY?' Tanner enquired, as an elderly woman's shrivelled-up face appeared from behind a cheap PVC front door. 'My name's Detective Chief Inspector Tanner, and my colleague, Detective Constable Townsend.'

'My husband's not in,' she immediately stated, giving their ID's nothing more than a courtesy glance. 'He's out with my son. Don't ask me where, cus I don't know. You can check inside if you don't believe me.'

'Er...thank you, Mrs Appleby,' Tanner replied, raising a curious eyebrow at Townsend, 'but we're not here for your husband, or your son, at least we don't think we are.'

'Then it's a good job they're not in then, isn't it!'

'You called about having had some items of clothing stolen?'

The woman's eyes narrowed with accusatory reproach. 'That was this morning.'

'Yes, sorry about that. We've been a little busy of late. May we come in?'

'To do what?'

'To see where they were taken from. One of my constables mentioned something about a washing line?'

'Do you have a search warrant?'

'Do we need one?'

'You do if you want to come inside.'

'But...Mrs Appleby, only a few seconds ago you said we were welcome to.'

'That was to prove I was tell'n the truth about my husband. Anyway, didn't you say you were a Detective Chief Inspector?'

'Er...that's correct.'

'Then don't you 'ave more important things to be getting on with than going around investigating stolen clothes?'

'We're actually here in connection with the missing twelve-year-old boy. You may have heard about him on the news?'

In the blink of an eye the woman's expression transformed from one of wary suspicion to that of deep motherly concern. 'Why on Earth didn't you say that before? That poor boy! Of course you can come in!'

As the woman turned to start hobbling her way back inside, Tanner and Townsend were left stranded on the porch, gazing at each other with similar expressions of mystified bemusement.

'Are you coming or not?' came her commanding voice, echoing out from inside the house.

'Er...yes, of course,' Tanner replied, motioning for Townsend to follow him into a damp-smelling hallway that almost immediately led through to the most basic of kitchens beyond.

Stepping outside onto a small concrete patio, Tanner took a moment to take in the terraced property's modest rectangular garden, in particular an old picket fence at the end, past which he could see what looked to be a footpath with the glint of a river beyond.

'Here's where the clothes were taken from,' the woman stated, stopping beside a large rotary washing line to their left.

'Is that the River Thurne?' Tanner questioned, lifting himself up onto the balls of his feet as the white triangular tip of a sail drifted silently into view.

'It is,' she confirmed, following his gaze. 'You can see it more clearly from the bedroom upstairs.'

'And is that a public footpath?' he continued, making his way down the garden to stare over the short waist-high fence.

'Unfortunately,' she nodded. 'You hardly ever see anyone walking on it, though. Only at Easter and during the summer holidays.'

'So, just about anyone could climb over your fence to gain access to your garden?'

'Well, yes, but no one ever has, at least not to my knowledge, not until now, that is.'

'What sort of clothes did you have out?'

'Oh, you know. The normal.'

'I don't suppose you could be more specific?'

The woman gazed up at the grey over-cast sky. 'Three pairs of jeans, some t-shirts, a purple hoodie, and a matching baseball cap. My son's stuff, mostly.'

'I don't suppose the hoodie had anything written on it?'

'Just that Nike tick-thing, same as the baseball cap.'

'And how old is he?'

'And why, may I ask, do you want to know that?' the woman demanded, folding her arms over her ample chest.

'Let me rephrase that. Do you think the clothes would fit your average twelve-year old boy?'

'Good God, no! My son's twenty-eight! He's also over six-foot tall and spends his life either eating me out of house and home or lifting weights with his father. He couldn't have fitted into your average twelve-year old's clothes when he was eight, let alone now!'

- CHAPTER TWENTY FOUR -

'IT WASN'T THE missing boy, then,' Townsend observed somewhat obviously, following Tanner out of the house.

'Not unless he's grown rather dramatically over the last couple of days.' Tanner replied, reaching his car to skirt around its elongated bonnet. 'There were also some larger-than-average footprints left in the mud on the other side of her somewhat inadequate fence, which hopefully means it was Samuel Tunk.'

'Why hopefully?'

'Because there can't be all that many six-foot-two ex-pro wrestling convicts wondering the Broads wearing purple Nike hoodies with matching baseball caps, at least I hope there aren't.'

Unlocking the car, Tanner was about to put a call through to the office when he saw the same ostentatious Bentley Continental he'd now seen for the third time that day, parked discreetly under the branches of a nearby weeping willow.

Tucking his phone away, he turned to catch Townsend's eye. 'Do me a favour, will you? Give the office a call? See if they have any news on either the boy or our prime suspect. Then give them an update as to what Samuel Tunk has hopefully decided to start wearing. I'm just going to have a very quick chat with our Mr Jeremy Blackwell.'

Leaving Townsend to make the call, Tanner

marched over to confront the person he could see pushing open the car's long heavy door.

'Is that you, Mr Blackwell?' he called, as an immaculately dressed man stepped gracefully out.

'Chief Inspector? What a remarkable surprise!'

'May I ask what you're doing, following us around like this?'

'I wasn't aware I was. I just happened to see your car, so I thought I'd stop to say hello.'

'And earlier, outside the station? I'm fairly sure I saw you there as well.'

'I came in to provide the requested DNA and fingerprint samples. I was going to bring my father in as well but, perhaps unsurprisingly, he didn't feel up to the task, so I arranged for one of your forensics officers to visit him instead.'

'And then I saw you speeding away?'

'I had another appointment; the joyful task of identifying my brother's body.'

Tanner opened his mouth only to close it again. 'Was it him?' he asked, in a more respectful tone.

He watched Jeremy respond with a nod of his head.

'OK, well, thank you for doing that. It couldn't have been easy.'

'Someone had to. I certainly didn't want my father doing it.'

'I understand, so thank you again.'

'Did the woman you were talking to know anything?' Jeremy continued, lifting his gaze to the terraced house where Tanner's car was parked.

Tanner scowled back at him, his mouth remaining firmly closed.

'The woman you were just talking to,' he repeated, ignoring Tanner's ignominious glare. 'Does she know where my nephew is?'

'Sadly, no.'

'Had she at least seen him?'

'Look, Mr Blackwell, I understand that you want to find him, but following me around isn't going to help.'

'As I said before, I wasn't following you.'

'Uh-huh.'

'What about Samuel Tunk?' Jeremy continued, spitting out the man's surname as if it was poison. 'Had she seen him?'

Tanner narrowed his eyes. 'Are you here in search of your nephew, or the man convicted of murdering your sister?'

'My nephew, naturally. But if I were to find Mr Tunk as well, then I wouldn't complain.'

'I see. And what would you do if you did happen to find him before we did, may I ask?'

Jeremy shrugged his shoulders. 'I'd ask him a few questions, I suppose.'

'Wrong answer, I'm afraid. The correct response would be to give him an extremely wide berth before putting an immediate call through to either myself or one of my colleagues.'

'Well, yes, I would, of course,' Jeremy continued, pretending to search his pockets, 'but I don't seem to have your number.'

Levering out his wallet, Tanner let out an unamused sigh. 'In all seriousness, Mr Blackwell, if you do see him, please don't think you'll be able to tackle him on your own. By all accounts, he's considered to be a particularly dangerous individual.'

'The man murdered my sister and her entire family, and thanks to the corruption that seems to run rife through the British Police, and the frankly ridiculous way our legal system works, he's now been allowed to murder my brother, probably my nephew as well. So yes, thank you Detective Chief Inspector

Tanner,' he continued, taking the crisp white business card being offered, 'I'm fully aware of just how dangerous he is.'

Seeing the rage burning deep within his smouldering eyes, Tanner felt obligated to try and calm the man down. 'I understand how you must be feeling, Mr Blackwell. I lost a family member in similar circumstances myself. But at the moment we don't know that it *was* Mr Tunk who killed your brother. We also don't have any reason to believe that your nephew is anything but alive and well. The best thing you can do at this precise moment in time is to stay home and sit tight. For all we know, Edward is making his way to you as we speak, which won't be much use if you're not there when he arrives.'

'There's no need to try and placate my feelings, Mr Tanner. I'm not a child!'

'My point is that you're not helping us find either Edward or Mr Tunk by following me around all the time. If anything, all you're doing is slowing up the process.'

'I think you're underestimating my abilities.'

'I see,' Tanner replied, an amused smile playing at the corners of his mouth. 'You fancy yourself as some sort of private detective, do you?'

'Oh, I'm fairly sure I don't have the level of intelligence needed for such an intellectually demanding job.'

Tanner felt his hackles immediately rise. 'Please don't patronise me, Mr Blackwell. Like you, I'm not a child.'

'Then I suggest you stop trying to dissuade me from doing all that I can to find the man who's murdered half my family.'

'I thought you were looking for your nephew?'

Jeremy dug his hands down into the pockets of his

tailored pin-striped suit. 'Neither of us may be prepared to admit it, but I think we both know that my nephew is already dead.'

A cold silence fell over them, broken moments later by the shrill sound of Townsend's voice, calling for Tanner's attention behind him.

'Go home, Mr Blackwell,' Tanner continued. 'We'll call you when we have some news.'

'As will I,' Jeremy replied, flicking defiantly at the corner of Tanner's crisp white business card.

Shaking his head, Tanner turned on his heel to make his way back to his car where he could see Townsend staring at him with a look of earnest intent. 'That's all we need,' he muttered to himself. 'A self-appointed vigilante.'

'Sorry to have interrupted, boss.'

'No problem. We were done anyway. What's up?'

'There's been a call. Someone's been seen taking food from the post office at the end of Thurne Dyke.'

'When was this?'

'Only about twenty minutes ago. The owner said he was fairly sure it was Samuel Tunk.'

- CHAPTER TWENTY FIVE -

'FOR CHRIST'S SAKE,' moaned Tanner, glancing fitfully into his rear-view mirror. 'I've got no idea what he's hoping to achieve.'

'What who's hoping to achieve?' asked Townsend, swivelling around to see a Bentley Continental about twenty metres behind them.

'Jeremy Blackwell's following us – again,' Tanner replied, flipping the mirror up so he wouldn't have to keep looking at him. 'He's hoping we're going to lead him straight to Samuel Tunk.'

'And what if we did?'

'He said he'd like to ask him some questions.'

'Wouldn't we all?'

'Reading between the lines, I think he meant that he'd like to beat the living shit out of him for murdering his brother and sister.'

'That's if he did murder his brother.'

'Unfortunately for Tunk, I think the general consensus of opinion is that he did.'

'Does that include us?'

Tanner didn't answer; his attention focussed on the road ahead.

'What about his nephew, Edward? Isn't he trying to find him as well?'

'He appears to have reached the conclusion that he's already dead.'

It was Townsend's turn to fall silent.

'I'm still hoping he isn't,' Tanner eventually added, knowing what Townsend must have been thinking.

'But you think it's more likely that he is?'

Tanner flipped the mirror back down only to find Jeremy Blackwell's Bentley Continental was now directly behind him. 'Looks like he's given up on the idea of being discreet. The guy's right up my arse!'

Townsend turned to try and catch Tanner's eye. 'I take it that's a yes?'

Deciding he may as well leave the mirror where it was, Tanner returned his attention to where he was going, and to Townsend's as yet unanswered question. 'Unfortunately, the man's right. The longer the boy remains missing, the more likely it is that he's already dead.'

- CHAPTER TWENTY SIX -

TWENTY MINUTES LATER, Tanner pulled up outside Thurne Dyke Post Office to see a uniformed police officer talking to a small elderly man just inside the doorway. Assuming the man to be the owner, he climbed quickly out to cast a glowering eye over at Jeremy Blackwell, rolling his car onto a grass verge behind them.

'Persistent bugger, isn't he,' he heard Townsend remark, climbing out the other side.

'Annoying pain-in-the-arse, more like.'

'Isn't there something we can do to stop him from following us around all the time?'

'Short of sticking a nail into one of his tyres, I'm not sure there is.'

'Couldn't we arrest him for attempting to pervert the course of justice?'

'I think his intention is to *accelerate* the course of justice.'

'What about a restraining order?'

'Nice idea, but the only thing he's done wrong is to drive a little too close to the back of my car. I think we're just going to have to put up with him for a while. With any luck, he'll get bored after a day or two and find something more entertaining to do. Shall we see what the owner knows about the man he saw shoplifting?'

'Can you give me a minute?' Townsend requested,

his eyes still focussed on the Bentley as its driver stepped slowly out.

'If you're thinking about having a word with him, you'll be wasting your time.'

'Nothing like that.'

'Suit yourself,' Tanner responded, with a dismissive shrug.

Leaving Townsend loitering beside his car, Tanner made his way inside the quaint village post office only to find himself walking straight into the police constable he'd seen earlier, hurrying out the other way.

'Detective Chief Inspector!' the constable exclaimed, jumping back with a start.

'So I've been told,' Tanner replied, his mind attempting to put a name to the face. 'Preston, isn't it?'

'It's actually Pearson, boss.'

'Don't call me boss.'

'Sorry, boss.'

Tanner rolled his eyes. 'Is the owner in?'

'He's just over there,' the constable continued, directing Tanner's attention towards an elderly man wearing a beige cardigan, shuffling his way towards the counter at the end. 'A Mr Harold Padgett.'

'I don't suppose there's any chance that he caught the shoplifter, and he's now safely locked up inside the cellar doing a jigsaw puzzle?' Tanner enquired, his eyes drifting towards a nearby shelf piled high with a myriad of brightly coloured Broads themed souvenirs.

'Er...no,' the young PC replied, giving Tanner an odd sort of a look. 'He got away. I've taken the owner's statement, if you'd like to see it?'

'Thank you, but now that I'm here, I may as well have a word with him myself.'

With the constable returning to his duties, Tanner made his way down to the counter to find the owner perched on a stool behind it, a pencil tapping against his chin as he stared pensively down at a folded newspaper. 'Mr Padgett?'

'Yes?' the man replied, squinting up, his hands searching for a pair of glasses.

Tanner dug out his formal ID. 'Detective Chief Inspector Tanner, Norfolk Police.'

'Sorry, you'll have to speak up,' Padgett replied, cupping a hand around an elongated ear. 'Unfortunately, my hearing isn't what it used to be. Neither is my eyesight for that matter,' he added, leaning forward to read the ID Tanner was holding out.

'Detective Chief...' Tanner began, only to end up letting out a sigh of bored capitulation. 'DCI Tanner, Norfolk Police.'

'Oh, right. I was just talking to one of your officers, at some length I may add. Did he forget to ask me something?'

'I was keen to have a quick word with you myself, if that's OK?'

'Sure! No problem! Fire away!'

'The man you caught shoplifting. You said you thought he was the missing convict, Samuel Tunk?'

'That's correct.'

'Are you sure it was him?'

'Your young constable asked me that exact same question.'

'And...'

'Didn't he tell you?'

'Er...' Tanner began, realising it would have probably been sensible to have glanced through the constable's notes first, '...perhaps if you could tell me again?'

Padgett scowled at him over the rim of his glasses. 'I do have better things to do other than repeatedly answer the same question.'

'Yes, I can see,' Tanner replied, taking in the crossword puzzle the man was halfway through.

'I'm not one-hundred percent sure it was him,' Padgett eventually replied, 'but I'm fairly sure.'

'Even though your eyesight isn't what it used to be?'

'It is when I've got my glasses on.'

'Which you had on at the time?'

'Well, no, but...'

'So, you're not sure?'

'He was certainly big enough to have been him.'

'Did you see what he was wearing?'

'Just a raincoat.'

'Colour?'

'Black, I think.'

'And which way did he go when he left.'

'Towards the river,' the old man continued, 'pointing with his hand.'

'Did you see him climb into a boat?'

'I didn't see one head out, so I can only assume he didn't, but I can't say for certain. All I know is that by the time I got outside he was gone.'

'I don't suppose there was anyone else with him?'

'If you're referring to the missing boy, your young constable asked me about him as well.'

'Again, if you could tell me, it would be appreciated.'

Padgett let out a discontented sigh. 'No, there was nobody with him, at least not inside the shop. Whether or not there was someone waiting for him outside, I don't know. All I do know is that there was nobody there by the time I'd made my way outside, which I admit did take me a while. Unfortunately, like the rest of me, my legs aren't...

'...what they used to be,' Tanner sighed.

Hearing the demanding tone of his mobile, Tanner reached inside his coat. 'If you'll excuse me for a moment.'

'By all means.'

'Tanner, speaking!' Tanner continued, turning away.

'Hi boss, it's Vicky.'

'Yes, Vicky, what've you got for me?'

'A young lady, out in reception.'

'Does she have a name?'

'Gina Booth. She said she's here for a job interview.'

'Christ! I'd forgotten all about her.'

'Shall I tell her to come back another time?'

'No, it's OK. I'm not far away, besides, we need all the staff we can get, and from what I remember, she's immediately available.'

'You'd better not advertise that to our male members of staff.'

'Why's that?'

'Oh, nothing. I just think they might struggle to get any work done.'

'I'm still not with you.'

'Don't worry.'

'OK, well, if you can ask her to wait – maybe make her a coffee – I should only be about twenty minutes.

'Sorry about that,' continued Tanner, ending the call to return his attention to the shop's owner, 'but I think we were just about done anyway.'

'Don't you want to see the CCTV footage?'

Tanner's eyes darted up to the ceiling. 'You have security cameras?'

'My son fitted them for me last year,' Padgett

continued, pointing them out.

'Can you play the videos back for me now?'

'I could, I suppose, but I'd have to dig out the manual to remind myself how.'

'Were they on at the time?'

'They're always on, at least they should be.'

'OK, well, unfortunately, I have to go.' Tanner replied, digging out another business card. 'When you work out how, could you email the video files over to me?'

Taking the proffered card, the old man took a moment to focus his eyes on it. 'I'm sure that will be fine, although I can't say I'm very good with email either. I'll have to give my son a call, but don't worry, I'm sure he'll be able to help.'

- CHAPTER TWENTY SEVEN -

STEPPING OUT OF the shop, Tanner looked up to see Townsend, staring down at his phone whilst leaning against his car, an amused smile playing over his lips. 'Good to see you've been keeping yourself busy.'

Jumping to his feet, Townsend straightened his face. 'Just checking my messages, boss. How'd it go inside?'

'The owner is about as old as the hills; not that there are many of those around here,' Tanner replied, glancing surreptitiously over his shoulder.

'Was it Tunk?'

'He seemed to think so, but I'm not so sure. The guy could barely see his hands in front of his face. Anyway, he reckons he should have some CCTV footage for us to look at. He just needs to get hold of his son to email it over.'

'What about the boy?'

'He said he didn't see him, although that's not saying much.'

'Did he at least see which way the man went?'

Tanner stopped beside the driver's side door. 'You know, you wouldn't have to ask all these questions if you'd come inside with me, taking notes as you should have been.'

'Yes, I know. Sorry about that, boss. It won't happen again.'

Tanner gave the young DC a disapproving scowl before looking away. 'The man said he thought he saw him heading for the river but didn't see a boat pull away. So, if it was him, he's on foot, which means he couldn't have gone far.'

'If it *was* him,' Townsend repeated.

'Anyway, I need to get back to the office. I have a new recruit waiting to be interviewed, and we could certainly do with an extra pair of hands.'

'Anyone nice?'

'I've no idea,' Tanner continued, tugging open the door, 'but her CV reads well. More importantly, she's immediately available.'

Townsend raised an intrigued eyebrow. 'Was that on her CV?'

'Was what on her CV?'

'That she's immediately available?'

'Er...I think so. Why?'

'I assume it had her phone number on it as well?'

'Oh, right. I see what Vicky was talking about now.'

'What was that?'

'Nothing important,' Tanner replied, tugging open the door to see Jeremy Blackwell jogging back to his car. 'Looks like we still have our shadow.'

'Not for long,' Townsend smirked, following his gaze. 'When he was snooping around outside the shop, presumably trying to overhear what you were saying, I took the executive decision to let the air out of his tyres.'

- CHAPTER TWENTY EIGHT -

LEAVING JEREMY BLACKWELL endeavouring to work out why his car could barely move, they left the post office to arrive back at the station less than twenty minutes later.

With Townsend trailing behind, Tanner entered reception to glance quickly around. Seeing Vicky perched on the edge of one of the cheap plastic seats, having a good old natter with a dark-haired woman facing away from him, assuming it to be the job applicant he was supposed to be interviewing he went bounding forward wearing his very best smile.

'Hi Vicky,' he interrupted, his head turning to stare into the sparkling blue eyes of a particularly attractive young woman. 'Miss...er...Booth, isn't it?'

'Gina,' the woman replied, pushing herself up to hold out a hand.

'Chief Detective Inspector – I – I mean, Detective *Chief* Inspector Tanner, at your...er...' Tanner heard himself splutter, feeling his skin prickle with heat with the realisation that he'd very almost said, "at your service." 'I see you've met my colleague,' he managed to continue, 'Inspector Detective...'

Vicky rolled her eyes. 'Detective Inspector Gilbert, otherwise known as Vicky. And yes, she has, thank you!'

'She hasn't met me yet,' came Townsend's exuberant voice, shoving past Tanner with his hand extended.

'I wasn't aware you counted,' Tanner grimaced, rubbing his shoulder.

'Constable Detective Townsend,' the young DC grinned, enthusiastically shaking the rather startled young woman's hand, 'but my friends call me Mark. I understand you're immediately available?'

'Well, at the moment, I suppose I am,' Gina replied, returning a smile that could launch a thousand ships only to sink them shortly afterwards when the captain forgot to look where he was going. 'I suppose it depends on how the interview goes.'

'Speaking of which,' Tanner interrupted, pushing Townsend to one side, 'if you'd be kind enough to follow me, we'll be able to get that process started.'

Ushering the candidate through to the main office, they'd only just made it past the kitchen when he saw Sally push herself up from her desk to come hurrying over.

'Yes, Sally, how can I help?'

Taking a brooding moment to look Gina up and down, Sally turned her attention back to Tanner. 'I've just found out that the murder victim's wife and his brother, Jeremy, had been having an affair.'

'Are you sure?'

'Maybe not one hundred percent, but their phone records show they've been in regular contact over the past six months. They're friends on Facebook as well!'

'And being friends on Facebook means people are having an affair?'

'Well, no, but their constant communication suggests *something's* been going on.'

'OK, well I suppose you'd better make sure that our bods in forensics check to see if either Jeremy Blackwell's prints or DNA have been found at the scene,' Tanner replied, without sounding particularly convinced.

'Do we have them on file?'

'We should do, at least he told me he's provided them. Let me know what you find.'

Sally gave Tanner an obedient nod before spinning away, but not before sending what appeared to be daggers into Gina's eyes.

'Sorry about that,' Tanner apologised, both for the interruption and for Sally's apparent hostility. 'As you probably know, we've managed to find ourselves in the middle of a murder investigation,' he continued, ushering her towards his office.

'I heard about it on the news,' Gina replied. 'I must admit, I was half expecting you to cancel.'

'To be honest, if I'd remembered, I probably would have!' he laughed, reaching the door. 'Anyway, we're here now, so we may as well continue.'

'OK!' Tanner began, closing the door behind them. 'So, Miss Gina Booth!'

'It's actually Boothe, with an e,' Gina replied, levering herself down into the seat being offered.

'Oh, right, I see. I wasn't aware there was a difference?'

Gina returned to him a coy smile. 'I must admit, it is subtle. Do you have a copy of my CV?'

'I think so,' Tanner replied, skirting around his desk to plonk himself down into his chair. 'At least, it should be on the system somewhere.'

Waking up his computer to discover his inbox had over a dozen new emails, none of which had been there when he'd last looked, he cursed quietly to himself. About to close the window to start searching for the candidate's CV, another one popped up, this one with the subject, "CCTV Footage from Thurne

Dyke Post Office."

'Could you give me just one minute?' he asked, glancing briefly over. 'There's an email here I need to look at.'

'Of course!' she replied, smiling back.

Opening the attachment, Tanner took a moment to watch a short grainy video of a large man lumbering his way past an aisle piled high with a familiar array of tourist souvenirs. The moment the man looked up at the camera he stopped the footage to stare at the screen. There was no question about it. The person featured was without a doubt the very man they were looking for.

'Sorry about that,' he eventually continued, closing the window. 'Now, where were we?'

'You were looking for my CV.'

'That's right.'

'I have one here, if it helps?' Gina responded, removing a document from her handbag to hold out for him.

'Thank you!' he smiled, taking it from her to begin leafing through. 'You may as well start by telling me a little about yourself.'

'Well, I was born here, in Norfolk,' she began. 'Raised here as well, so I've got a good grasp of the area. Until recently I worked as a PC for the MET and I've just completed my National Investigators Exam.'

'And you have a degree in Law?'

'From Cambridge,' he heard her add, a clear note of pride in her voice.

'We actually have another trainee with a Law degree from Cambridge. Timothy Henderson. Perhaps you know him?' Tanner asked, still studying her CV.

'Er...the name doesn't ring a bell. He might have been in the year above.'

'Actually, now that I think about it, he may have studied at Oxford, *or possibly a slightly less well known university off the coast of Borneo*,' Tanner continued, under his breath.

Glancing up to find Gina staring at him as if he had one more head than he was supposed to, he returned to her an unassuming smile. 'So...' he continued, placing the CV down, 'I suppose the main question is what made you want to join the police? With a Law degree from Oxford...'

'Cambridge,' Gina corrected.

'Sorry, with a Law degree from Cambridge, I'd have thought you could have found yourself a comfortable enough office job working for one of the country's top law firms.'

'I'm not really sure,' she shrugged. 'I suppose I've always had a strong sense of right and wrong. I went to university with the intention of becoming a lawyer, but to be honest, I found the whole subject a little dry. Also, my grandfather works for the MET.'

'Oh, right!' Tanner exclaimed, sitting up. 'Anyone I know?'

'Actually, I believe you do. Matthew Bardsley, or should I say Commander Bardsley?'

'You're Matthew's granddaughter?' Tanner eventually asked, having spent a good moment staring at her with his mouth hanging open.

Gina nodded back with a discreet smile. 'He recommended that I applied for a position here when he heard you'd become the station's DCI. But I was looking to move back to Norfolk anyway. London's OK, but to be honest, I missed the Broads, and I feel it's important that I'm here for a while.'

Tanner raised an inquisitive eyebrow. 'May I be so bold as to ask why?'

'My father hasn't been well recently,' she replied,

shifting awkwardly in her chair.

Tanner paused for a moment. 'I'm sorry to hear that.'

'He had a heart attack out of the blue. At first the doctor said he might not have long to live, so I took a sabbatical. Since then he's had a bypass operation and is making a good recovery, so I'm ready to get back to work, I'm just keen to stay closer to home this time around.'

'Right, well, that makes good sense.'

A knock at the door had Tanner glancing up to see Townsend's face appear.

'Sorry to disturb you, boss,' he began, his eyes flickering briefly at Gina, 'but there's been another report of items being stolen, this time food from a market stall in Potter Heigham. The stall owner again thinks it was Samuel Tunk.'

'Potter Heigham?' Tanner repeated, pushing his chair back to make his way over to the map of the Broads attached to the wall behind where Gina was sitting. 'And where was the post office we were at earlier?'

'Thurne Dyke.'

'And Jason Blackwell's body was found at Acle Dyke,' Tanner continued, placing a finger against the map before stepping back to fold his arms.

'Looks like he's heading north,' suggested Townsend.

'The question is, does he have a particular destination in mind,' Tanner mused, still staring at the map, 'and if so, can we second-guess were he's likely to be next?'

'I think he might be following Weavers' Way,' came the unexpected sound of Gina's voice.

Tanner glanced around to find her looking over his shoulder. 'Sorry, what was that?'

'That he might be following Weavers' Way,' she repeated, her attention focussed on the map, 'which I think would make good sense. Most of it is what's left of the Great Yarmouth to Aylsham railway line that was closed down in the 1950s. These days its only really used by hikers during the holiday season, so it would be a good way for your suspect to navigate from one end of the Broads to the other without being seen.'

'I don't suppose you know roughly where it goes?'

'The route should be marked,' she replied, nudging herself forward to study the map. 'Yes, look, it's here,' she continued, her finger tracing a thin green dotted line. 'It starts at Great Yarmouth, runs over to Acle, then heads up to Hickling, passing Stalham, North Walsham, and Aylsham to end up at Cromer on the north coast.'

'So, if he was here at Thurne Dyke,' said Tanner, stepping forward to join her, 'then at Potter Heigham, I assume he'd now be somewhere up near Hickling Broad?'

'I'd have thought so,' she replied with a sagacious nod, 'but only if he continues to follow the footpath. If he decides to hop on a bus instead, he could be anywhere.'

'It would also depend on if it was Tunk seen stealing food from the market stall,' interjected Townsend.

'Well, it was definitely him at the post office,' said Tanner. 'I've just seen the proof. Was the stall's owner sure it was him?'

'At first he said it was, but when I pushed him on it he said he wasn't sure.'

'I take it they don't have CCTV?'

'I doubt it. The street the market's on might do, though. Do you want me to check?'

'Don't worry. I need to speak to the stall's owner in person anyway. We can find out then.'

A knock at the door had the three of them turning to find Sally staring first at Gina, then Townsend, with an antagonistic glare.

'Yes, Sally?' Tanner asked impatiently, his attention immediately returning to the map.

'I just came in to say that neither Jeremy Blackwell's fingerprints nor his DNA are on the system, or at least I can't find them there.'

'Don't worry, they'll turn up somewhere. They've probably just been miss-filed.'

'I've also asked around the office,' she continued. 'Nobody saw him come in to provide them.'

Sally's insistent tone had Tanner returning to look back at her. 'OK, if he really didn't come in when he said he did, then that's something we'll have to ask him about, but at the moment we've got bigger fish to fry. Our brand new Trainee Detective Constable here has put us onto a new path, one that leads all the way from Great Yarmouth to the top end of Norfolk.'

Gina threw Tanner a look of hopeful expectation. 'Does that mean I've got the job?'

'I'll need to check with your referee, but as he's a family friend, I can't see that being a problem.'

'Oh, right. Great!' she replied, supressing a victorious smile. 'When do you want me to start?'

'To be honest,' Tanner continued, 'I thought you already had!'

- CHAPTER TWENTY NINE -

'I THOUGHT YOU made an excellent choice, offering Gina the job like that,' commented Townsend, as Tanner led him through the main office towards reception.

'I suppose you were impressed with her in-depth knowledge of the Norfolk Broads, and her seemingly natural ability to realise why our prime suspect would be keen to travel by foot along Weavers' Way, as I was?'

'To be honest, I was more impressed by her legs,' Townsend whispered, leaning his head towards Tanner with a conspiratorial grin. 'Did you see them?'

'It may come as an unfathomable surprise to you, Townsend, but I didn't think to look.'

'You mean, you didn't get a chance?'

'I mean, I had other things on my mind, like finding a missing twelve-year-old boy and a psychotic serial killer, for example.'

'Yes, of course. Me too!'

Tanner scowled at him before pushing open the main office doors.

'When we get back,' Townsend began, following behind, 'I don't suppose I'd be able to take a quick look at her CV?'

'There aren't any pictures of her legs on it, if that's what you're after.'

'I was thinking more about her phone number.'

'For Christ's sake, Townsend. Give it a rest, will you?'

'It's not my fault!' he exclaimed. 'It's my hormones. They're completely out of control. I've been this way since I was a teenager.'

'Then I suggest you try to find some way to rein them in. Believe it or not, we've got work to do.'

'I suppose I could have a quick cold shower. That normally does the trick. I would invite you to join me, but it looks like you've got other matters to contend with.'

'Huh?'

'Superintendent Forrester's about to walk in the door, and it looks like he's got his grumpy trousers on.'

'Shit,' cursed Tanner, coming to a halt to see Townsend was right, Forrester could clearly be seen marching towards the glass entrance door wearing a particularly morose expression. About to reverse to slip discreetly out the back, he glanced up again to realise he'd already been spotted.

'Do you think it could be about what you said at the press conference?' Townsend queried, offering him a spurious frown.

Cursing again, Tanner resolved to meet both the situation, and the person, head-on. 'You better wait by my car. Hopefully, I won't be long.'

'And if you are?'

'Then it may be necessary to call an ambulance. Actually, judging by the look on his face, you might want to just skip straight to giving Dr Johnstone a call.'

- CHAPTER THIRTY -

'SUPERINTENDENT FORRESTER!' TANNER exclaimed, biting the bullet by leaping forward to open the door for him. 'What a pleasant surprise!'

'Don't give me that bullshit,' came his superior's less than affable response. 'I've spent the entire fucking day stuck in the most tediously dull meeting imaginable only to discover that you'd given a press conference advising the entire population of Norfolk to board up their windows, just in case a recently released homicidal maniac breaks in to stab them all to death whilst watching Teletubbies with their children.'

'Er...that's not *exactly* what I said.'

'It was close enough, Tanner!' Forrester replied, grabbing hold of Tanner's elbow to steer him outside. 'What the hell were you thinking?'

'Not a huge amount.'

'No kidding!'

'I simply decided to tell the press what they were probably going to write anyway.'

'Then you're just going to have to hold another one to let them know you were joking.'

'Well, I could, of course, but I'm not sure they'd believe me. Besides, with any luck, we'll have the man in question back behind bars before we'd be able to agree a time.'

Forrester opened his mouth to continue berating Tanner before appearing to change his mind by closing it again. 'Is that true?'

'What I said to the press, or what I just told you about Samuel Tunk?'

'For once in your life, can you please give me a straight answer?'

Tanner glanced over the car park to see a photographer busily taking photographs of them. Suppressing the urge to wave, he turned back to face his superior. 'We believe Samuel Tunk has been able to go largely unseen by keeping himself to a little used footpath called Weavers' Way. So far we've had at least one, possibly two sightings of him shoplifting food. The first was at Thurne Dyke, where he was caught on CCTV. The other was about twenty minutes ago, from a market stall owner in Potter Heigham. I was heading over to have a chat with him before I saw you. If that turns out to have been Samuel Tunk as well, and he's still following the same footpath, we're going to know pretty much where he's going to be, and when he's going to be there.'

'Do you have enough to arrest him?'

'To arrest him, yes.'

'But not to charge him?'

'We've yet to find any physical evidence to place him at the murder scene, but we have at least found a motive. The mother of the family Tunk was convicted of both raping and murdering was none other than Jason Blackwell's older sister.'

'Christ! I'd no idea!'

'There's no reason for you to have known. Throughout the trial, she was only referred to by her married name, Sarah Jackson.'

'OK, but that still doesn't give Tunk a motive to set about murdering the rest of his family.'

'After the trial, Jason began visiting him in prison. Every week, apparently.'

'Please, God, tell me you're joking?'

'Unfortunately not.'

'What the hell did he do that for?'

'His father is of the opinion that it was to help him come to terms with what happened to his sister. I can't imagine what he would have said to him, but whatever it was, it couldn't have been good.'

'You think it could have been enough to make Tunk want to track him down and murder him the moment he was released?'

'Taunting, maybe even threatening the life of a convicted psychopath, one who hasn't a single thing to do with his time other than to plan a suitable end for his tormentor. Frankly, yes, I do.'

'What about the boy?'

Tanner looked away. 'I think the chances of finding him alive are becoming less likely by the hour.'

The two men parted briefly to allow a uniformed policewoman to enter the building, saluting them both as she did.

'OK,' Forrester continued, the moment she'd gone, 'so, what's the plan?'

'As I said, I'm on my way to see this market stall owner. If I'm able to confirm that it was Samuel Tunk he saw, I'll be giving the order for everyone to stop what they're doing to begin searching the area in question.'

'You don't think it's worth doing that now?'

'Not until we know it was him. I simply don't have the manpower to risk sending everyone out if it isn't.'

- CHAPTER THIRTY ONE -

REACHING THE MARKET in Potter Heigham to find most of the stall owners packing up for the day, Tanner left his XJS parked on the pavement to begin diving from one stall to the next, asking if anyone knew the person who'd called the police. Eventually being pointed in the direction of a large burly man he could see throwing a long wooden table into the back of a van as if it weighed no more than a bag of flour, he ran up to call out his name. 'Excuse me, Mr Jacobs?'

Seeing him turn to glare around, Tanner came jogging to a halt. 'It is Mr Jacobs, isn't it?'

'What's it to you?' the man replied, lifting his chin with a suspicious eye.

'DCI Tanner, Norfolk Police,' Tanner replied, pulling out his ID. 'It's about the call you made earlier. You said you saw someone stealing food from your stall, and that you thought it was the person we're looking for, Samuel Tunk?'

'Yes, and...?'

'I just need to know if you think it was definitely him?'

'Let me guess, you don't believe me.'

'Not at all. We just need to be sure, that's all.'

'Well, the guy was bigger than me, and to be 'onest, it's not often I see anyone who is.'

'Did you see his face?'

'No, but as I said...'

'What about what he was wearing?'

'Just a black coat, I think.'

'I don't suppose it could have been a purple hoodie, by any chance?'

The stall owner shook his head. 'I'd 'ave noticed if it was, but it did have a hood.'

'Was it on or off?'

'On.'

'So, all you really saw was someone wearing a dark coat with the hood pulled over his head?'

'As I said, he was bigger than me. I can't imagine who else it could've been.'

'What are you, six-foot?'

'Six-two, more like.'

'And there's nobody else in Norfolk who's taller than that?'

'Listen, mate, I didn't say he was taller than me, just bigger!'

Tanner turned his head to roll his eyes with mounting frustration. 'I don't suppose you know if there are any CCTV cameras around here?' he continued, glancing up at the surrounding buildings.

'What, in Potter Heigham?' the man laughed.

'Did you at least see which way he went?'

'Down that way,' Jacobs replied, pointing to a footpath disappearing into a nearby clump of trees. 'If you find 'im, tell 'im I'd like my carrots back. They don't grow on trees, you know.'

'They don't?'

'No, mate, they grow in the fuck'n ground!'

Leaving the man howling at his own joke, Tanner ambled wearily over to where the path disappeared into the treeline, at the edge of which was a wooden signpost.

'Weavers' Way,' he read, stopping where he was to

stare into the shadows beyond.

As he continued to look, the clatter of a bicycle had him stepping cautiously back to see a breathless woman come charging out, her skin as white as a sheet.

Breaking free of the trees, she skidded to a halt to stare back at the path.

'Are you OK?' Tanner asked, endeavouring to catch her eye.

'I j-just saw him,' he heard the woman stutter, her body shaking as her mouth gasped desperately at the air.

'You just saw who?'

He watched her turn to stare round at him, her eyes as wide as discs. 'That man who was on the news, the one who murdered all those people. He's just back there!'

'Are you sure?' Tanner demanded, searching the woman's face.

'What?'

'Are you sure it was him?' Tanner repeated, urgency rising in his voice.

'No question! No question at all! I was nearly stupid enough to ride straight into him!'

- CHAPTER THIRTY TWO -

IT WASN'T UNTIL nearly twelve o'clock at night when Tanner finally arrived home to hear Christine's welcoming voice, singing out to him from the back of the house.

Entering the main living area to find her curled up in the corner of their L-shaped sofa, a book in one hand and a steaming drink in the other, he sent her a resilient smile. 'You didn't need to wait up.'

'I couldn't go to bed, not when I knew who you were out looking for.'

Tanner peeled off his coat to make his way over to the kitchen. 'Well, don't worry, we didn't find him.'

'I thought you said you were nearly runover by a cyclist who herself had almost ridden straight into him?'

'Yes, well, that's what she said,' Tanner replied, washing his hands in the sink, 'but despite immediately closing off the entire area to bring down every man, woman, and police dog to look for him, we didn't find a single trace. So, either she was seeing things that simply weren't there, or our elusive Samuel Tunk was able to teach himself some remarkably effective disappearing tricks during his ten years in prison.'

Drying his hands he glanced at the fridge. 'I don't suppose there's anything to eat?'

'Your dinner's in the oven. I can heat it up for you,

if you like?'

'Thanks, but I'm peckish more than anything.'

'I can make you a sandwich?'

'It's OK,' Tanner replied, pulling a plate out from a cupboard with peevish agitation. 'I think I can manage.'

Christine put down her book to push herself up. 'Here, let me do it for you.'

'I know this may come as a shock to you, but believe it or not, I do have the ability to make myself a fucking sandwich,' came Tanner's antagonistic response.

As an unwelcome silence crept its way over the room, he cursed angrily at himself to tug open the fridge. 'Sorry,' he eventually said, rubbing at his eyes. 'It's been a long day.'

Feeling Christine's hand rest gently on his shoulder, he let her nudge him gently out of the way.

'Ham and cheese?' came her soothing voice.

'That would be nice, thank you.'

'I left the rum out for you on the breakfast bar. There's a glass there as well.'

Turning to see them standing alongside each other, he found himself smiling with benevolent gratitude. 'So, it's true. You really do love me.'

'You know I do,' came her purring response.

By the time he'd managed to pour himself a drink, a perfectly prepared sandwich had already appeared before him.

'Bread, butter, ham, cheese,' Christine announced. 'Nothing more, nothing less.'

'Looks good!' he replied, downing the rum.

'How was the rest of your day?'

'You know, it's been so long since it started, I'm not sure I can remember.'

'I saw you on TV, talking to the press.'

'Uh-huh,' he replied, picking up one half of the sandwich to take a generous bite.

'I must admit,' she continued, 'I was a little surprised by what you said: telling everyone that there was a crazed homicidal maniac on the loose.'

'Don't worry, you weren't the only one.'

'You shouldn't let the press get to you like that.'

'Was it that obvious?'

He glanced up from the plate to see Christine nod back in response.

'Well, don't worry, I'll let Cooper do it next time.'

'Not seriously?'

Tanner half-smiled at her before electing to change the subject. 'Did I tell you that I held my very first interview today?'

'Not that I remember.'

'She's another Cambridge graduate, like Henderson, just more attractive. Hopefully, more intelligent as well.'

'I thought you said Henderson went to Oxford?'

Tanner shrugged with indifference. 'To be honest, I'm rarely able to remember which one is which.'

'Was she any good?'

'Well, she was born and bred right here in sunny Norfolk, which has already proven useful. More to the point, she's immediately available.'

'I bet that set the cat among the pigeons.'

'Am I the only person on the planet who thinks the phrase "immediately available" refers to someone's ability to start a job without having to give notice to an existing employer?'

'I think you must be.'

'Anyway, you're right of course. Townsend could barely keep his eyes off her. Neither could Sally, for that matter, although I suspect for different reasons.'

'And you?' Christine queried, folding her arms.

'Oh, I'm far too old for that sort of thing. Besides, I don't have the candidate's immediate availability.'

'Not at the moment, but that could easily change, especially if you're unable to start coming home a little earlier than ten minutes before midnight.'

'Don't worry. Once Samuel Tunk is back where he should be, I'll be making the executive decision to be home by five.'

'You mean, until the next body is discovered, wrapped around some poor boat owner's propeller.'

'That's not going to happen.'

'Oh, really! How come?'

'Because, next time I'll delegate the work out, leaving me behind my desk, preferably with my feet resting on top of it.'

'We'll see,' she laughed, taking the now empty plate to place inside the dishwasher. 'I don't suppose there's been any sign of the missing boy?'

Tanner shook his head. 'Every call we get seems to lead back to Tunk.'

'Do you think that means...?'

Tanner glanced up to find her gazing at him with a look of motherly concern. 'The longer he remains missing, without a single person calling in to say that they've seen him, I'm afraid the more likely that scenario becomes.'

- CHAPTER THIRTY THREE -

NIGEL JACOBS COULD finally feel himself drifting off to sleep when he heard the yelling start all over again.

'You must be fucking joking,' he cursed quietly to himself, turning onto his back to stare up at the hire boat's white plastic ceiling. 'What the hell are they going on about this time?'

Lifting his heavy bulbous head off the bed, he stared over at his wife lying next to him, her long dark hair spilling over her pillow like a greasy black oil slick. When he realised she was snoring, he rolled his eyes. 'How can you possibly sleep through this?' he asked her out loud, half-hoping his question would jolt her awake.

It didn't.

Curious to know if he could hear what the family on board the boat next to theirs were arguing about this time, he lowered his head back down. From what he could make out, it was a continuation of what they'd been screaming at each other about since they'd arrived; how the husband didn't lift a finger to help out with the children whilst the wife, apparently, did nothing all day but message her friends. It was when he heard their two children start bawling their eyes out did he push himself up to fumble around for his phone.

'For fuck's sake,' he cursed, staring down at the

screen where the illuminated time seemed to be mocking him. It had only just gone midnight. They'd gone to bed before eleven, meaning it had taken him over an hour to get to sleep, only to be woken the moment he had.

Rubbing his eyes, he glared down at his wife's head again. She'd always had the insanely annoying ability to fall asleep the moment her head touched the pillow, leaving him staring up at whatever ceiling he happened to be lying under at the time, miserably cursing the day she was born. Even more irritating was the fact that once she had drifted off, it would be virtually impossible to wake her up, whereas with him, the slightest noise would have him lying awake for hours on end, as would no doubt be the case now, the only difference being that whatever was going on next door was far from a slight noise.

With his phone resting idly in his small chubby hand, he checked to see if he'd had any social media notifications. With nothing new since the last time he'd looked, he was about to throw back the duvet to search the hire boat's rudimentary kitchen for something to eat when he heard the argument begin to abate.

After a few moments, the only sound was the mesmerizing noise of the river, lapping gently against the boat's cheap fiberglass hull. Even his wife had stopped snoring.

Breathing deeply, he lowered himself down until his head sank slowly into his pillow. With his phone back behind his head, he drew in another breath before closing his eyes. And there he lay, his mind waiting to find the spiralling corridor that would lead him down into a deep, untroubled sleep.

A woman's scream cut the night's air like a sharpened axe, disappearing a second later to leave nothing but the sound of his heart thumping hard inside his chest.

With his eyes wide open again, he remained completely still, tuning his ears for the slightest of sounds. The scream had definitely come from the boat next door, but now there was nothing but the noise of the gently lapping river.

'Did you hear that?' he eventually asked, tilting his head to look at his wife. 'Seriously?' he questioned, realising she was still sound asleep. 'How could anyone sleep through that?'

With the only response being her rasping breath, he shook his head from side to side. 'And the Olympic gold medal for the person who can sleep through absolutely bloody anything goes to my wife. Congratulations! All those years spent stuffing your face in front of the TV has finally paid off.'

Heaving his vast weight up onto his elbow, he took a moment to listen again, but there was still nothing but the sound of his heart beating and the water lapping.

I didn't dream that, did I? he soon began to question, turning his head in the direction of the boat moored up next to theirs.

Closing his eyes, he listened again. It was only then that he heard the muffled, almost indiscernible sound of what he instinctively knew to be someone sobbing. Then came the snap of the boat next door, snagging up against its mooring lines like a horse pulling impatiently at its reins.

'What the hell is going on over there?' the question directed down to his still sleeping wife.

Looking away, he took a moment to think what to do. Should he call the police, telling them that he'd just heard a terrifying scream? Obviously not. The last time he'd bothered to call them was in the middle of the night some two years before, when his neighbours were playing music so loud that the contents of his fridge were able to keep time. In that instance he was told that it wasn't their problem, and that he needed to contact the council, as if someone would have been there to answer the phones at one o'clock in the morning. No doubt the police would say something similar now.

Knowing he'd never be able to get back to sleep, not in a million years, he threw off his half of the duvet to climb out of bed as quietly as possible, not so much to prevent disturbing his wife, but more to keep his presence a secret from anyone who may have been lurking outside.

Tugging on some clothes, he spent a few moments scrabbling around for a torch before picking his way to the exit at the back end of their boat. There, he slid the hatchway open as quietly as its rusty hinges would allow to poke his head out into the night's cold damp air.

With the torch switched on, he cast its beam over the long narrow roof of their boat to the larger one moored upriver from theirs. He then traversed the beam onto the grassy bank, over to the surrounding trees, then to the deserted river slipping silently past like sickly sweet treacle.

With neither sight nor sound of a single soul, he lifted himself out to begin creeping carefully along the narrow walkway.

Reaching the bow, he stopped to focus the beam on his neighbour's boat. As far as he could see there wasn't a single light on. The only sign that there might have been someone on board was that the hatchway at the back was open.

'Hello?' he called quietly out, his voice jarring against the night's unsettling hollow silence. 'Is anyone there?'

There was no response.

Unsure what to do next, he swung the torch back to the trees, then to the boat. Still unable to either see or hear anyone he clambered over the railings, stepping gently down to the slippery grass bank below.

Waiting in earnest for the boat to finish rocking, he inched his way towards the neighbouring one ahead. The moment he came alongside it, he used his torch to try and peer through its rectangular aluminium-framed windows, but with the curtains tightly closed, he was unable to see so much as a glimpse of anything inside.

'Hello?' he called once more. 'Is anyone on board?'

With still no response, he returned to the boat's aft end to try and look through the open hatch. Unable to see any further than its shadow-filled stairwell, he took a furtive glance behind him before placing a tentative foot onto its side to heave himself up. As the boat lurched suddenly towards him, he climbed quickly into the cockpit to be met by a stark metallic clicking sound, drifting up from somewhere inside.

Crouching immediately down, he aimed his torch's beam through the open hatchway. There was nobody there. Just a half-open door, swinging silently on its hinges as the boat continued to rock gently to and fro.

Breathing hard, he considered calling out again, but there was something about the silence that held his mouth closed.

With the torch's beam focussed directly ahead, he inched his way through the open hatchway to descend slowly down the companionway steps. The moment he reached the floor below, he brought the torch to bear on the still half-open door. Holding his breath, he nudged it open with his foot.

It was just an empty toilet.

Letting out a relieved sigh, it was then that something occurred to him. What if everyone on board was simply asleep, and he was now creeping around their boat like some sort of deranged pervert? After all, the only reason he'd thought to leave the comfort of his bed was because he'd heard a scream, or at least he thought he had. But what if it hadn't been a scream, at least not a human one? What if it had been a fox instead, or the mating call of some weird nocturnal animal he'd never heard before?

With a sickening sense of shameful dread, he jolted his head around, half-expecting to see some pyjama-clad eight-year-old boy, staring curiously up at him whilst waiting desperately to go to the loo. With no such child there, he turned the torch off to begin re-tracing his steps back the way he'd come, his body flinching every time the flooring creaked under his vast cumbersome weight.

As he placed his foot onto the first of the companionway steps, he took hold of the handrail when he saw another door ahead, one that was slowly beginning to swing silently closed. Realising his body's weight on the step was pulling the boat over, just enough to start closing the door, he stepped quickly down. As the door swung back the other way to clunk loudly against something solid behind it, he screwed up his eyes to curse silently to himself.

Hearing nothing to indicate that someone had been woken up, he drew in a breath. It was then that he reached the conclusion that his best bet was to simply get off the boat as quickly as possible, even if that did mean waking everyone up in the process. As long as he was back on board his own boat before anyone saw him, he'd be in the clear.

About to execute his plan of retreat, something

caught his eye. It was the lower half of a woman's leg, lying on a bed in the cabin ahead. Assuming it must have belonged to the woman he'd seen when the family had moored up, he recalled the moment he'd been ogling her slim curvaceous body when she'd been helping to secure their boat to the bank. The thought of her lying on the bed, possibly naked, just behind the already half-open door he was standing in front of had his mind reeling with a string of lurid lascivious thoughts.

Remaining completely still, he listened again, all the while debating whether or not he should risk nudging the door open a little more to discover just how much of her he'd be able to see. He knew such a voyeuristic opportunity would be unlikely to present itself to him ever again. With that at the forefront of his mind, he steadied himself to begin manoeuvring his vast physical mass around the companionway steps.

With his fingers resting on the surface of the door, he nudged it gently away to lean his head over to one side. When he saw the woman's slightly parted unblemished thighs, he pushed it open a fraction more to find himself gulping involuntarily at the smooth pale curves of her fully exposed buttocks.

As a surge of raw animalistic passion began swelling between his legs, he felt his thumb click the torch back on.

Leaving its imposing beam aimed at the floor, his free hand began clawing its way between his bloated fat stomach and the elasticated waistband of his already bulging tracksuit bottoms. Only when he'd taken hold of himself did he ever-so slowly bring the torch to bear on the part of her body he'd become so desperate to see, and only then did he stumble back in terror, the torch clattering against the floor as the boat returned to its former state of all-consuming blackness.

- CHAPTER THIRTY FOUR -

SALUTED BY A uniformed police officer, a fluorescent yellow jacket zipped up to his nose, Tanner offered him only the briefest of nods before trundling his XJS slowly past. As he came rolling to a halt behind a police forensics van, he screwed up his eyes as an exhausted numbing sensation buzzed its way through the core of his brain. With his mind desperate for sleep, and his body craving for the bed he'd been tucked-up in just half an hour before, he blinked his eyes open to stare blankly at the square plastic analogue clock illuminated on the Jag's varnished wooden dashboard. It took him a full moment to work out which was the long hand and which was the short, and that the time was indeed half-past one in the morning.

Stepping slowly out to find himself surrounded by whirring blue lights and distant indiscernible chatter, he took a moment to rub the palm of his hand against his forehead in what proved to be a forlorn bid to wake himself up.

Once he'd managed to orientate himself towards the sound of voices, he began trudging past an eclectic mix of emergency vehicles, each parked awkwardly over the damp uneven grass, to eventually walk straight into a beam of light being pointed directly into his face.

'Turn that fucking thing off!' he snapped, lifting a hand to try and see which idiot was pointing it at him.

'Sorry, boss,' came young Townsend's voice. 'I saw you pull up, so I thought I'd come and find you.'

'OK, well, thank you, but I've got no idea why you thought I could have been lost. I mean, the place is lit up like a bloody Christmas tree. I'd have to have been blind not to have found my way, which I may well be now, thanks to that bloody torch of yours.'

Townsend responded by turning it off, leaving them standing in the inky black shadow cast by the ambulance they were standing next to.

'Now I can't see a bloody thing!' Tanner continued.

'Which was why I brought the torch, boss.'

'Then I suppose you'd better turn it back on again, hadn't you!'

Doing what he was told, Townsend proceeded to lead the way towards where two white boats could be seen, nestled beside each other against a secluded grassy bank.

'The bodies were found inside the nearest,' Townsend commented, stopping to lift up a line of Police Do Not Cross tape for Tanner to duck under. 'A man and a woman.'

'Have you been on board?'

Townsend shook his head. 'Forensics beat me to it.'

'What about Dr Johnstone?'

'His car's here, so I assume he is.'

'Is anyone else on site?'

'Vicky's over there,' he pointed, 'talking to the guy who found them. I think Cooper's still on his way.'

'And the new boy, Henderson?'

'I haven't seen him, but if he's barely able to get into work on time, I can't see how he'd make it to a near-deserted stretch of water at such an early hour.'

Tanner cast his eyes briefly over at Vicky, then at the river running silently past. 'I suppose I'd better take a look on board. If you could see to having this tape extended to include both boats? Then tell Vicky to make sure our witness doesn't decide to motor away before I've had a chance to have a word.'

- CHAPTER THIRTY FIVE -

SEARCHING HIS POCKETS for some disposable gloves, Tanner stepped lightly over the all too familiar aluminium platforms to heave himself up into the boat's spacious cockpit. There, he hooked a pair of plastic covers over his shoes before descending the companionway steps.

With the back of Dr Johnstone's head looming into view, he squeezed past a forensics officer to navigate himself through to the cabin at the back.

'Good evening Chief Inspector,' he heard Johnstone say, in his normal upbeat tone, 'or should I say good morning. At this hour, it's always a little difficult to know which one is which.'

'What've we got?' Tanner replied, too tired for the normal pleasantries.

'Not much room for a start. Barely enough to swing a cat.'

'Surprisingly, I was referring to the couple lying on the bed, being that neither are moving and they're both covered in a disproportionate amount of blood.'

The flash from a forensics officer's camera had Tanner blinking his eyes into an irritated scowl.

'Looks like someone got out of bed on the wrong side,' Johnstone responded, taking a moment to study Tanner's face.

'When you're forced to get up at one o'clock in the morning to find yourself staring at two dead bodies, whilst some over-enthusiastic police forensics officer goes around gleefully taking pictures of them, I'm fairly sure a right side doesn't exist.'

'Yes, well, fair enough,' Johnstone replied, signalling the forensics officer under discussion to give them a minute. 'Anyway, as you can see, it's a man and a woman, I'd say both in their mid to late thirties, probably killed by a knife, certainly attacked by one. The man has a series of stab wounds to the chest, the woman to the front and sides of her neck, which would appear to have opened the carotid artery, exterior jugular vein, and the trachea, otherwise known as the windpipe. Unfortunately for her,' he continued, leaning his head forward with a curious frown, 'I suspect she died from asphyxiation before having the chance to pass out through loss of blood.'

'Because her windpipe was severed?' Tanner questioned, trying not to look at the gaping wounds beneath her blood-covered jaw.

'More likely from the contents of her body's blood supply being pumped down into her lungs,' Johnstone speculated, his head hovering over her attractive ashen grey face. 'If you look closely, you can see the acute angle at which the jugular vein was cut.'

'I'd rather not, if it's all the same to you.'

'Anyway, what is clear that they were both killed, and not by each other I may add.'

'Was it the same person as before?'

Johnstone took a contemplative moment to push his glasses up the ridge of his nose. 'I'll be able to give you a better idea when I get them back to the lab, but from what I've seen so far, the shallow depth of the stab wounds – at least the majority of them – would suggest that it most likely was.'

Tanner took an irritated moment to stare over at

him. 'You're not still trying to convince me it was a woman, are you?'

'I seem to remember my previous report suggesting that the stab wounds could have been caused by someone who was perhaps weaker than your average man, leading naturally to the possibility that it could therefore have been a woman. I certainly didn't say it was.'

'Either way,' Tanner replied, digging his fingers into the corners of his eyes, 'it doesn't help. Not when our prime suspect is a six-foot-two ex-pro wrestler who by all accounts has lost nothing of his physical stature, despite having spent the last ten years in solitary confinement. It certainly won't when either yourself or one of your colleagues is in the dock being cross-examined by the defence attorney, questioning how it was possible that Samuel Tunk could have been responsible when he could probably crush a man's skull between his hands without breaking into a sweat.'

'Are you suggesting that I alter my report in order to accommodate the findings of your investigation?'

'No, of course not!' came Tanner's terse response.

'If it's any help, I'd say that it was a less frenzied attack than the last one. It doesn't look like anything's been taken either, at least nothing obvious.'

'Do we at least know who they are?'

Slipping his tablet out from under his arm, the medical examiner began swiping at the screen. 'David and Lisa Rutherford. Their home address is in Ipswich. But that's only based on identification found on their driving licences.'

'Do the photos match?' Tanner continued, tugging out his notebook.

'As far as I can tell.'

'And time of death?'

'I'd say between one to three hours ago. As always, I'll be able to give you a more accurate idea when I get them back to the lab.'

- CHAPTER THIRTY SIX -

BARGING HIS WAY past yet another overall-clad forensics officer, Tanner could feel his brain becoming increasingly numb as he clawed his way up the short companionway steps.

As he emerged into the night's cold uninviting air, he stopped to stare down at the river, unable to do anything but replay what Johnstone had said; that whoever had murdered both sets of victims was unlikely to have been the man who had been, up until then at least, their prime suspect.

Endeavouring to recall the faces of the two women he'd so far spoken to during the course of the investigation, and what possible motive either one of them could have had for murdering the couple lying dead beneath his feet, he caught sight of Vicky, picking her way over the raised platforms towards him.

'Are you done with the witness?' he asked, catching her eye.

'Uh-huh,' she nodded, coming to a halt beside the boat's gently undulating side.

'Anything?'

'Only that it looks likely that we're going to find his fingerprints plastered all over the crime scene. There's a forensic technician with him now.'

'Anything about who may have killed them?'

'He didn't see anyone near the boat. All he heard

was a scream, which is why he climbed on board to investigate, or at least that's what he said.'

'I assume he's still here?'

'He's being treated for shock. His wife as well, but only because she woke up to find herself surrounded by paramedics poking at her to see if she was still alive. Apparently, she slept through the whole thing.'

'Lucky her,' Tanner lamented.

'You'll find him on board his boat, if you want to have a word.'

'I suppose I'd better. Any sign of either Townsend or Cooper?'

'Not yet, but the new boy is here.'

'Really?'

'He's over there, on the other side of the tape. The one staring blankly at the ground with his hands in his pockets.'

'I see him,' Tanner replied, shaking his head.

'Do you want me to get him to do anything?'

'Not really.'

'How about me?'

Tanner glanced absently about, as if he'd lost something he knew was important but had forgotten what it was. 'How many suspects do we currently have who are women?'

'Apart from the first victim's wife, Abigail Blackwell, I wasn't aware we had any.'

'Me neither. Johnstone seems to be under the impression that we should, though.'

'The stab wounds again?'

'He just informed me that they have the same characteristics as that of the previous victims,' Tanner nodded, 'being that the majority would appear to be shallow in depth.'

As if to ask a question, Vicky opened her mouth, only to close it again to look slowly away.

'Which leaves us with a problem,' Tanner continued.

'If it isn't Tunk, then who is it?' she responded, her gaze drifting back to the boat.

'According to Johnstone, either a weaker than average man or someone who isn't, hence the question about female suspects, preferably one who has a substantial enough motive for needing to kill both the eldest heir to the Blackwell estate, the woman he just happened to be sleeping with at the time, and now a seemingly random couple staying on board what to me looks like your larger-than-average Norfolk Broads cruiser.'

'Maybe they're not just some random couple?'

'Which is why I was looking for the others. If they ever do show up, I want one of you to run a search for a David and Lisa Rutherford, both living in Ipswich. We specifically need to know if there's any connection – any at all – to either Jason Blackwell, the girl he was found lying in bed with, or any of the other members of the Blackwell family.'

'Including Jason's wife?' Vicky replied, supressing a yawn with the back of her hand as she removed her notebook to make a quick note of the victims' names.

'Especially Jason's wife!' Tanner exclaimed, 'not to mention the woman who was his official girlfriend, the one who turned up at the scene carrying a suitcase. What was her name again?'

Tanner waited patiently for Vicky to leaf back through the pages of her notebook.

'Julia Ward,' came her eventual response.

'That's the one. If either of them has even the vaguest connection to what's left of the couple down there,' he continued, pointing at the hatchway with his chin, 'then I suggest we pull them in for immediate questioning.'

Catching Vicky stealing a look at her watch, he paused to blink down at his own. 'Jesus Christ! It's nearly two o'clock!'

'I can head back to the office to start now, if you like?' he heard Vicky offer, but by the drawn-out tone of her voice, it was fairly obvious what she was really asking.

'That's kind of you, but I think it would make more sense to head home. You can make a start in the morning.'

'How about you?' she asked, tucking her notebook away with renewed vigour.

Tanner looked up at the line of emergency vehicles, then over at the other boat. 'I need to have a chat to the witness first. Anyway, if you could tell donkey-boy over there to go home, Townsend and Cooper as well – if you see them – I'll no doubt see you bright and early in the morning.'

- CHAPTER THIRTY SEVEN -

DESPERATE TO GO home himself, Tanner reached the other boat only to find the cockpit empty and the hatchway closed.

Hoping the occupants hadn't already gone back to bed, he knocked gingerly on the boat's grubby plastic side to call out in a loud whisper, 'Hello? Is anyone home?'

With no immediate response, he was beginning to think they had when his voice was eventually met by the fiberglass hatchway sliding open to reveal the reddish face of an overweight middle-aged man, puffing and panting as if he'd just completed a marathon.

'DCI Tanner, Norfolk Police,' Tanner announced, holding up his formal ID.

Tanner watched as the man's entire face seemed to visibly sag.

'I thought you lot were done with me,' he eventually said.

'I'd just like to quickly go over what you saw, if that's OK?'

'What – again?'

'It won't take long,' Tanner replied, forcing a smile at him to replace his ID with his notebook.

'Yes, of course. Sorry. Do you need to come in?'

'I'm fine here, thank you. I take it your name is Nigel Jacobs?'

'That's correct.'

'And that you heard a woman scream?'

'Uh-huh.'

'May I ask what time that was?'

Jacobs let out an impatient sigh. 'I've already told this to at least two of your colleagues.'

With his pen poised over his notebook, Tanner lifted his eyes to meet the man's already wavering glare.

'About twelve o'clock,' Jacobs eventually continued.

'At which point you decided to sneak on board to take a look?' Tanner asked, beginning to wonder if everyone in Norfolk thought it was OK to hang out on board other people's boats without gaining the owner's permission beforehand.

'I did call out first!' he exclaimed. 'I looked through the windows as well, at least I tried to, but I couldn't see much. The curtains were all closed.'

'But you still went inside, even though there was no evidence that anyone was actually on board.'

'I just said, I heard a woman scream.'

'So you decided to climb out of bed to tiptoe over, and when you saw that there was nobody on board you thought you'd take a look inside anyway?'

'That's not what I said!'

Tanner raised a questioning eyebrow at him before returning his attention back to his notebook. 'Well, that's what my notes say.'

'You're making it sound like I'm some sort of Peeping Tom.'

Tanner continued making notes.

'What are you writing now?' Jacobs demanded, craning his neck in an effort to see.

'What you said: that you're some sort of Peeping Tom.'

Jacob's stood bolt upright to lock his arms over his wide flabby chest. 'I'd like to speak to your superior officer, please.'

'I *am* the superior officer,' Tanner growled, lifting his head with a callous smile.

'I went on board because it sounded like someone had just been murdered, and as it turned out, I was right!'

'Fortunately for you, else you'd be facing a charge of unlawful entry.'

'Next you'll be accusing me of murdering them.'

'Did you?'

'I didn't even know them!'

'Sorry, was that a yes or a no?'

'It was a no, obviously!'

'Did you touch anything whilst you were having a little rummage around? One of the bodies, perhaps?'

'No!'

'Are you sure about that? Our forensics team will know if you did.'

'I didn't!'

Tanner took a breath to quietly return to his notes.

'I sincerely hope you're not writing down that I just confessed to murdering them?'

'Did you see anyone near the boat, apart from yourself, of course?' Tanner continued.

'Nobody.'

'Did you hear anyone?'

'Not a soul.'

'What about earlier?'

'All I've heard all day was them constantly shouting at each other. They'd just started up again when I heard the woman scream. Are you sure it wasn't her husband who killed her?'

'Before stabbing himself multiple times in the chest?' Tanner replied, with belligerent sarcasm.

'How was I to know that?'

'Sorry, I thought you said you found them?'

'I did, but...'

'But you were too busy staring at the dead woman's naked body to notice?'

Jacob's face darkened with blood.

Tanner shook his head. 'Anyway, can you tell me anything else, anything at all that you think might help?'

'Only what I told you; that they were constantly shouting at each other.'

'Did you hear what they were arguing about?'

'Not clearly. I was more worried about their children than trying to hear what they were saying. God knows what it must have been like growing up with that going on all the time.'

Tanner stopped where he was to stare at the man. 'What did you say?'

Jacobs gave him a curious look. 'That I couldn't hear what they were saying. Not clearly, at least.'

'You said they had children.'

'Yes, of course. Sorry. Two girls aged five or six. I must admit, up until now, I'd somehow managed to completely forget about them.'

- CHAPTER THIRTY EIGHT -

Wednesday, 27th April

WAKING WITH A start to find Vicky glaring at him from the other side of his desk, it took Tanner a full second to realise where he was.

'Don't you have a home to go to?' he heard her ask, lifting his stubble covered chin off his chest to gaze slowly around his office.

'I – I must have fallen asleep,' he eventually croaked, his tongue sticking to the inside of his mouth like flypaper.

'I take it you didn't know that Christine's been trying to contact you?'

'Christine?' he queried, staring wildly about for his phone, only for a jarring pain in his neck to bring his head grinding to a halt. 'How do you know?'

'Because she called me at seven-thirty this morning, asking if I'd seen you.'

'Oh – right,' Tanner muttered, seeing his phone next to a half-empty bottle of rum. 'I didn't know she had your number,' he continued, shifting himself forward to surreptitiously slide the bottle off the desk to drop down into its deepest drawer.

'We're members of the same WhatsApp group. The one called Why Men Are So Useless That They Can't Even Be Bothered To Call Their Pregnant Girlfriends

To Let Them Know Where They Are.'

'Don't tell me you're pregnant as well?'

'So despite having barely had a wink of sleep myself,' Vicky continued, ignoring his glib remark, 'I came in early to see if you were here.'

Tanner rubbed at the temples of his now throbbing head as he remembered what he'd discovered that had forced him back to the office.

'The couple we found last night,' he began, pushing himself up to drag himself over to his coffee machine.

'What about them?'

'They had children. Two girls, aged five or six.'

Vicky fell into a stunned silence. 'How did you find out?' she eventually asked.

'The guy who found the bodies.'

'But – why didn't he tell me?'

'I've no idea. Johnston and the forensic technicians helped me search the boat and the surrounding area. The ambulance crew lent a hand as well.'

'I take it you didn't find them?'

Tanner shook his head. 'I came back here to fill out a missing persons' report, then to scrawl out a quick press release. I must have fallen asleep before I finished.'

The office fell silent as Tanner got up to begin clattering about with his coffee machine.

'You should have told me,' came Vicky's eventual response. 'I'd have come back to help.'

'I didn't see any point. It was obvious what had happened. They'd been taken, just like the Blackwell boy, leaving us with four bodies, three missing children, and not a single solitary idea as to who's responsible.'

Unable to look Vicky in the eye, Tanner's head fell

forward in despondent futility. 'I should never have taken this job,' he eventually muttered. 'I'm clearly not fit for purpose, not when my idea of handling a crisis is to hide inside my office to spend the night getting blind fucking drunk.'

'Come on, John! It's hardly your fault!'

'The uncontrollable drinking, or the inability to find the missing children?'

The sound of voices had him glancing through the partition window to see Townsend and Sally, pushing through the doors to the main office.

'For a start,' Vicky continued, following his gaze, 'it was my fault for not having found out myself, being that it was a blindingly obvious question to have asked.'

'Don't worry. I didn't think to ask either. He only mentioned them as a side-note.'

Seeing more staff members begin traipsing their way up the office thoroughfare, Tanner took a quiet moment to finish making his coffee. 'Anyway,' he eventually continued, 'the children *are* missing, and it's my job to find them.'

'Do we know that for a fact?'

'Do we know *what* for a fact?'

'That they're missing? Isn't it possible that they weren't even on board at the time?'

'Where else would they have been?'

'Staying with a relative?' Vicky shrugged. 'Their grandparents, perhaps?'

'Hardly likely.'

'But possible, nonetheless.'

Tanner slumped down into his chair to do nothing more productive than stare down at his cup.

'Don't we at least need to check?' Vicky continued. 'Preferably before we head outside to announce to the world that they're missing?'

Tanner placed his cup down to pull himself up straight. 'You're right, of course,' he eventually conceded.

'We also need confirmation that the couple are who we're assuming them to be. It wouldn't do any harm to have something back from forensics as well.'

'I'll give Johnstone a call,' Tanner replied, reaching for his desk phone. 'I suppose it's possible that he's been able to officially identify the bodies. Whether he has or not, I think we're going to have to proceed on the basis that they are who we think they are. Also that the children are missing, at least until someone tells us otherwise.'

'What do you want me to do?'

'Try to get in contact with their family. Ask Sally to help. We need to at least make them aware of the situation before going any further. We also need to ask if they have any idea where the children might be. Some photographs would be useful as well. Then I want you to let the vultures outside know that I'll be holding another press conference.'

'When for?' she asked, taking frantic notes.

'As soon as we have something to offer them, other than how old we think the children are. Then if you could get someone to print up some pictures from the scene last night. I'll be holding an office-wide briefing in exactly fifteen minutes, so if anyone needs to make themselves a drink, let them know that now is the time.'

- CHAPTER THIRTY NINE -

'OK, LISTEN UP everyone!' Tanner bellowed from the far end of a bustling office, the sound of his voice jarring against the pulsating ache in his head.

As he felt the contents of his stomach suddenly churn, as if they'd just been shovelled into a cement mixer, he took a much needed moment for his audience to settle.

'As I'm sure most of you know by now, at around one o'clock this morning we were called to the scene of another murder, a man and a woman, once again found inside a boat.'

Tanner waited for the expected round of whispered remarks to circle the room.

'We're still awaiting reports from both our medical examiner's office and forensics, so a certain amount of what you're about to hear is based on assumptions we're being forced to make due to the urgent nature of the investigation. The first is that the victims are David and Lisa Rutherford, a married couple from Ipswich. Both were attacked with a knife. The medical examiner's on-site prognosis was that the stab wounds were similar in form and depth to those found at the previous murder scene. If that does prove to be the case, then it looks likely that Samuel Tunk is no longer our prime suspect, as the attacker was most likely to be either a man lacking upper body strength or, perhaps more likely, a woman. This, of course, means that we spent all of yesterday looking for the wrong bloody person!'

The frustrated tone in Tanner's voice left his audience submissively silent.

'Unfortunately,' he continued, the skin under his collar prickling with heat, 'the bad news doesn't stop there. After speaking to the person who found them, we eventually discovered that they had children; two girls, each aged between five and six, neither of whom could be found on board the boat, or anywhere else for that matter.

'So, here we are. Four dead people and no less than three missing children, without a single bloody clue as to who's responsible. And when word gets out to the press, journalists from up and down the country are going to be crawling out of whatever rock it is that they live under to start making their way over. I wouldn't be surprised if some came out of retirement, just for the chance to cover the story. So I think it goes without saying that we need to find those children, and just hope to God that they're alive and well when we do.'

From the back of the room came Cooper's hand, followed by his questioning voice. 'What about Samuel Tunk?'

'Fuck Samuel Tunk!' came Tanner's biting response, the words flying out of his mouth before he had a chance to stop them. 'If he wasn't responsible for either the murders or for taking the children, then what possible interest is he to us?'

'Even though a man of similar build was seen fleeing the scene of the last murder, the same person who had a direct connection to Jason Blackwell, being that he was the brother of the woman Tunk was convicted of murdering, and that Jason was known to have spent at least six months visiting him in prison. More so that he remains a convicted psychopath who was only released on a technicality?'

'Thank you, Cooper. Your thought-provoking summary is greatly appreciated. And of course you're right, which is why he *was* our prime suspect. But if Dr Johnstone's post-mortem report comes back to say that the attacker was most likely to be a woman, then it doesn't matter what the previous evidence suggests, especially when it's nothing but circumstantial hearsay and creative conjecture. Even if we were to find his fingerprints plastered all over the scene, it would certainly be challenging to secure a conviction when our very own medical examiner takes to the stand to tell a jittery jury that it was most likely *not* to have been a man who killed them!

'So anyway,' he continued, taking a breath, 'the children need to be found, and sooner rather than later.'

'But we still need to work out who's been going around murdering people inside their boats.'

'Do we, Cooper? How strange. And there was me thinking we could let them get away with it.'

'I'm only saying that you seem more concerned with finding the missing children than you do the person who murdered their parents.'

'Yes, I see. Out of curiosity, which do you think is more important, finding three children who at least stand a chance of still being alive, or figuring out who killed four adults who are all most definitely dead?'

'I wasn't aware that whoever killed them has decided to stop.'

'And I wasn't aware that I was giving them carte blanche to continue. Now, do you mind if I carry on with the briefing?'

'Be my guest,' Cooper replied, folding his arms

over his portly stomach to offer Tanner a malevolent grin.

Lifting his eyes to the clock marking time against the opposite wall, Tanner drew in what he hoped would be a calming breath. 'So, as I was saying, our priority *is* to find the children. With that in mind, I'll be holding another press conference in less than twenty minutes to let the entire world know that they're missing. Meanwhile,' he continued, forced to re-engage Cooper's unwelcoming glare, 'I had hoped you'd be willing to lead a search party to help find them?'

'Of course. Anything to help.'

'And if Townsend can lend a hand?'

A quick glance down to the front of the office found the young DC rolling his eyes.

'Excellent!' Tanner continued, with over-exaggerated delight, lifting his own to find Vicky. 'Did you have any luck getting hold of the victim's relatives?'

'I spoke to the male victim's father, down in Colchester,' she replied. 'I told them we weren't sure, but that there was a possibility we'd found his son and daughter-in-law. He confirmed that they were here, staying on board their boat for a couple of weeks, but was convinced it wasn't them, being that he'd only spoken to them the day before. When I asked if he'd be willing to see if he could identify the bodies, he said he'd give them a call first, to prove it wasn't them.'

'I assume you asked about his grandchildren?'

'He said he hadn't seen them, at which point I told him that there was a possibility they were missing, asking if he'd be able to send us some photographs. He said he would, but only if he was unable to get hold of his son.'

'And...?'

'An email came through from him about ten minutes ago. I've already asked Sally to print out the attached photographs.'

The office fell into an unsettling silence.

'OK,' Tanner eventually continued, wringing his hands with nervous anxiety, 'at least that helps confirm what we already suspected. As soon as this briefing is over I want every available officer out looking for the missing children. Whatever you're currently working on will have to wait.

'Meanwhile, as DI Cooper has so kindly pointed out, we still have a murderer to find, preferably before they kill anyone else. Presuming our medical examiner is correct, and that our most likely suspect is a woman, that currently leaves us with two possibilities. The first is the person who arrived at the scene of Jason Blackwell's murder carrying a suitcase, a Miss Julia Ward.'

Tanner stopped for a moment to direct his audience's attention to one of many photographs attached to the whiteboard behind him.

'According to her, and despite Jason Blackwell being found with another woman, she was his girlfriend. Her motive for murdering them is fairly obvious. If it *was* an unpremeditated crime of passion, it's possible that she'd forgotten about Jason's son, and only took him when she realised he could be a potential witness. More concrete evidence is in the form of her fingerprints and DNA being found all over the crime scene. However, I'm not sure that will be much use in court, as her defence attorney will simply point to the fact that they were bound to be, being that she lived on board at the time. Of course, we don't have a single clue as to why she would have felt it necessary to murder David and Lisa Rutherford as well, nor for her to have taken their children. Her alibi for the first murder is that she'd spent the weekend with her parents. Did anyone have the chance to confirm that?'

Tanner glanced around to see Sally, raising her hand beside Townsend.

'I spoke to them,' she replied, lifting her voice. 'They confirmed what she'd said: that she had been there that weekend. Whether or not she'd asked them to say that or not, I don't know. Assuming she had been, I also don't know what time she arrived back.'

'You haven't attempted to track her movements?'

'Er...no, but I'm more than happy to.'

'OK, make that your first priority. If you could then give her a call to ask her what she was doing last night, between the hours of eleven o'clock and one in the morning, that would be useful.'

Seeing her nod, Tanner returned his attention back to the room.

'At the moment, the only other female suspect we have is Jason's estranged wife, Abigail Blackwell, who I believe has a far more compelling motive, being that her now deceased husband is, or at least was, the heir to Blackwell Pharmaceuticals. According to Google, Jason has a net worth of approximately twenty-five million. Being that she was still married to him at the time of his death, it seems likely that she'll inherit the lot. We also know that she's struggling to make ends meet, and that she blamed her husband for the demise of her modelling career. According to her, he refused to let her have an abortion when she fell pregnant, saying he'd cut her out of his will if she did. Allegedly, he then embarked on a series of affairs whilst constantly refusing her demands for a divorce. On top of all that, it took a little coercing, but she eventually admitted to having paid him a visit on the night he was killed, and both her fingerprints and

DNA have been found all over the crime scene.

'If what our medical examiner said last night remains in his final report; that the same person was responsible for the murder of all four people, as with Julia Ward, we don't have any idea why Abigail Blackwell would have felt it necessary to attack and kill last night's victims, nor why she would have taken their children. The only possible motive I can think of is that the victims somehow knew what happened, either by having witnessed the event, or via some other means. If they did, and they knew the identities of both the victims and their assailant, it's possible that a blackmail attempt was made. If that was the case, then I'd have thought the most likely suspect would be Jason Blackwell's wife, simply because of her newly expected wealth. Either way, we need to start digging into the lives of each. If we can establish a connection between either Julia Ward or Abigail Blackwell and our latest victims, no matter how tenuous that connection might be, then I think we'll be one giant step closer to not only identifying our murderer, but also locating the whereabouts of our missing children. I've already tasked Vicky with the job of starting that process. If I could ask Sally to join her. I'll leave the two of you to decide how many uniformed officers you need.

'Right, if nobody has any questions, that's it for now,' Tanner concluded, bringing his hands together.

Taking a sultry moment to watch his audience slowly disperse, his eyes were left resting on a solitary figure, standing awkwardly in the middle of the room with a hand half-raised in the air.

Instantly recognising her as being the young woman he'd interviewed the previous day, he stepped briskly over to begin wracking his brain for her name. 'Gina Booth – isn't it?'

'It's Boothe with an "e",' she corrected, returning to Tanner a nervous smile.

'With an "e",' he repeated. 'Of course! Sorry. With everything going on at the moment, I'd somehow managed to forget that I'd asked you to start today.'

'I think that's understandable. To be honest, I wouldn't have thought to bother you had it not been for one small problem.'

'What's that?'

'I don't seem to have a desk,' she replied, glancing about.

'Oh – right – yes, of course. A desk! Something else I'd managed to forget. Um...' he continued, endeavouring to follow her furtive gaze. 'I don't suppose you'd be willing to work out in reception. At least there are plenty of chairs out there.'

Seeing her staring open-mouthed at him from the corner of his eye, he turned to offer her a mischievous grin. 'Sorry, that was my rather peculiar idea of a joke. Bear with me and I'll see what I can do.'

- CHAPTER FORTY -

LEAVING GINA WITH the duty sergeant to help sort out a desk, Tanner couldn't help but notice the gaggle of reporters, already assembled in the front car park.

Before girding his loins to address them, he knew he had one more job; to update Forrester on the previous night's events, preferably before it appeared on his Twitter feed.

'Good morning, sir, it's Tanner,' he began, closing the door to his office.

'Yes, Tanner, how can I help?' came his superintendent's reply, the rumble of traffic humming quietly in the background.

'Is now a good time?' he continued, half-hoping it wasn't.

'I suppose that depends. If it's to ask for a pay rise, then probably not.'

'Then I suppose I'd better call back next month.'

'What is it Tanner? I'm expecting another call.'

Tanner poured himself another much needed coffee. 'I'm afraid we found another murdered couple in the early hours of the morning. Very similar to the last, I'm afraid. Regretfully, the victims' children are missing as well.'

There was a sullen pause from the end of the line, broken only by the distinctive thud of a car door slamming.

'How old?'

'Five and six. Two girls.'

'Are you sure they're not staying with family or friends?'

'We're about as sure as we can be.'

'Shit!'

'I'm about to give a press conference, asking if anyone's seen them.'

'What about the victims?'

'They've yet to be formally identified, but it seems likely that they're Mr and Mrs Rutherford from Ipswich, visiting the Broads for a boating holiday. Johnstone seems confident that the same person is responsible. He's also still pushing the theory that the attacker is likely to have been a woman.'

'Remind me why that was again?'

'The shallow depth of the stab wounds, or at least the majority of them.'

There was a pause from the end of the line as the ambient background noise changed from distant traffic to the sound of people answering phones.

'Is that really enough to conclude that it was a woman?' Forrester eventually continued.

'Either that, or a man lacking upper body strength.'

'What about Samuel Tunk? Are you sure it still couldn't have been him?'

'Not if the recent reports of his physical size are to be believed.'

'How about his mental state?'

'Sorry, sir, I'm not with you,' Tanner replied, glancing down at his watch before gazing out of his window at the dozens of journalists waiting for him.

'Surely there are other reasons to explain the depth of the stab wounds, other than pure physical strength.'

'Are you asking if it was a frenzied attack?'

'More that the motive for the murders could have a bearing. If it was a crime of passion, then I'd be looking for consistently deep puncture wounds. However, had it been a more perfunctory cold-blooded attack, I'd have thought the depth of the wounds could easily have been more varied.'

Tanner sank slowly down into his chair to stare down at his coffee. Forrester was right. If Tunk had conducted the attacks as part of some long-considered plan, then they could have easily been undertaken with cool professional interest, as opposed to the raw animalistic fury normally associated with murder.

'You're saying I'm back to square one, again,' he eventually said, his voice dropping with despondent despair.

'You're not back to square one,' came Forrester's terse reply, as the background noise disappeared completely. 'You're simply going to have to keep Tunk on your list of suspects, that's all. Who else do you have?'

Tanner let out a heavy sigh. 'Jason Blackwell's wife and the girlfriend he'd been cheating on at the time.'

'Well, at least three suspects are better than none.'

Instead of responding, Tanner turned to look blankly at his computer's monitor.

'Anyway,' Forrester continued, 'as I said, I'm expecting another call. What time is your press conference?'

Tanner glanced down at the time displayed on the bottom corner of the screen. 'About five minutes ago.'

'OK – well – good luck, and make sure to let me know how you get on.'

'I doubt I'll need to. I'm fairly sure you'll see the whole thing played out on every news channel across the entire country.'

- CHAPTER FORTY ONE -

THE MOMENT TANNER stepped outside, the awaiting press pack burst into life as at least two-dozen cameras began taking what must have been the exact same picture of him, whilst a dozen more heckled out a seemingly endless series of incomprehensible questions.

With what he felt to be the patience of a saint, Tanner waited for them to settle down before attempting to open his mouth.

'I'm more than happy to take your questions at the end,' he began, feeling far more relaxed than he'd been expecting, 'but for now I'd like to start by saying good morning, and to thank you all for coming.'

As some of the more familiar faces began casting a few surprised glances around at each other, Tanner smiled to himself before continuing. 'I will be updating you at the end as to where we currently stand with the murder of Jason Blackwell and the woman he was found with, together with his missing son, Edward, but for now I need your help.

'Unfortunately,' he continued, feeling the weight of their eyes resting on his, 'it would appear that whoever murdered them has done so again.'

Closing his mouth, he braced himself for the expected rampage of demanding questions, but instead he was met by a peculiar silence.

Beginning to wonder if they'd heard what he said,

he pulled in a breath to continue. 'The couple were found on board their boat in the early hours of the morning. They've yet to be formally identified, so we're not at liberty to say who they are, but we do need your urgent help to locate their children.'

With his audience still remaining strangely quiet, he picked up the pile of leaflets that Vicky had left on the table for him. 'Their names are Susan and Isabella, aged five and six,' he continued, handing the pile to the nearest reporter, 'and were last seen on board their parents' boat moored up at the entrance to Catfield Staithe. As with Edward, the other missing child, there is no reason for us to believe that they've been harmed, but I'm sure it goes without saying that we need to find them as soon as possible, so anything you can do to help get the word out that they're missing would be gratefully appreciated.'

'Any sign of Samuel Tunk?' came a voice Tanner instantly recognised as belonging to the belligerent reporter from the Norfolk Herald.

'While Mr Tunk does remain a suspect, there are currently two other people we're in the process of talking to.'

'That didn't answer my question.'

'Sorry, my mistake. Unfortunately, we've yet to locate Mr Tunk, but as I said, or at least hinted at, he's no longer considered to be our prime suspect.'

'You're saying that a previously convicted psychopath, one who was released the morning before Jason Blackwell and his lover were found brutally killed, the same person who was found guilty of having murdered his sister, *isn't* your prime suspect?'

Tanner closed his eyes to roll them discreetly inside his head. It had been a good run, but it had been fairly obvious that it wasn't going to last.

'We are still keen to talk to Mr Tunk,' he eventually replied, re-opening them to stare about, 'and again, if anyone has any information that would help us locate him, the phone number remains the same. But as I said before, at this precise moment in time, he isn't our prime suspect.'

'If *he* isn't, then would you mind telling us who *is*?'

'At this stage in our investigation we're unable to say.'

'Do you know if there's any connection between the two sets of victims, or do you think they were picked purely at random? I'm only asking as I'm fairly sure that our readership would like to know if they should continue to be on the lookout for an as yet unidentified psychopath, one waiting for an opportune moment to butcher them inside their beds before making off with their children, for seemingly no other reason than there was nothing to watch on TV?'

'We believe there is a strong likelihood that the victims do share a connection, but with the latest incident having only taken place...' he made a point of looking at his watch, '...less than ten hours ago, we are still at the very earliest stage of the investigation. Our forensics department is still in the process of collecting evidence from the scene, and we're still awaiting a provisional post-mortem report from our medical examiner.'

'Despite that, you've still decided to change your mind about Samuel Tunk?'

'We haven't simply "changed our minds",' Tanner bit back, feeling the tentative hold he'd had on his temper ebbing quickly away. 'We go where the evidence takes us.'

'But I thought you just said you didn't have any, being that you hadn't heard back from either your forensics department or your medical examiner?'

'Our thoughts regarding Samuel Tunk are based on evidence already uncovered from the crime scenes.'

'So what you're really saying is that you don't have any real idea if it was Samuel Tunk or not, neither do you know if he's following some sort of methodical plan, or if he's simply choosing to spend his newfound freedom going around murdering just about as many of us Norfolk residents as possible before being caught, which, by the sounds of it, could be a while?'

Clasping his hands firmly behind his back to begin wringing them raw, Tanner fixed the eyes of the obstinate reporter to offer him a razor sharp smile. 'Sorry, what was your name again?'

'Sid Fletcher, Norfolk Herald,' the tall, greasy looking man replied through a crooked smile.

'That's right. Well, Mr Fletcher,' Tanner repeated, 'as I've said I think three times now, Mr Tunk continues to remain a suspect. I'll leave you and your highly educated readership to speculate if it was him or not. You're also free to suggest what motives he might have, if he's likely to kill again, how often, and when. Meanwhile, if you could find time to mention something about the missing children, Edward, Susan, and Isabella, being that they all may have witnessed their parents being murdered, and could well now be hiding, scared out of their wits that the same thing could happen to them, I'm sure the rest of us would be eternally grateful.'

- CHAPTER FORTY TWO -

WINDING UP THE conference to leave the reporters bellowing out an endless series of increasingly nonsensical questions, Tanner turned on his heel to make his way back inside, only to nearly walk straight into Townsend, heading out the other way.

'I thought you were out looking for those missing children?' he asked, his mind still reeling from his exchange with the belligerent Norfolk Herald reporter.

'We're – er – just leaving now,' Townsend replied, his skin flecking with colour.

'But I told you to head out immediately. That was half an hour ago!'

'Yes, I know. We had to print up some more copies of the leaflets.'

'That doesn't take half an hour.'

'Then the toner ran out of ink, and nobody seemed to know where the cartridges were kept.'

'Couldn't you have asked Sally?'

'She was on the phone.'

'What about the duty sergeant?'

'I couldn't find him.'

Tanner shook his head with bemused disbelief.

'Then we couldn't find any paper,' Townsend continued.

'Alright, enough! Are you at least ready to leave

now?'

'I think so. I'm just waiting for Cooper.'

'And where is he?'

'The last time I saw him he was chatting to the new girl.'

'You must be fucking joking,' Tanner muttered, shoving his way past to burst through to the main office, just in time to see Cooper leap off the corner of Gina's desk to begin hurrying towards the exit.

'What the *hell* do you think you're doing?' Tanner demanded, deliberately blocking his way.

'I was – er – waiting for Townsend to fix the printer.'

'I see. And you didn't think for one single moment that it may have been useful to try and help him?'

Cooper gave his shoulders an apathetic shrug. 'I did offer.'

'You do still remember that there are three children missing, I hope?'

'Yes, of course.'

'And yet there you are, chatting up the new girl, apparently with the only thing on your mind being whether or not she'd allow you to climb inside her pants.'

'I was showing her how to use the database.'

'And that was more important than helping Townsend fix the printer?'

Instead of replying, Cooper did nothing but glare back at Tanner with an ever darkening face. 'Do you want me to go or not?'

'I wanted you to go half an hour ago!'

'Then would you mind getting out of my way?'

Tanner held Cooper's eyes for a moment longer before stepping to one side.

'*Fucking idiot,*' he cursed to himself, as Cooper disappeared through to reception.

Spinning around, he scanned the room looking for Vicky.

Unable to see her, he made his way over to speak to Sally instead.

'How's it going?' he asked, standing beside her desk to continue staring about.

'I've spoken to someone at Wroxham Station. They promised to send me over CCTV footage from yesterday. That should at least give us an idea as to when Julia Ward arrived back from her parents. I've also requested access to her email, phone, social media, and bank accounts, and am in the process of doing the same thing for Abigail Blackwell.'

'OK, good. I don't suppose you've seen Vicky?'

Sally glanced quickly around. 'She said she was looking for you.'

'But I'm right here!'

'Look, there. Coming out of the kitchen.'

'OK, thanks. Don't forget to keep me posted.'

Lurching around, he marched over to meet Vicky to stare down at the steaming mugs held at the end of each of her arms. 'Do you really have time for that?'

'Sorry, I offered to make Gina a drink.'

'Christ! Not you as well?'

'Not me as well – what?'

'I've just caught Cooper chatting her up, now here you are, making her a bloody coffee!'

'Oh, right. Well, I shouldn't worry about Cooper if I were you. I think you'll find that I got there first.'

'What?'

'I asked Gina out this morning. We've got a table booked at The Bittern for eight o'clock tonight.'

Tanner opened and closed his mouth a few times, his mind struggling to find a suitable politically correct response. 'I'm – I'm sorry...' he eventually began. '...I didn't realise you were a...'

'You didn't realise I was a...what?' she replied, her eyes boring into his.

'You know...a...a...'

'A gay?'

'I wasn't going to say that,' Tanner spluttered in response, his eyes darting about the room, hoping to God that nobody was listening to their conversation. 'I was going to say a *lesbian*,' he continued, whispering the last word as if saying it any louder would conjure up a malevolent spirit.

Vicky's face finally cracked into a cavorting grin. 'The look on your face!'

'What?'

'I'm winding you up, you idiot.'

'Oh – right,' Tanner replied, becoming even more desperate that nobody had overheard. 'Good one.'

'Thanks. Besides, even if I was a lesbian, I'm not sure she'd be interested.'

'And why's that?' Tanner found himself asking, joining Vicky in staring over at her.

'Because she has what looks to me like an engagement ring on the third finger of her left hand, and there's a picture of a particularly good-looking young man on her desk who I'd say was her brother, if it weren't for the fact that they were snogging.'

'It could still be her brother,' Tanner mused, raising an intrigued eyebrow.

'Either way, I think it's evidence enough that she's straight.'

'It's a little circumstantial, but I'm not going to argue with you.'

Realising the awkwardness of the conversation had at least allowed him to forget about the press conference, as well as his run-in with Cooper, he turned his attention back to Vicky. 'I heard you were looking for me?'

'I've managed to find a connection between the most recent victims and Jason Blackwell's estranged wife.'

'Go on.'

'The man who was killed, David Rutherford. He's a director at TDK.'

'Sorry, am I supposed to have heard of them?'

'TDK Model Management? It's one of the UK's top modelling agencies. Abigail Blackwell used to work for them, at least she did before she became pregnant.'

'You're not seriously suggesting that she murdered him because he fired her?'

'You asked for a connection.'

Tanner looked absently away. 'I suppose I did.'

'Besides, her motive could have been something completely different.'

'Like what?'

'Like you said during the briefing: he'd somehow found out that she'd killed her husband and was attempting to blackmail her.'

'He kicked her out of his modelling agency and now he's trying to blackmail her?'

Vicky offered Tanner a sheepish shrug. 'It *is* possible.'

'I suppose,' he responded, without sounding in the least bit convinced.

'I can head out to have a chat with her, if you like?'

'No. I'll go. I need you here to keep digging. If we're going to bring her in on a multiple murder charge, we're going to need a little more than some outlandish theory that she murdered her husband to get her hands on his money before killing someone else in an effort to keep hold of it.'

- CHAPTER FORTY THREE -

ABOUT TWENTY MINUTES later, Tanner rumbled his XJS around the broad brick-paved circular driveway where Abigail Blackwell lived, gazing up at the ostentatious Tudor-style mansion. Apart from the bullet-grey Aston Martin, now parked facing forward, with all the windows and curtains closed it seemed as if there was nobody home. It was only when he stopped alongside the Aston that he realised the boot was open, poking out of which could be seen a couple of distinctively patterned Louis Vuitton suitcases.

Reversing to leave his car parked directly in front of it, Tanner climbed quickly out to make his way over to the entrance, only to find the person he'd driven over to see come hurrying out the other way.

'Mrs Blackwell!' he exclaimed, stopping where he was to cast a voyeuristic eye over the skimpy white skin-tight dress she was wearing. 'Are you going somewhere?'

With only a brief look of surprise, Abigail dropped a set of keys casually into her black and gold Gucci handbag before pulling the door closed behind her. 'I'm going to see a friend, but don't worry, Chief Inspector, he only lives down the road.'

'Of course,' Tanner replied, stepping to one side with a subservient nod. 'I was just hoping to ask you a few more questions.'

'I take it that means you still haven't found my son?'

'Not yet,' he replied, watching her wiggle her way past with an additional suitcase being rolled along behind her. 'But I can assure you that we're still doing everything we can to find him.'

'I should hope you are!' she replied, reaching the car's open boot to glare back.

'Did you hear the news – that another couple had been found?'

Abigail shook her head with a distinct lack of interest. 'The last thing I heard was that you were looking for that Skunk character.'

'Samuel Tunk,' Tanner corrected, watching her haul the suitcase up into the boot. 'I don't suppose you know him?'

'Don't be ridiculous.'

'Well, your husband did.'

With her hand resting on the boot's lid, she sent Tanner a questioning look. 'Why would Jason have known a convicted murderer?'

'Don't you know?'

'If I knew I wouldn't be asking.'

'Samuel Tunk was the man who raped and murdered your husband's sister. That's why he was in prison.'

'I – I didn't know.'

'He didn't tell you?'

'He never talked about his sister. I thought I told you that?'

'I assume that means you didn't know he used to visit him in prison, either?'

Abigail's face was now a mask of total bewilderment. 'But – why would he have done that?'

'We don't know. Nor do we know what he said. But whatever it was, it's difficult to imagine that it would have been anything pleasant.'

'Is that why he killed him; for what he said to him in prison?'

'Oh, sorry, we don't think Tunk was responsible. At least not anymore.'

'That's not what you said on the news just now.'

'So you did watch it?'

'I caught the tail end,' she replied, turning away to close the Aston Martin's boot, 'as I was walking out the door.'

Tanner took a step back to watch her navigate her way around to the driver's side. 'If you'd watched all of it, you'd have heard that we have two more suspects in mind.'

'Please don't say one of them is me,' she responded, tugging open the door. 'I've already told you that I was at a party the night my husband was killed.'

'Not before stopping by to see him.'

'Which I've already explained.'

'You've also yet to tell us where you were last night, between the hours of eleven and one?'

'You haven't asked!'

'I'm asking now.'

'I was here,' she immediately continued, her eyes boring into Tanner's. 'Where else would I have been?'

'Not attending another party?'

'Since news came out of my husband's death, my social diary's been surprisingly empty, which is why I'm going to stay with a friend for a few days. Besides, why on Earth would I decide to murder some random people who I don't even know?'

'I wasn't aware we'd given out the victim's names. In fact, now that I think about it, I know we didn't.'

'It doesn't make the slightest difference who they are.'

'Even if one of them was the co-founder of your former modelling agency?'

'I'm sorry?'

'David Rutherford, of TDK Model Management. I assume you knew him?'

Abigail's eyes danced erratically between Tanner's. 'I – I did – yes – but not very well.'

'May I ask how well?'

'Oh, hardly at all. I was introduced to him when I first started working there, at an office party.'

'And that was it?'

'I'd occasionally see him at fashion shows and photoshoots.'

'Did he take an active role in managing the agency's roster?'

'If you're seriously suggesting that I murdered him for no other reason than because he had me taken off their books, you're wrong. He was their Chief Financial Officer. He had nothing to do with us lowly models.'

'But you said he'd sit in on the photoshoots?'

'I said he *occasionally* would, but I'm fairly sure it wasn't for professional reasons.'

'Then why would he?'

'Why d'you think?'

'I've no idea.'

'Put it this way, it wasn't to help with the lighting, not unless it was to give him a better view.'

'Are you saying he was some sort of pervert?'

'No, Chief Inspector, I'm saying he was a man.'

'A man who you barely knew?'

'That's right!' she retorted, planting her hands down on her hips. 'Now, if there's nothing else?'

'Not at this precise moment in time, but I will need the address of where you're going, especially as it looks like you'll be staying there a while.'

Abigail continued glaring at him for a moment longer before shaking her head with belligerent capitulation. 'Fine!' she eventually stated, diving into her handbag to pull out her phone. 'Have you got a pen, or should I text it to you?'

'The old fashioned way is fine,' he replied, retrieving his notebook with an accommodating smile.

Making a note of the address, he put his notebook away to remain standing where he was.

'May I go now?'

'By all means,' Tanner replied, taking a single backwards step.

'Then you'll need to move your car.'

'Oh, sorry,' he smiled. 'My mistake.'

Drifting over to it, he climbed inside to close the door, only to hear the demanding sound of his phone.

'Tanner speaking!' he replied, inserting his keys into the ignition.

'It's Vicky,' came the detective inspector's breathless voice. 'Sally's managed to gain access to Abigail Blackwell's email and social media accounts which have unearthed a couple of things I thought you should know.'

'Go on,' Tanner replied, turning to look out of the driver's side window to find the person under discussion glaring at him over the bonnet of her car with a look of indignant expectation.

'Firstly, it looks like her husband changed his will, excluding her from the bulk of his estate.'

Tanner fell momentarily silent. 'Any idea when that was?'

'Only about two months ago.'

'Are you sure?'

'He emailed her a copy with the revisions highlighted.'

'Great. There goes another suspect,' he moaned, hunching his shoulders over to start the engine.

'Hold on, there's more.'

'I can't see how there can be. The only realistic motive she ever had for killing him was for his money. If she knew she wasn't going to get a penny, then she's hardly likely to risk spending the rest of her life being locked up for doing so.'

'As I said, I hadn't finished,' came Vicky's chastising voice. 'The day after she received the email she took out a life insurance policy. Not for herself, mind. It was for her husband. And it wasn't for peanuts, either.'

'How much?'

'Two-and-a-half million.'

The sound of the Aston Martin's horn blasting rudely out had him once again turning to stare over at the woman behind the wheel, now vigorously gesturing for him to move. 'Hold on, Vicky, I'll call you straight back.'

Ending the call, a thin smile tugged briefly at the corners of his mouth, leaving him reaching inside the glovebox before climbing slowly out.

'What the hell do you think you're doing?' Abigail demanded, lowering the Aston's driver's side window.

'Would you step out of the car, please?'

'I'll do no such thing!'

'Very well,' Tanner continued, digging out the handcuffs he'd found in the glovebox. 'Mrs Abigail Blackwell, I'm arresting you for the murder of Jason Blackwell, Deborah Betton, David Rutherford and his wife, Lisa Rutherford.'

'You can't be serious?'

'You do not have to say anything, but it may harm your defence if you do not mention when questioned something which you later rely on in court.'

'Stop, please! This is just stupid!'

'Anything you do say may be given in evidence,' Tanner continued, ignoring her remarks of protest. 'Now, you can either step out of the car and place your hands above your head, or I can call for an armed police unit who I'm sure will be happy enough to force you.'

- CHAPTER FORTY FOUR -

LEADING VICKY INTO one of the station's interview rooms to find Abigail Blackwell, deep in conversation with an overweight middle-aged man who looked as if he'd been stuffed into the grey three-piece suit he was wearing, Tanner set his coffee down on the table to catch the eye of his brand new prime suspect. 'I see you've managed to find yourself a solicitor.'

'You better know that I've advised my client to remain silent,' the solicitor in question interjected, sitting back in his chair as beads of sweat clung to his round puffy face, 'for the time being, at least.'

'Oh, right! So you think she's guilty?'

Tanner watched Abigail jolt her head around to stare at the man sitting next to her. 'You do know that's what the jury will think if you choose to remain so?' he continued, catching her eye.

Abigail blinked twice before opening her mouth.

The second she did, the solicitor lunged forward to place a steadying hand on her arm.

'My client is fully aware of her rights, thank you.'

'I've no doubt she is, but does she understand them, or more to the point, does she know what a jury will think when they hear she refused to answer our questions, especially when there was no apparent reason for her not to?'

'I'm sorry,' the solicitor continued, 'I didn't catch

your name?'

'Detective Chief Inspector Tanner,' Tanner replied, taking the seat nearest to the wall. 'And you are?'

'Mr Harold Graves. I'm here at Mrs Blackwell's request, that is until such a time as you admit your mistake and offer her a formal apology in front of the hordes of press parked outside, the same ones you so insensitively paraded her in front of on your way in.'

Inviting Vicky to take the seat next to him, Tanner smiled first at Abigail, then at her gleeful solicitor. 'Shall we begin?'

'By all means!'

Tanner started the recording device mounted to the wall to speed his way through the formalities. Once done, he asked Vicky for the file she'd brought in with her to lever out a photograph.

'Is this your husband, Mrs Blackwell?'

As Abigail leaned forward to stare cautiously down at the image, Tanner spoke directly into the recording device. 'The suspect is being shown a photograph of the body of the male victim found on board a boat moored up at Acle Dyke on Monday, 25th April.'

Tanner gave her a few more moments to answer before continuing. 'If it goes on the record that you refused to answer any of our questions, Mrs Blackwell, a jury will be left with little choice but to assume that the only reason you didn't was because you're guilty, and doing so would have forced you to admit that you were.'

With his eyes boring into Tanner's face, Graves' hand returned to Abigail's forearm. 'Do I really have to remind you that an individual is innocent until proven guilty? Subsequently, it's not my client's job to prove something that has already been established, which is exactly why she has the right to remain silent.'

'In theory, your solicitor is correct,' Tanner continued, holding Abigail's now wavering gaze, 'but if you're not prepared to answer questions that will help to maintain your innocence, then we'll be left with no choice but to charge you with the four counts of murder you were arrested for. Taking into account the violent nature of the crimes, the chances are that you'll have to remain in police custody until the trial begins, which could take months. Oh, and don't forget, during that time the British press will be free to print whatever they like about you, which, from my own experience, is unlikely to be anything good. By the time you eventually end up in the dock, even if the jury reaches the conclusion that you didn't answer our questions because you were innocent after all, they'd have heard so much about what motivated you to kill your husband and the three other victims that they'd have concluded you're guilty before the trial even starts. So, I ask you again, Mrs Blackwell, is that a photograph of your husband; yes or no?'

Abigail glanced fitfully around at her solicitor, whose only response was to fold his arms over his barrel-like chest.

'Yes!' she finally replied, sending daggers into Tanner's eyes. 'That is my husband, but I didn't do *that* to him!'

'She speaks!' Tanner exclaimed, with mock astonishment. 'For a minute there I was beginning to wonder.'

'Whilst I am,' she continued, her eyes burning with indignant rage, 'when you're forced to let me go, I will be suing you – personally – for wrongful arrest *and* character defamation. And the longer you keep me here for, the more I'll be demanding!'

'We'd better push on then, hadn't we?' Tanner

replied, happy to meet her penetrating gaze before returning his attention to the file.

'Do you remember how you met your husband?' he eventually continued, taking a series of documents out.

'Seriously?' Graves questioned.

'Sorry, was that one too difficult?'

'I'm not in the least bit interested in how challenging your questions are, Mr Tanner, only if they are leading, repetitive, or in this case, completely irrelevant.'

'Am I allowed to ask your client what it was about him that she found most attractive?'

'You're allowed to ask her as many pointless questions as you like,' Graves continued, making a point of looking at his watch. 'You're the one on the clock.'

'Does that mean she's allowed to answer?'

'That's entirely up to her.'

'Mrs Blackwell?'

Abigail shrugged with indifference. 'Jason was a very attractive man, especially when he was younger. I don't think there were many women who would have disagreed.'

'Can you remember who asked who out?'

Abigail hesitated. 'I'm not sure either of us did. We met at a party during Paris Fashion Week.'

'Was that when you first had sex?'

'Jesus Christ!' the solicitor said, burying his head in his hands with theatrical drama. 'You don't have to answer that.'

'It doesn't bother me,' Abigail replied, arching her back as if recalling the experience. 'It was the first night we met.'

'You seduced him?'

'If I remember correctly, he seduced me. He told

me the punch was alcohol free whilst encouraging me to drink about five gallons of the stuff.'

'Did you know who he was at the time?'

'We were formally introduced, but I didn't connect his name with Blackwell Pharmaceuticals until later.'

'At which point you married him?'

'Ah...yes...of course,' Graves interrupted. 'You're attempting to establish a motive for my client to have murdered her husband; to inherit his vast sprawling estate. Well, I've already seen a copy of his will, and my client barely gets a mention.'

'Yes, we know,' admitted Tanner, falling sullenly silent.

Graves held his gaze for a moment longer before raising his hands somewhat dramatically in the air. 'Then what on Earth was all that about?'

'She didn't tell you?'

'Tell me what?'

'Your client took out a life insurance policy in Jason Blackwell's name,' Tanner eventually replied, 'the day after he emailed her a copy of his revised will, the one which, as you so rightly said, she barely gets a mention.'

'I was angry,' came Abigail's sultry voice, as her solicitor turned to look around at her. 'And can you blame me?'

'So you took out a life insurance policy on his behalf for the somewhat hefty sum of two-and-a-half million?'

'I had no choice. He was refusing to agree to a divorce. If anything happened to him before he did, I'd have been left with nothing.'

'Did he have any adverse medical conditions?'

'Well, no, but...'

'Then why did you think something might happen to him?'

'Because of how much he drank!' she stated. 'When you combine that with the fact that he was stupid enough to live on board a boat without having ever had the good sense to learn to swim first, the man was an accident just waiting to happen, and I couldn't take the chance that one day it would, not until he'd agreed to a divorce.'

'I see. Well, that makes sense, I suppose, the only problem is one of time.'

'Time?'

'If he wasn't prepared to divorce you, the only way you'd be able to get your hands on the money you seem to be in such desperate need of is if he either got so old he had a heart attack, or so drunk that he fell off his boat and drowned, neither of which were guaranteed to happen any time soon. The quickest solution would be to simply stab him and the woman you found him in bed with at the time, to then attempt to make it look as if they'd been attacked by the psychotic lunatic who'd coincidentally been released from prison the morning before.'

'I didn't kill my husband! Certainly not for something as ridiculous as money!'

'So it was because you found him in bed with someone else?'

'I've already told you. I couldn't give a shit who he slept with.'

'But you did pop round to see him the night he was killed?'

'That was to ask for a divorce, and I've told you that as well.'

'Perhaps it was the first time you'd actually seen him in bed with another woman? It may be one thing to hear your husband having sex with someone else, but quite another to see him doing so.'

'This is very entertaining,' interjected the solicitor,

'really it is, but it fails to include what I think you're going to need if you're to have any chance of a conviction. Something called evidence. Perhaps you've heard of it?'

Tanner smiled at him. 'I was just coming to that. Fortuitously, the forensics report came in just as your client did.'

'Then why haven't I seen a copy?'

'Because we've only just printed it out,' Tanner continued, pushing a bound document over the table.

Tanner waited a few moments for the solicitor to leaf his way through it. 'As you'll see on page four,' he eventually said, 'samples of your client's fingerprints and DNA were found on board the victim's boat no less than fifty-seven times.'

'Which only proves she'd been on board at some point,' Graves muttered, his eyes still scanning the pages, 'which is hardly surprising. I mean, the boat *did* belong to her husband. I believe she's already admitted to having been on board on multiple occasions.'

'They were concentrated in the kitchen, and the cabin in which the bodies were found.'

Graves looked up from the report to send Tanner a look of scolding disapproval. 'This isn't enough. Not by a long way. You need to have something that puts her at the scene of the crime when it actually happened.'

'Then may I bring your attention to section three, paragraph two.'

The room fell silent as Graves returned his eyes to the document.

'I assume you've got to the part where your client's DNA was found on the bodies,' Tanner continued. 'Not just the male victim's, either.'

With the solicitor remaining stoically silent, it was

left up to Abigail to speak. 'Sorry – but – what does that mean?'

'Forensics have discovered traces of your DNA on your husband,' Graves replied, still studying the report, 'as well as the female victim he was found with.'

Abigail stared wildly over the table at Tanner. 'But – I didn't even know her!'

'Surprisingly, Mrs Blackwell, you don't need to know someone in order to murder them.'

The solicitor turned over a page to continue reading. 'OK, I admit, finding my client's DNA on both victims is more substantial evidence than finding her fingerprints on the fridge, but it's hardly conclusive. It's certainly not enough for a conviction, not when you take into account the fact that my client had been on board before the incident took place, and the ease at which DNA can be transferred from one object to another. The female victim could have picked it up from any part of the boat where my client had previously been. To be honest, I'd be more surprised if she hadn't. But putting that aside for now,' he continued, closing the file to shove back over the table at Tanner, 'from what I understand, my client was dragged in here to be questioned about *four* counts of murder, not just the two that have so far been mentioned.'

'The other victims were found last night.'

'So I've been told. I've also been made aware of who they are, and that my client just happened to know the male victim, being that he was the co-founder of the modelling agency she used to work for. But again, if that's the only evidence you have, that she just happened to know one of the victims through a previous employment, then I'm going to be demanding that you release her immediately.'

Tanner simmered silently in his seat, his eyes steadily boring their way into the solicitor's.

'Well?'

'I suggest we take a break,' came his eventual response.

'I assume that means you don't?'

Leaning his head in towards the recording device, Tanner glanced down at his watch. 'Interview suspended at 12.35 pm.'

'You mean interview terminated, surely?'

Switching the device off, Tanner pushed his chair back to stand. 'We're still in the process of collecting evidence, Mr Graves. For that reason, it may be worthwhile telling your client that if we feel unable to charge her after the initial twenty-four hour holding time, we'll be requesting a ninety-six hour extension, which I'm confident will be granted. Bearing that in mind, it may be wise for the two of you to make yourselves as comfortable as possible.'

- CHAPTER FORTY FIVE -

'I THOUGHT THAT went rather well,' commented Vicky, doing her best to keep up with Tanner as he stomped his way down the narrow hallway.

'I assume you're being sarcastic.'

'A little, perhaps.'

'Well, there's a time and a place, and this is neither.'

'Fair enough. So, what's the plan?'

'Unfortunately for us, her solicitor is right. We don't have enough evidence to charge her, and despite what I said, I'm not even sure we have enough to get an extension.'

Coming to a halt in front of the main office doors, he glared down at his watch. 'And that leaves us with only twenty-two hours to come up with some.'

With Sally hurrying out the other way, they stood aside to let her through.

'How'd it go?' she stopped to ask, her eyes fluttering up at Tanner's.

'Not great. I don't suppose there's been any more sightings of Samuel Tunk?'

Sally's forehead rippled with confusion. 'I didn't think we were looking for him anymore?'

'With the way the interview's going,' Tanner muttered, 'it may be necessary for us to re-think that.'

'Then I may have something that could help,' she

continued, retrieving a thick file from under her arm.

'A knife with the handle covered in Abigail Blackwell's fingerprints, together with the blade bathed in her husband's blood?'

'Not exactly. You know how I discovered that Abigail Blackwell had been having an affair with her husband's brother?'

'I remember you saying that they were friends on Facebook.'

'And that they'd been constantly chatting on the phone?'

'I wasn't aware the word "constantly" had been used, but go on.'

'I think she'd been sleeping with David Rutherford as well!'

Taking the file being offered, Tanner gave her a look of dubious curiosity. 'Are there any men out there who you think she *hadn't* been sleeping with?'

'I'm only going where the evidence takes me,' she replied, in a defensive tone. 'If you look at the file, you'll see that they've been exchanging emails and Facebook messages all the way back to when she first started modelling for TDK, right up until the week before she left. From what I can work out, she was having a relationship with him even before she met her husband. It also looks like he ended it a few months ago.'

Tanner fell silent as he skipped through the pages.

'If they had been,' Sally continued, 'it may offer another explanation as to why she murdered them before taking their children.'

'Go on,' he replied, stopping to read one of what did appear to be over a hundred email exchanges.

'Maybe she was in love with him first, but he married someone else instead. She could have then married Jason on the re-bound. If that was the case, it's possible she thought the children the Rutherford's had together should have been hers.'

'You're saying she murdered her husband for the money she'd get from his life insurance to then do something remarkably similar to her former lover, that time to take possession of his children?'

'As I said, it's possible.'

Closing the file, he handed it to Vicky. 'OK, look, it's an interesting theory, but I'm not sure it has the legs to stand up in court, or anywhere else for that matter. I certainly wouldn't want to hear what her solicitor would say if I was to suggest it. What we really need is something that places her at the scene of at least one of the crimes.'

'I thought forensics discovered her DNA on the woman found in bed with her husband?'

'They did, but it was only a particle of skin, which as her solicitor rather annoyingly pointed out could have been picked up from anywhere. I don't suppose forensics have come back with anything from the second scene?'

'Nothing that's come through to me.'

'Me neither,' added Vicky, checking her phone.

Tanner let out a frustrated sigh. 'If we can't find the necessary evidence, then we'll be left with no choice but to try and make her confess, which will be difficult, especially with that solicitor of hers telling her to remain silent all the bloody time. I don't suppose there's been any news on the missing children?'

'We've had a few calls,' Sally replied, 'but nothing of substance.'

'I assume Cooper and Townsend are still out looking?'

She nodded in response. 'Have you had a chance to ask the suspect about them?'

'Not yet,' Tanner replied, realising he perhaps should have.

'Well, if you want her to confess, it may be an idea to.'

'How do you mean?'

Vicky looked up from her phone. 'I think Sally may have something there. If we can get her to start talking about her son – what he was like – that sort of thing, I'd be surprised if she doesn't become emotional, especially if she has done something to hurt him. She may not appear to, but every mother has a special connection to their children. Even if they don't like them very much, deep-down they still love them. If we push her hard enough, she may just admit to having taken him, the others as well. And if she does that...'

'It's worth a shot, I suppose,' Tanner replied, his mind already thinking of possible questions. 'Sally, can you chase forensics for me? We really need something from the second crime scene, even if it's just an interim report. Meanwhile,' he continued, looking at Vicky, 'I suggest we grab ourselves a coffee and get back to it.'

- CHAPTER FORTY SIX -

'ANYONE FOR COFFEE?' offered Tanner, joining Vicky in placing two steaming mugs onto the table.

'Oh – um – thank you,' came Graves' somewhat hesitant response, leaning forward to take hold of the nearest.

Re-taking his seat, Tanner turned the recording device back on to formally re-commence the interview.

'I'd like to start by asking your client about her son,' he eventually began.

'I was wondering when he was going to get a mention. I take it you haven't found him yet?'

'We're still looking.'

'I believe my client has already told you that she doesn't know where he is.'

'I don't suppose you'd allow her to speak for herself, for a change?'

With an indifferent shrug, Graves leaned back in his chair to rest his coffee mug on top of his bulging waistcoat.

'Mrs Blackwell?' Tanner prompted.

'As my solicitor just said, I don't know where he is.'

'I must admit, I've always been a little surprised by your seeming lack of interest in his welfare. Don't you care about him at all?'

Abigail sat up straight to glare over the table at

him. 'Of course I care! But I've already told you; Jason forced me to have him, leaving me with a child I didn't want instead of a career I actually did.'

'Yes, of course. That must have been very difficult for you.'

'It was, thank you! I never wanted children, not even when I was one. I was never cut out to be a mother, and yet there I was, forced to bring up a child who was about as abnormal as the rest of the Blackwell family.'

'You mean he was gifted in some way?'

'I wouldn't use the word "gifted", exactly. Retarded would probably be a more accurate description.'

'Are you saying that your son has some sort of cognitive disability?'

Abigail clamped her arms over her chest to send Tanner a defiant glare.

'Mrs Blackwell?'

'OK,' she eventually continued, 'I suppose calling him retarded is a little unfair, but there's definitely something not right with the boy.'

'Is there any chance you can be a little more specific?'

'He sleeps with his eyes open, for a start.'

'I'm – er – not sure you can describe someone as having a cognitive disability just because they sleep with their eyes open.'

'It's not just that. He didn't utter a single word until he was five. Even now he barely speaks. All he does is read. He never liked to be picked up, either.'

'Anything else?' Tanner enquired, expressing little interest in having to listen to a mother moan about her unwanted son.

'I've never once known him to laugh, and the only interest he's ever had is killing things: ants, flies, wasps. Basically, anything that crawled about on more than four legs. He'd burn them all with a magnifying glass. He even killed a frog once. He skewered it with a garden fork before dangling it over a bonfire, whilst it was still alive, as well.

'It wasn't just me who thought he was odd, either,' she continued, her eyes darting between Tanner's. 'I had countless teachers dragging me into school to tell me that he'd do nothing more productive in class than to draw pictures of people murdering each other. If you want my opinion, he's the one you should be having this conversation with, not me.'

'Can we please be serious, Mrs Blackwell?'

'I am!' she stated, leaning forward. 'His school became so concerned about him they even advised me to have him psychologically evaluated.'

'And did you?'

'Reluctantly, yes.'

'OK, so, what was the result?'

Closing her mouth, her gaze dropped down to her hands. 'They said his behaviour was normal for a child whose parents had separated,' she eventually mumbled. 'But that doesn't mean there isn't something wrong with him.'

'If you ask me, he sounds like what you'd expect from a boy who spent their entire childhood being treated like some sort of unwanted fashion accessory.'

'You're blaming me?' she snapped, her steely eyes returning to his.

'I didn't bring you in here on a charge of being a bad parent, Mrs Blackwell, I arrested you under suspicion of murdering your husband, the woman you found him in bed with, your former employer, and the poor man's innocent wife.'

'Forgive me for interrupting,' the solicitor interjected, 'but you don't know that my client did discover her husband actually in bed with another woman, on the night in question or at any other time. She certainly hasn't admitted as such. And this idea that she murdered David Rutherford for no other reason than he was the co-founder of a modelling agency she used to work for is simply laughable.'

'But your client did know him.'

Graves let out an exasperated sigh. 'I thought we'd already established that?'

'She met him before she met her husband.'

'Yes...and? So what?'

'At which point they started what appears to have been a long-standing carnal relationship.'

'Do you have proof of that,' Graves enquired, holding Tanner's gaze, 'or is it simply more time-wasting conjecture?'

Tanner returned his attention to his suspect. 'We've found emails and text messages sent between the two of you dating back over fifteen years, Mrs Blackwell,' he began, sliding the file Sally had given to him over to her solicitor, 'some of which should come with a warning for explicit content.'

Opening the file, Graves began leafing through its contents. 'Again, Chief Inspector, it would have been useful to have known about these a little sooner.'

'We've only just discovered them ourselves.'

'And I'll need time to establish whether or not these do prove that they were having an affair, but either way,' he continued, closing the file to push back over the desk, 'even if they do, they hardly prove that she killed him. It doesn't even suggest motive.'

'But it does prove that your client lied to us. She told me only about two hours ago that she hardly knew the man, which leaves me with two questions: firstly, why she thought it necessary to, and perhaps more importantly, what else has she been lying about?'

'Assuming, for the time being at least, that they *were* having some sort of extramarital relationship, I'd have thought the reason for her not wanting to tell you was fairly obvious, being that it was a private matter, one few people would want to have broadcast to the world at large. And just because she elected to withhold one piece of information, doesn't automatically mean she's been lying about anything else.'

'But it does cast a shadow of doubt over everything she's said so far.'

'Again, Chief Inspector, my client is innocent until *proven* guilty. None of what you've come up with so far even comes close to doing that. So, unless you have something more substantial to present, I'd appreciate it if you could have the decency to admit your mistake and let her go. Perhaps then you'd have time to find her son. Hopefully, those other children as well. You may then get a chance to work out who *really* killed all those people, preferably before they start doing so all over again.'

- CHAPTER FORTY SEVEN -

A KNOCK AT the door had Tanner glancing around to see Sally's head appear, beckoning him out with a furtive look.

Apologising for the interruption, Tanner pushed his chair back to head out into the corridor.

'What is it?' he eventually demanded, holding the door closed with his hand.

'Sorry,' Sally began, 'but Christine's been asking for you.'

'You mean she's here?'

'She was on the phone. She wants you to call her back.'

Tanner shook his head in frustrated consternation. 'Didn't you tell her that I was in the middle of interviewing a suspect?'

'She said it was urgent.'

'If it's to ask what I want for dinner tonight,' he muttered, digging out his phone to see that he'd missed two calls, both from her, 'I may be needing your help in opening a Tinder account.'

Suspending the interview once again, Tanner hurried out to the back of the building, his mobile phone held firmly against his ear.

'Hey, darling,' he eventually said, forcing himself to sound upbeat, 'Sally says you've been trying to contact me?'

'I heard on the news that you've arrested Abigail Blackwell.'

'That's correct,' he replied, curious to know where this was going. 'I was in the middle of interviewing her, which was why I couldn't take your call.'

'It's just that one of my friends phoned,' he heard her continue. 'Melissa? We had lunch together a few months ago?'

'Uh-huh,' Tanner replied, hoping she'd get to the point.

'We read Psychology together at university, after which she went on to become a child psychologist.'

Tanner's mind harked back to what Abigail Blackwell had said. 'Is this about the missing boy?'

'That's why she phoned.'

'You mean – she knows where he is?'

'Er...I don't think so.'

Tanner let out an irritated sigh. 'Then why was she calling?'

'She wants to speak to you. Apparently, she was on a panel of psychologists who conducted an evaluation of him a couple of years ago.'

'Did she say anything else?'

'She said she couldn't tell me.'

'Well, I'm a little busy at the moment.'

'She wouldn't have called if it wasn't important.'

'Tell you what, if you give her my number, she's free to give me a call, but I can't promise I'll answer.'

'Will do,' Christine replied, 'although, I must admit, I already have.'

'You already have...what?'

'Given her your number.'

Tanner rolled his eyes.

'Sorry,' he heard her continue, 'I didn't think you'd mind.'

'OK, well, as I said before, she's free to call, but if I

don't pick up she'll have to leave me a message. Anyway, I've got to go. See you tonight.'

Ending the call, he spun around to head back inside when the phone's screen lit up in his hands.

'I knew she'd want to ask what I wanted for dinner,' he laughed, bringing the phone back to his ear. 'Hey, darling, if it's about what I want to eat tonight, I'm happy with whatever's in the fridge.'

'I'm sorry?' came the uncertain sound of a woman's voice.

Wrenching the phone away from his ear, Tanner stared down at the screen to see that it wasn't Christine after all.

'Sorry about that,' he apologised, 'This is John Tanner speaking. May I ask who's calling?'

'Dr Melissa Redbridge. Christine was kind enough to give me your number.'

'Right, yes, of course. How can I help?'

'It's about one of the missing children, Edward Blackwell?'

'So she said.'

'Did she tell you that I was one of the child psychologists who met with him?'

'She did,' Tanner continued, making his way back inside, 'but to be honest, we already know about this. His mother told us about ten minutes ago.'

'I assume she told you what the results were from the official report.'

'The "official" report?' Tanner repeated, stopping where he was.

The woman's voice fell momentarily silent. 'I don't suppose it would be possible for you to come to my office to discuss the matter in private?'

'Well, yes, I could, I suppose, but to save time...couldn't you just tell me now? Our conversation isn't being recorded, it that's what's worrying you.'

There was another pause before the psychologist's voice came back over the line. 'There were three of us who were asked to evaluate him on behalf of Social Services. Dr Phillip Alexander, Dr Thomas Hodge, and myself.'

'Go on,' Tanner prompted, digging out his notebook.

'It was supposed to have just been me. The other two were called in at the last minute. I found out later that they both knew Alfred Blackwell, the boy's grandfather. Apparently, they all went to Oxford together.'

'Are you saying that the evaluation wasn't perhaps as impartial as maybe it should have been?'

'Far from it! As far as I was concerned, it was obvious that the boy was displaying clear signs of having an extreme form of antisocial personality disorder, otherwise known as ASPD, which isn't good at the best of times,' the psychologist continued. 'Far worse if the subject is a ten-year-old boy.'

'Am I to assume that the other two doctors disagreed?'

'They both said he was more likely to have had only a mild form, which was nothing unusual in a child whose parents had been separated. After much heated debate, I eventually gave in, but if I'd known that the only reason they were there was because Lord Blackwell had asked them, I most definitely would not have.'

'Are you honestly trying to tell me that you think Edward Blackwell murdered his own father?'

'Not in so many words.'

'But you are saying it's possible, though?'

'Based purely on my own psychological evaluation, yes, I am.'

- CHAPTER FORTY EIGHT -

ENDING THE CALL, Tanner re-entered the building to find Vicky back behind her desk.

'What was all that about?' she asked, as he reached her chair.

Disappointed to find that she'd been doing nothing more productive than watching the news on her computer, Tanner cast an anxious eye over at the vans parked outside. 'One of Christine's psychologist friends wanted to have a word.'

'About what?'

'She was one of three who were asked to evaluate Edward. According to her, the other two weren't as impartial as perhaps they should have been, being that they were only there because Lord Blackwell had insisted on it.'

'And what does that have to do with our investigation?'

'She would appear to be in agreement with the boy's mother.'

'You mean she thinks Edward Blackwell, a twelve-year-old boy, stabbed his own father to death?'

'She didn't say he had, she only said that she thought it was possible.'

'But that's ridiculous!'

'Maybe, maybe not. Do you remember what Dr Johnstone said about the stab wounds?'

'That he thought it possible they were made by a

woman.'

'Or a man lacking upper body strength.'

Vicky leant back in her chair. 'OK, I suppose I can just about believe that the boy could have murdered his own father. I'm sure we'd have all liked to have done that at some stage in our lives. But the woman he was with as well?'

'According to the psychologist,' Tanner continued, pulling out his notebook, 'the boy had an extreme form of ASPD.'

'And that means he's a crazed psychopathic lunatic, does it?'

'Surprisingly, she didn't use the term "crazed psychopathic lunatic", but from what Christine's told me, whether someone is classed as being a psychopath or a sociopath, they're all considered to have ASPD, at least in some shape or form.'

'And what about the other couple?' Vicky continued. 'What possible reason could he have had for killing them?'

'I must admit, I don't know,' Tanner replied, hearing a phone ring in the background.

'It sounds to me like this psychologist you've been talking to needs counselling herself. Are you sure she is who she says she is?'

'Having only just got off the phone with her, I haven't had much of a chance to find out.'

'OK, let me have a look,' said Vicky, pulling herself towards her desk. 'What was her name again?'

'Dr Melissa Redbridge,' Tanner replied, referring to his notes.

'I don't suppose she has a haggard face with a mop of tangled grey hair, the latter of which looks like it's been dragged through a hedge backwards?'

'Er...I'm not sure. Why?'

'Because there's a particularly deranged-looking

woman currently being interviewed on Channel 4 news who would appear to have the exact same name.'

Leaning over her desk, Tanner stared at her monitor to see that there was indeed a woman meeting Vicky's description being interviewed over the internet, the name Dr Melissa Redbridge highlighted along the bottom of the screen. It was when another headline appeared underneath, telling the audience that she was a child psychologist currently working with Norfolk Police, that Tanner began fuming quietly to himself.

'Looks like she's attempting to promote a book,' commented Vicky, as the woman produced one from under her desk. *Inner Secrets of Your Child's Mind.* 'Are you sure she's not simply trying to muscle her way into the investigation to simply sell a few more copies?'

Cursing, Tanner looked furiously away, only to find his brand new detective constable standing quietly behind him, her hands held innocently in front of her as she stared down at the floor. 'Yes, Gina?' he asked, in a curt, irritated tone.

'Sorry to bother you,' she began, looking cautiously up, her face far paler than he remembered, 'but a call's come through. A body's been found at Braydon Marsh,' she continued, unable to hold Tanner's eyes. 'It sounds like it might be the missing boy.'

- CHAPTER FORTY NINE -

TANNER STOOD RESTLESSLY behind a line of blue Police Do Not Cross tape, his Wellington boots sinking slowly down into the surrounding marsh.

'Is it the boy?' he eventually demanded, the question directed at Dr Johnstone, stooped over what appeared to be a half-submerged body lying face-down in an area of thick congealed mud.

He waited impatiently as the medical examiner sank slowly down onto his haunches.

'Was that a yes or a no?'

'Listen, John,' Johnstone replied, glaring back, 'I know you're under a lot of pressure at the moment, but I've only just arrived myself.'

'Can't you at least hazard a guess?'

'That's hardly my job.'

'How about making an exception?'

Standing back up, Johnstone let out an ungratified sigh. 'Well, it's a human being, roughly five-foot-two with short dark hair. Judging by its condition, I'd say it hasn't been here all that long. On that basis, I'd say that there's a fair chance that it could be. However, until we dig it out and get it back to the lab, that's about as much as I'm prepared to say.'

As Johnstone turned his attention back to the body, Tanner remained where he was, staring blankly out over the grim unforgiving Norfolk marsh as an unwelcome sense of being utterly alone gnawed steadily down into the depths of his soul.

The sound of a distant phone had him glancing around, only to realise that it was his own, reverberating from inside the faded threadbare sailing jacket Jenny had given him for Christmas all those years before.

'Tanner speaking,' he said, digging it out to begin traipsing his way back to his car.

'Hi, it's Vicky. I just thought I'd call to see how you were getting on?'

'Johnstone's taking a look now,' Tanner replied, glancing fitfully over his shoulder.

'Is it him? Is it the boy?'

Reaching his car, he turned back to where the medical examiner could still be seen, crouching over where the body lay. 'We won't know for sure until he's been dug out and taken back to the lab, which I suspect could be a while. But being that there can't be all that many five-foot-two people with short dark hair whose bodies have been left lying face-down in the middle of a Norfolk marsh, I think it's probably safe for us to assume that it is.'

The line fell momentarily silent. 'I'm sorry, John,' he eventually heard her say. 'I know you were hoping to find him alive.'

'We all were, weren't we?'

'Yes, of course.'

'Anyway, at least it throws out the theory that our book publishing child psychologist was trying to sell us on. How've you been getting on?'

'I think it's possible that I may have some good news.'

'That would be a first.'

'Forensics have emailed over a preliminary report for the second murdered couple. Once again they found traces of Abigail Blackwell's DNA.'

'On the bodies or just the boat?'

'Both.'

It was Tanner's turn to fall momentarily silent. 'So, it is her,' he eventually said.

'Looks like it,' he heard Vicky reply, 'but it could still be considered circumstantial, being that her DNA could have been transferred from a previous encounter with the suspect.'

'That's hardly likely, though, is it.'

'I suppose not,' came Vicky's somewhat hesitant response.

'OK, I'm heading back now. I suggest we re-commence the interview as soon as I arrive. I can't wait to hear what she has to say for herself when we tell her what forensics found, and that her son's body has been discovered lying face-down in the middle of Braydon Marsh.

- CHAPTER FIFTY -

'SORRY ABOUT THAT,' Tanner apologised, leading Vicky back into the windowless interview room, its stagnant air filled with the aroma of stale coffee and evaporated sweat. 'Now, where were we?'

'You were about to let my client go,' Graves began, 'after presenting her with a written apology.'

Tanner rested his hands on the back of his chair to gaze sagaciously up at the ceiling. 'I don't *think* that was it.'

'You mean, you've managed to find some actual evidence?'

'Something like that,' he replied, offering first Graves, then Abigail, a spurious smile. 'Shall we begin?'

Having formally re-started the interview, he opened the file he'd brought in with him to begin leafing through its contents. 'We've had a report back from forensics regarding the scene where the bodies of David and Lisa Rutherford were found.'

'I don't suppose I'm going to be allowed to see a copy?'

'Tell me, Abigail,' Tanner continued, deliberately ignoring Graves' request. 'Did you ever step on board your former lover's boat?'

'Don't answer that!' the solicitor snapped.

Tanner stopped to offer him a disapproving scowl.

'Mr Graves, I do hope we're not going to have to go through all this again?'

'I'm more than happy for my client to reply, Chief Inspector, but only after I've had a chance to review the contents of the forensics report being referred to.'

'You mean this one?' Tanner queried, gesturing down at it with a whimsical smile.

'She's not answering anymore of your questions until I know what's in that report, especially when you're so obviously trying to trick her into incriminating herself.'

'I was only asking if she'd been on board Mr Rutherford's boat before.'

'I assume you've managed to unearth some evidence that would suggest that she had?'

'Apart from her DNA being found all over it, not really,' he replied, closing the report to push over towards him. 'On their bodies as well, as it happens,' he added, leaving Graves to begin leafing his way through it whilst offering his suspect a whimsical smile.

'Yes, is the answer,' Abigail finally replied.

'Sorry, but it's been so long since I asked, I've forgotten what the question was.'

'You asked if I'd been on David's boat before, just like you did my husband's, the answer to which is yes. I've been on board both their stupid boats. But as hard as it may be to believe, that didn't mean I killed either them *or* the brainless twig-bitches they just happened to be screwing at the time.'

'By "brainless twig-bitches" I assume you mean Miss Deborah Betton and David Rutherford's wife, Lisa?'

'Sorry to interrupt,' came the solicitor's voice, glancing up from the forensics' report, 'but is this really it?'

'Is *what* really it?' Tanner replied, unable to hide his growing irritation.

'Is this the extent of your new so-called "evidence", a few microscopically small samples of my client's DNA discovered on board Mr Rutherford's boat when, once again, she's admitted to having been on board.'

'That is correct, and although the incredulous look on your face would suggest that it isn't enough, I think you'll find that it is, especially when it's combined with everything else we've discovered.'

'You mean, what you consider her motive to have been for murdering no less than four people; because she was married to the first, was having an affair with the second, and the other two because they just happened to be there at the time,' the solicitor laughed.

'We're actually thinking more because of the two-and-a-half million pound life insurance policy she'd taken out against her husband only one month before, and because David Rutherford must have somehow found out what she'd done and was endeavouring to blackmail her.'

'I see. And you have evidence to prove that Mr Rutherford *was* trying to blackmail her, do you?'

'Besides,' Tanner continued, forced to side-step the question, 'there aren't four victims, there are five.'

'Oh, right. Sorry, I must have miss-counted.'

'Another body's been found,' Tanner continued, endeavouring to catch Abigail's eyes, 'lying face-down in the middle of Braydon Marsh. We've yet to make a formal identification, but at the moment we're proceeding on the basis that it's your son, Edward Blackwell.'

As the room fell into a sullen silence, he studied her face as she continued to stare down at her hands, searching for any signs of an emotional response. But there was none. Her mouth didn't twitch, her nostrils didn't flair. Even her eyes failed to blink.

'Did you hear me, Mrs Blackwell?' Tanner was forced to ask. 'We've found the body of your son, dumped in the middle of some God-forsaken marsh.'

'I keep telling you, Chief Inspector,' came her solicitor's voice once again, 'my client has the right to remain silent.'

'Even after she's just found out that her son is dead?'

'Besides,' Graves continued, 'you haven't asked a question for her to answer.'

Tanner sat back in his chair to draw in a pacifying breath. 'Fair enough, I suppose. Mrs Blackwell, when was the last time you saw your son, alive that is?'

'And that, as you well know, Chief Inspector, is a leading question.'

'How can that possibly be a leading question?'

'Because it presupposes that the last time she saw him was after he'd been killed, the assumption being that she was responsible.'

'Then I suppose I'd better rephrase it. Mrs Blackwell, when was the last time you saw your son? Was it when you went to see your husband on board his boat, the night he was killed?'

'It was,' she nodded, her eyes never leaving her hands' ever-whitening knuckles.

'And that was when you took him, because he saw what you did, stabbing his father and the woman he was screwing in a fit of uncontrollable jealous rage...'

The solicitor sat forward in his chair. 'Chief Inspector, please!'

'...fuelled by the fact that he'd written you out of his will,' Tanner continued, 'after stating with absolute categorical certainty that he was never going to agree to a divorce? So you were left with little choice but to take out a two-and-a-half million pound life insurance policy against him. All you had to do to get your hands on that so-desperately needed money was to kill him in such a way that it made it look as if it was someone else.'

The solicitor slammed a fist hard against the table. 'Chief Inspector, I must object!'

'It was then that you heard news of Samuel Tunk's release. You knew he'd raped and murdered your husband's sister. You may have even known Jason tormented him in prison. Either way, there you were, staring at him inside his boat, watching him being ridden like a donkey by some "twig-bitch" of a tart. It was only when you'd finished the deed that you remembered your son. Maybe you turned around to find him staring at you, the knife held in your shaking hand, still dripping with his father's blood? Or maybe you found the boy lying awake in his bed? Whichever it was, you couldn't risk him being a witness, so you took him with you, only to realise that there was only one way to guarantee that he'd never be able to tell anyone what he'd seen you do.'

'You need to stop this little rant of yours, Chief Inspector,' stated Graves, 'or I'll be forced to report your outrageous conduct to Professional Standards.'

'Then you get a call from your lover, Mr David Rutherford. Somehow he managed to find out what you'd done. Maybe he saw you, or maybe you made the mistake of telling him your plans after too many glasses of wine? Either way, it was an easy enough problem to fix.'

'Either you charge my client, Chief Inspector, right now, or I'm walking her out the door.'

'After all, you'd done it before,' Tanner continued, 'and such things are always just so much easier the second time around, don't you think?'

'Right, that's it. Up you get, Mrs Blackwell. We're leaving!'

Tanner stared up at Graves with a look of bewildered amusement. 'Was it something I said?'

'The evidence of what you did say is sitting on that recording device,' Graves remarked, pushing himself up from his chair, 'which I'll be directing your superiors towards the moment I get back to my office.'

Watching his limp-limbed suspect being hauled to her feet by her now perspiring solicitor, Tanner joined them by rising to his. 'Mrs Abigail Blackwell, I'm hereby charging you with the murders of Jason Blackwell, Deborah Betton, David and Lisa Rutherford, as well as your son, Edward Blackwell.'

Graves stopped where he was to stare open-mouthed at Tanner. 'You can't possibly be serious?'

'Due to the horrific nature of these crimes,' Tanner continued, finally able to stare into his suspect's face, 'you'll have to remain in police custody until the initial hearing is held at the local magistrates' court. It will be for the judge to decide if bail will be permitted before your trial takes place.'

As he finished his sentence, he watched Abigail's eyes glaze over as her legs collapsed underneath her, leaving her toppling backwards into her solicitor's short stubby arms.

'You haven't heard the last of this,' came Graves' breathless voice, desperately trying to prevent his client from falling to the floor.

'I sincerely hope not,' Tanner replied, taking a satisfying moment to watch him struggling with her weight. 'And do please make sure to let us know if you need a hand escorting her to the holding cell. I'd hate for her to get hurt on the way, leaving you telling everyone that we were the ones responsible.'

- CHAPTER FIFTY ONE -

LEAVING VICKY TO fill out a charge sheet, Tanner instructed the duty sergeant to help escort Abigail Blackwell to the holding cell before heading back to his office. It was as he was closing the door, hoping for some desperately needed solitude, when he heard Sally's voice calling out his name.

'What is it?' he replied, with curt irritation, pivoting around to face her through the already half-closed door.

'My uncle's been trying to get hold of you.'

'Right, well, if he calls again, do me a favour will you? Tell him I'm in a meeting.'

'He's holding on line two for you now.'

'Shit!'

'Sorry, boss. He asked to hold, so I assumed it was important.'

'Don't worry. He's probably due an update anyway. I don't suppose Cooper and Townsend have had any luck finding the remaining children?'

'They just called in.'

'And...?'

Sally shook her head, her eyes holding his for a moment before sinking to the floor.

'Then maybe it's time we began searching Braydon Marsh,' he sighed, turning to stare at his desk phone where a red light could be seen flashing with demanding impatience. 'Anyway, I'd better pick up your uncle's call before he drives over to pay us a more personal visit.'

'Superintendent Forrester, it's Tanner speaking,' he said, the moment Sally had left. 'Sorry to have kept you.'

'No problem,' he heard his superior say. 'Just calling to see how everything's been going.'

Tanner momentarily paused before opening his mouth. 'We found the boy, sir.'

Expecting to be asked if he was alive or dead, Tanner waited in solemn silence, the phone's receiver held hard against his ear. But the tone of his voice must have been answer enough, as no such question came.

'His body was discovered just before one o'clock this afternoon,' he eventually continued, 'in the middle of Braydon Marsh. Johnstone hasn't given us much to go on, but that's probably because he was found submerged in mud. I suspect it will be a while before they'll be able to dig him out. Longer still before we have a cause of death. I also think the mud will make finding usable DNA evidence unlikely.'

'Does the boy's mother know?' Forrester eventually asked.

'I told her about ten minutes ago, inside interview room one.'

'And...?'

'I've just charged her with five counts of murder.'

There was a momentary pause before Forrester's voice came back over the line. 'Don't you think it would have been wise to run that by me first?'

'Oh, I'm sorry,' came Tanner's terse reply, 'for a minute there I thought I was the station's DCI?'

'You are, of course, but only since last month, and

taking into account the family involved, it may have been sensible to have asked me before doing so.'

'The fact that they're some of the richest people in the country makes a difference, does it?'

'It's got nothing to do with how much money they have, as you well know. It's the interest the British press has in them that makes it an issue. Such people can barely buy some milk from their nearest corner shop before journalists start lining up to take photographs of them, and that's before half their family's been murdered.'

Tanner smouldered with indignant resentment. He knew Forrester was right. The fleet of news vans parked bumper-to-bumper outside was proof of that. 'Fair enough, I suppose, but if I'd known I was going to have to ask your permission every time I wanted to do something, I doubt I'd have taken the job.'

'We're not talking about ordering staples, Tanner. This is about charging Lord Blackwell's daughter-in-law with multiple counts of murder. And I'm not saying you had to ask my permission. I was simply suggesting that it may have been prudent to have consulted with me before doing so.'

Tanner opened his mouth to tell him that the very next time he was about to charge some biblically rich guy's daughter-in-law with five counts of murder he definitely would, before changing his mind. He knew the evidence they held against her was unlikely to stand-up in court. He also knew that the only reason he'd charged her was because he'd lost his temper. So, instead of saying anything at all, he closed his mouth to await the next obvious question, which came just a few moments later.

'Anyway, that aside for now, what evidence do you have?'

Tanner dug his fingers into his eyes. 'Her DNA has

been found at the first two crime scenes. On all four bodies as well.'

'That sounds positive. What about motive?'

'She'd taken out a two-and-a-half million pound life insurance policy against her husband just one month before, after he'd written her out of his will and had refused to sign their divorce papers.'

'And for the other couple?'

'The suspect and the male victim knew each other. He was the co-founder of the modelling agency she used to work for. It also looks likely that they'd been having an affair which had come to an acrimonious end. It's possible he'd somehow managed to find out about what she'd done and was attempting to blackmail her.'

'What about the boy?'

'Being that he was on board his father's boat at the time, it seems likely that he was a witness.'

'You really think she could have killed him as well?' Forrester queried, his voice wavering with uncertainty.

'Well, she's openly admitted to having had little love for him. He was basically an unwanted child. The only reason she had him was because her husband threatened to cut her out of his will if she didn't.'

'How about a murder weapon?'

'All our energy's been spent trying to find the missing children.'

'Right, yes, of course.'

'Hopefully, we'll find the girls alive, but if they haven't turned up by tomorrow morning then I'm going to be ordering a search of the marsh, where the boy's body was found.'

Forrester exhaled sharply down the end of the phone. 'I suppose we better just hope and pray that it doesn't come to that. I assume you haven't mentioned any of this to the press?'

'Not yet.'

'How about the remaining members of the Blackwell family?'

'To be honest, I hadn't given them a second thought.'

'OK, well, I think it might be a good idea if they were told. I can't imagine they'd be particularly happy if the first time they hear about it is with their feet up watching the evening news.'

'I suppose I could give them a quick call.'

'Do you really think informing Lord Blackwell that his grandson has been found lying in the middle of a marsh, and that you've just charged his daughter-in-law with his murder, is something you should be doing over the phone?'

Tanner let out a petulant sigh. 'Then I suppose I'd better drive over there.'

'Yes,' Forrester responded, 'I suppose you had!'

- CHAPTER FIFTY TWO -

RESENTFULLY TAKING FORRESTER'S advice, Tanner arrived at the end of the Blackwell estate's tree-lined drive to find the place seemingly deserted. There wasn't a single car parked outside, the fleet of gleaming classic motorcycles he'd been admiring during his first visit were nowhere to be seen, and every single one of the stately home's windows appeared to have had either their curtains drawn or were covered by painted wooden shutters.

Assuming someone had to be home, even if it was only a lowly housekeeper, he made his way up a short series of smooth stone steps to its resplendent entrance to begin searching for some sort of a bell. With nothing in sight, he used its heavy black cast iron knocker to hammer against the door before standing back to listen. But the only reply came from the door knocker's sound, echoing back at him from the acres of parkland behind.

As the echo faded to be replaced by the lonely chatter of a single magpie, he hammered again, this time to be rewarded by the muffled sound of a door being slammed from somewhere deep inside the sprawling stately home.

Expecting to hear hurrying footsteps, he turned to spend a few moments watching a small herd of deer grazing lazily in the distance. When it became obvious that nobody was coming, he turned to look back at the house. 'There must be someone in!' he eventually exclaimed, fully aware that he was talking to himself.

Realising he should have had the good sense to call ahead before driving over, he cast a frustrated eye back at his car. 'Sod it!' he cursed, returning his gaze to the building to see if there was some way he'd be able to look around the back.

Stopping occasionally to peer through some of the firmly shuttered windows, he crept his way along the front of the building, past where Lord Blackwell had his motorcycle collection assembled before. When he eventually rounded the corner at the end, he came to a pair of giant black wooden gates set in the middle of a crumbling brick wall, so high that only the ivy that covered it seemed able to climb. Assuming the gates would be as locked as the rest of the house, he took hold of a circular wrought iron handle to lift and turn. With the gate creaking open, he raised a surprised eyebrow before poking his head through the slowly widening gap.

'Hello?' he called, his voice left to reverberate around the empty cobblestoned courtyard beyond. 'It's DCI Tanner, Norfolk Police.'

With no response, he stepped cautiously inside, taking a moment to stare around at a series of arched bricked stables, the rusting bonnets of old classic cars lurking out from the shadows of each.

Closing the gate behind him, his ears pricked at the eerie sound of a clanking chain, closely followed by at least one harshly whispered voice. 'I'm looking for Lord Blackwell, if he's about?' he continued, stepping cautiously forward. 'I did try the front door, but there was no reply.'

No sooner had the words left his mouth than an

elderly man emerged from the shadowy arch at the courtyard's furthest end, a pair of mud-splattered Wellington boots at the ends of his legs. It was only when he saw him open his mouth did he realise that it was the very person he'd come all that way to see.

'Chief Inspector?' Lord Blackwell's voice echoed out, busily tucking an old checked shirt into a pair of faded corduroy trousers. 'I'm most dreadfully sorry. I wasn't expecting you.'

'And I'm sorry for not calling ahead,' Tanner apologised, finding himself peering over the approaching man's shoulder, half-expecting to see someone else emerge from the shadows behind.

'How on Earth did you get in?'

The curious nature of the question had Tanner returning his attention to the man in front of him. 'Through the gate,' he replied. 'I think it's only classified as breaking and entering if it's locked,' he joked.

'I suppose it is, although I must admit, I could have sworn it was,' Lord Blackwell continued, his eyes narrowing as they studied Tanner's face. 'Anyway, you're here now. What can I do for you?'

Tanner took a moment to clear his mind. 'I'm afraid I've come with news.'

'Is it about my grandson?'

Unable to hold the man's eyes, Tanner gazed around, his mind searching for the most suitable words. 'Is there somewhere we could maybe sit down?'

'I'm not your average old-aged pensioner,' Lord Blackwell replied. 'Whatever you have to tell me, I'm quite capable of hearing it standing up.'

Tanner pulled his shoulders back to meet his penetrating gaze. 'A body was found this morning,' he began, pausing for just a fraction of a second to draw in a fortifying breath. 'We've yet to conduct a formal identification, but at the moment we're proceeding on the basis that it is your grandson.'

Tanner watched Lord Backwell's regal face tighten like a drum as he continued to stare, his eyes now blazing with fermenting rage.

'Right, that's it then,' he eventually said, his left eye twitching as he stared off into space. 'Thank you for having the balls to tell me in person, Chief Inspector,' he continued, re-engaging eye contact for the briefest of moments before turning to glance behind him. 'Now, if you don't mind, I have things I need to attend to.'

'Yes, of course,' Tanner replied, offering the man a sympathetic nod, 'but before I do, there's something else I need to tell you as well.'

'Go on then,' Lord Blackwell snapped, with an impatient huff.

'I've spent the best part of the day speaking with your daughter-in-law about the events surrounding the death of your son. Possibly your grandson as well.'

'You mean...*Abigail?*' he questioned, the anger falling from his eyes to reveal a look of perplexed incredulity.

'We discovered that she'd taken out a substantial life insurance policy against your son after he'd written her out of his will. He'd also been refusing her demands for a divorce.'

Lord Blackwell shook his head, as if clearing it of thoughts he was unwilling to entertain. 'I'm sorry, Chief Inspector, but you're way off the mark with that one. I've known Abigail for years. I can't imagine her killing anyone. Not on purpose, at least. Don't get me wrong, I'm sure she could if it was an act of passion, but for her to both plan and methodically carry out someone's murder? She doesn't have the intelligence, let alone the courage.'

'Naturally, your opinion is gratefully received,' Tanner replied, as magnanimously as his pride would allow, 'but we believe differently.'

'And you think she murdered Edward as well – her own son?'

'Until we hear back from forensics, our attention is focussed on what happened to *your* son, as well as the three other victims.'

'May I ask if there's any evidence to support such an outlandish theory?'

'Regrettably, we're unable to disclose the specific details of our investigation, certainly not with someone so closely related to two of the victims, as well as the person who's just been charged.'

'I take it that means you don't?' Lord Blackwell laughed, staring at Tanner with a look of mocking reproach.

'To be perfectly honest,' Tanner continued, bristling with a sense of embarrassed humiliation, 'what's beginning to interest me more is why you appear so keen to find out?'

'You've charged my daughter-in-law for the murder of both my son and grandson. Why do you think?'

'Yes, but when I told you that we'd found Edward, you didn't appear to have the slightest interest in finding out anything more about it. You didn't even ask how he died, let alone if we had any idea who may have killed him.'

'I didn't need to. Like everyone else on the planet, I already knew. The only person who doesn't would appear to be you.'

'Right, yes, I see. And who, pray tell, do *you* think it was?'

'Samuel Tunk, obviously!'

'I'm sorry, but why's that so obvious?'

'Because he's a deranged psychotic lunatic, one who'd already been found guilty of murdering my daughter and her entire family, who my son was then stupid enough to spend the next six months tormenting in prison. If that wasn't enough, Mr Tunk was released the morning of the day Jason was found dead.'

'Those are reasons for why he may have killed your son. I came here with the news that we'd found your grandson.'

'Are you really as stupid as you look?' Lord Blackwell questioned, tilting his head to stare at Tanner as if he was a circus curiosity.

Tanner returned to him an acrimonious smile. 'I suppose I must be. Presuming you think Tunk killed your grandson as well, what I fail to understand is why he didn't when he was still on board the boat? I mean, why take the child off only to murder him later?'

'How do you know he didn't?'

'Because our forensics team didn't find a single trace that he had. But for arguments sake, let's say he did. Why then would he carry the boy's body off to dump it in the middle of Braydon Marsh, some five miles away from where your son's boat was moored? Then there's the other couple, of course. Why would he kill them as well? We've found no connection. And again, why would he have taken their children?'

'I have no idea, but it's not my job to know, Chief Inspector, it's yours!'

'And yet here you are, telling me with absolute certainty that it was Samuel Tunk who took the life of your son.'

As Lord Blackwell sneered silently back, the sound of a clanking chain came echoing around the courtyard once again, immediately followed by the muffled curse of another man's voice.

Seeing the old man's eyes dart surreptitiously to his side, Tanner narrowed his own towards the shadow hanging under the arch from where he'd seen Lord Blackwell emerge. 'Who else is back there?' he questioned, his voice a curious whisper.

'Nobody! Now, as I said before, I have things I need to be getting on with, so if you'll excuse me.'

'And what *things* might they be?' Tanner demanded, remaining exactly where he was.

'Nothing that's of any concern of yours. I have no idea how you managed to get in, being that I'm fairly sure the gate *was* locked, even though you said it wasn't, but either way, I'd be grateful if you'd turn around and march yourself out the same way.'

Once again came the sound of a chain, but this time it was followed by what sounded like a muffled cry for help.

'Who the hell have you got back there?' Tanner questioned again, this time stepping forward.

'One more step, Chief Inspector,' Lord Blackwell replied, blocking his path, 'and I'll be on the phone to your superintendent, asking if he knows what you're doing here, breaking and entering into my private estate.'

'You know him personally, do you?'

'I've made it my business to know.'

'Then you'll be able to ask him yourself why I'm here, being that he was the one who sent me. If it had been my choice, I'd have relayed the sad news of your grandson's passing via text.'

Another muffled cry had Tanner surging forward, this time to have Lord Blackwell physically push him back.

'I'm warning you, Chief Inspector. There's nothing

back there that's of the slightest concern of yours.'

'And I'm warning you. I don't give a shit who you are. If you touch me again, I'll be arresting you for assault.'

'You're the one who broke into my estate.'

'And you're the one who left the gate open. Now, if you'll excuse me.'

'I'll be more than happy to step aside,' Lord Blackwell continued, his eyes boring into Tanner's like a pair of diamond-tipped drills, 'just as soon as you present me with the necessary search warrant.'

Another muffled cry had Tanner shoving past Blackwell with such violent force, the old man was left staggering backwards, cursing loudly as he struggled to stop himself falling to the ground.

'Who the hell do you think you are?' he heard him screaming out behind him.

'*I'm Detective Chief Inspector John Tanner*,' Tanner muttered quietly to himself, his jaw set firm as he marched his way over the cobblestoned courtyard. '*Who the fuck are you?*'

- CHAPTER FIFTY THREE -

AS TANNER STRAINED his eyes to see into the inky black shadow cast by the crumbling brick archway, it wasn't until he was a few feet away that he saw a figure begin to slowly emerge.

'If it isn't the last remaining heir to the throne,' he eventually said, gazing into Jeremy Blackwell's dark hollow eyes before taking in what he was wearing, an out of place brown leather butcher's apron, the front of which appeared to be stained with patches of dried-up blood. It was only when he realised that the man's hands were being held awkwardly behind him that he felt a faint twinge of concern.

Taking a precautionary backwards step, Tanner lifted his eyes to meet Jeremy's calculating stare. 'May I ask what you're doing here?'

'I think the more pertinent question is what *you're* doing here?' Jeremy retorted, a scrutinising frown framing a threatening sneer.

'He must have broken in,' said Lord Blackwell, coming to a breathless halt beside them, 'but don't worry,' he continued, digging out his phone, 'I'm about to call his superior officer to let him know that not only has one of his wayward DCIs gained illegal entry into our private residence, but decided to assault me in the process.'

The same distinctive sound of a rattling chain had Tanner tilting his head to gaze past Jeremy's head into the impenetrable shadow beyond. As curiosity overcame caution, he lurched instinctively forward, only to find Jeremy blocking his way to reveal what he'd been holding in his hands, a sharpened axe in one, a stick with a double-pronged end in the other.

Recognising the stick as being a particularly lethal-looking cattle prod, Tanner returned Jeremy's still sneering gaze. 'Just what exactly is going on here?'

'Nothing that's of any concern of yours,' he heard Lord Blackwell state beside him.

As Tanner's eyes became increasingly accustomed to the archway's low level of light, another figure began to slowly emerge, a vast naked hulk of a man, hanging by his wrists at the end of a black rusting chain. Only when he was able to see the man's profusely sweating face, his staring petrified eyes, and the gaffer tape flattened over his mouth, did he realise that it was none other than the previously released prisoner, Samuel Tunk.

'Is this your idea of justice?' he demanded, spinning around to face the prisoner's tormentors.

'Something like that,' Jeremy replied, feeling the weight of the axe in his hand, 'although, saying that, we've barely started.'

Tanner took a moment to stare around at the archway's damp crumbling walls, and the dust-covered cobwebs that stretched between each like ghostly lines of ethereal silk. 'Funny, but this doesn't look like the local magistrates' court.'

'The system didn't work last time, so we've decided to take matters into our own hands.'

'The system *did* work last time,' Tanner corrected.

'Ten years inside a cosy prison cell for the murder of my sister and her entire family? I'm sorry, Chief Inspector, but that sounds more like an extended holiday than the multiple-life sentence he was originally given. Besides, he's yet to tell us what he's done with Edward, which is where the axe and the cattle prod come in.'

'No!' Tanner exclaimed. 'That's where *I* come in!'

Seeing a cloud of confusion pass over Jeremy's face, Tanner turned to the man's father with an expectant glare.

'The Chief Inspector, here,' Lord Blackwell began, his gaze switching between Tanner and his son, 'came to tell us that they found Edward this morning.'

As the words echoed listlessly around the courtyard, Jeremy stared at his father with a look of anguished uncertainty. 'Is he...OK?'

Lord Blackwell shook his head to stare listlessly at the ground, leaving his son's face to begin twisting with a look of pure animalistic rage.

'So, all that's left to do is make him confess,' Jeremy eventually muttered, casting the cattle prod to the ground to take hold of the axe with both hands.

Hearing the chains links clanking together, Tanner turned to see Tunk twitching in the air, frantically trying to free his wrists from the hook he was suspended by.

'OK, that's enough,' Tanner stated, positioning himself between the axe-wielding Jeremy Blackwell and the pale blubbering body of Samuel Tunk.

'I suggest you stand to one side, Chief Inspector. It would be a shame to have to hurt you as well as that sad excuse for a human being, the one squealing like a pig behind you.'

'I'm afraid the Chief Inspector's right, Jeremy,' came Lord Blackwell's capitulating voice. 'I'm sorry, son, but we brought him here to find out where Edward was. We know that now. There's nothing more to be gained from this. We're going to have to let him go.'

Jeremy glared over at his father. 'You're not being serious?'

'I don't think we have much of a choice.'

'Right, well, fair enough, but he's still going to have to confess,' Jeremy retorted, his grip on the axe's handle tightening as he inched inextricably closer to Tanner, and the man he was endeavouring to protect.

'And just exactly how is he going to do that, with gaffer tape still covering his mouth?' Tanner questioned, remaining resolutely where he was.

'He's going to have to apologise as well,' Jeremy sneered, his focus now fixed on Samuel Tunk's bulging blood-shot eyes.

'I said that's enough!' Lord Blackwell ordered, charging forward to pull back on his raging son's arm.

'That psychotic bastard raped and killed our Sarah', Jeremy spat back in response, wrenching himself away. 'Then he murdered Jason. Now Edward as well? I'm sorry, father, but it's only right that he's made to suffer.'

'Please, Jeremy. Put the axe down before you do something you'll spend the rest of your life regretting.'

'Don't worry, I'm not going to kill him. I'm just going to fuck him up a little.'

Shoving past both his father and Tanner, Jeremy swung the axe behind him, his eyes fixed on Tunk's wide barrel-like chest.

As the axe's head arced ever higher, Tanner threw himself forward, lifting a hand to catch its handle, just below the now rapidly descending blade. But one hand was only enough to deflect it from its intended target.

Seeing it miss Tunk's chest by no more than an inch, Tanner watched in horror as the blade continued down, the handle being wrenched from his hand leaving the sharpened blade to plunge deep into his unprotected shoulder.

It wasn't until his now cursing assailant pivoted the axe head out that the pain came tearing through his body, as if his entire arm was being ripped from its socket.

As hot pulsating blood spurted up into his face, Tanner could do nothing but watch him wield it once again.

It was the harrowing cry from his father that made Jeremy suddenly stop, casting his eyes to his side. There, struggling to push himself up from the ground, lay Lord Blackwell, a blood-soaked hand clamped against the side of his ashen grey face.

'Father?' Jeremy questioned, his body turning slowly around.

'Stop – please,' the old man pleaded, his voice nothing more than a faltering whisper.

Jeremy's eyes drifted slowly down to the axe still clutched in his hands. As if being woken from a horrifying dream, he let it clatter to the ground, his eyes shifting to where Tanner lay. 'Jesus Christ! What have I done?'

Blinking blood from his half-blinded eyes, Tanner caught a glimpse of Tunk's huge hulking figure, heaving himself up behind Jeremy Blackwell. A split second later, one of Tunk's giant sinuous legs caught fast around the man's elegant neck, the foot on its end hooking around the other to begin closing the gap between calf and thigh like a steel industrial vice.

As Jeremy gasped frantically at the air, his hands clawing hopelessly at Tunk's ever-tightening leg, Tanner tried hauling himself up, desperate to do something to help. But he'd only been able to roll himself onto his uninjured side when came the stomach-clenching sound of splintering bones, deep within Jeremy's already broken neck.

Blinking blood from his eyes, Tanner stared up in horror to see Jeremy's body fall to the ground like a broken puppet. It was only when he realised what Tunk was planning next that a wave of fear began rampaging through his veins.

Using the body lying discarded at his feet as a human platform, Tunk lifted himself up, slipping the rope that bound his wrists over the hook he'd been suspended by. Once free from the chain, he stepped down from the body, ripping the gaffer tape from his mouth.

'So,' Tunk began, retrieving the axe from the ground to stare dementedly over at Tanner, 'you's a copper, is ya?'

As incoherent words began stumbling out of Tanner's juddering mouth, he tried desperately to push himself away.

'Don't worry, mate,' the hulking man continued, watching the heels of Tanner's shoes slip uselessly on the dust-covered ground. 'I'll do me best to make it quick.'

Lunging forward, Tunk swung the axe back before rotating it up and around, its trajectory aiming straight for Tanner's head.

Unable to look away, Tanner held up a useless hand to the rotating blade, his voice pleading pathetically out.

As that single terrifying moment stretched out for what felt like an eternity, the air was split by the crack of a gun, disappearing a moment later to leave nothing but an all-consuming silence.

Through the fingers of his still outstretched hand, Tanner saw the axe's blade hanging high above Tunk's anvil-shaped head. But the blade was now still, and the giant man's eyes were no longer staring into his, but at a point just beyond, as if his mind had been carried away by some fantastical dream.

It wasn't until Tanner realised that the side of the man's face was missing, and that the hulking body was falling slowly to the side, that he saw the smoking gun from the corner of his rapidly flickering eyes, and the frail unsteady hand clasped around its cold metal hilt.

- CHAPTER FIFTY FOUR -

THE SOUND OF agitated voices spiralling around his head had Tanner waking up to find himself being laid down onto what he somehow knew to be a stretcher. With the unsettling sense of being lifted into the air, he raised his head to try and examine his injury, only to find a thick white bandage had taken its place. The intense debilitating pain had also gone. All that remained was a dull pulsating ache.

As the stretcher was slid into the back of an ambulance, he took a moment to wonder how long he'd been unconscious for, who had called the emergency services, and what had happened to Lord Blackwell; the man who'd effectively saved his life?

The muffled sound of a phone ringing from somewhere nearby made him realise for the first time that he'd been stripped from the waist up, and that his clothes lay in a folded bundle on his pelvis, on top of which was also his mobile.

'Mr Tanner, can you hear me?' came an unknown female voice from somewhere to his side.

As he blinked in acknowledgment, a stern young woman's face came drifting into view.

'I'm going to insert a saline drip into a vein in the top of your hand, then you'll be taken to hospital.'

Tanner opened his mouth to speak, only to find his tongue was as dry as sandpaper. Closing it to swallow, he looked up into the paramedic's eyes. 'Do you mind if I answer my phone first?'

Tanner watched her scowl down at him with a disapproving glare.

'It could be important,' he continued, picking it up to do his best to offer her a congenial smile.

'If you must,' she eventually replied, 'but make it quick. You've lost a lot of blood. I'd hate for you to lose your arm as well.'

'Is that...er...likely?' he asked, with a note of alarm.

'I've no idea,' the woman replied, taking in the arm in question. 'All I know is that your blood pressure is far lower than it should be, which is why we need to get fluids into your body to help compensate.'

Left to hope that she'd only been joking about his arm, he dragged the phone limply towards his ear. 'Tanner speaking.'

'Hi darling, it's me,' came Christine's cheerful voice. 'You sound half asleep. I didn't wake you, did I?'

'Not at all. The paramedics had already done that for you.'

'The paramedics?' he heard her repeat.

'Don't worry. I'll explain later.'

'But you're OK, though?'

'Just about, although I may have to lose an arm.'

'You mean, you cut your finger on a Post-It note again?'

'Something like that. Anyway, what's up?'

'I'm not sure you've heard, but I wanted to tell you anyway. We found the missing children, or at least one of my colleagues did.'

Feeling a surge of emotion well up inside him, Tanner sucked in a juddering breath. 'Are they – are they – alright?' he asked, the words stumbling out of his mouth.

'Apart from being filthy dirty and starving hungry, according to him, they're OK.'

Clutching the phone to his ear, he forced his eyes closed to stop tears of relief from spilling down the sides of his face.

'Anyway, I thought you'd want to know,' he heard her continue.

'Of course, yes, and thank you. I can't tell you how much that means to me. I don't suppose they said who'd taken them?'

'I'm not sure. As I said, it was one of my colleagues who found them.'

Seeing the paramedic tap impatiently at her watch, Tanner started to finish the call. 'Anyway, I'd better go.'

'Before you do,' Christine continued, 'there's something else I wanted to ask.'

'Go on,' Tanner replied, just as Vicky's head appeared above him, her lightly freckled face staring open-mouthed at the bandages covering his shoulder.

'We've managed to arrange for the girls' grandparents to pick them up.'

'OK, yes, that's fine,' Tanner replied, acknowledging Vicky's presence with a nod. 'But we will need statements from them, at some point at least.'

As Vicky's eyes latched onto his, he watched her say the words, 'We need to talk.'

'I thought I'd take the other one home with me,' he heard Christine continue.

'And I need to hook him up to an intravenous drip!' demanded the paramedic, holding out her hand for Tanner's phone.

'Are you sure you're OK?' came Christine's voice again.

'Don't worry, I'm fine. Anyway, I have to go. I'll call

you later to let you know what time I'll be back.'

Ending the call, Tanner handed his phone to the paramedic with a sheepish smile. 'Sorry about that, but it was important.'

'As is your physical well-being,' she replied, returning the phone to his pile of clothes to take a firm hold of his wrist. 'Now, if you hold still, this should only take a moment.'

As the paramedic focussed her attention on finding a suitable vein, Vicky caught Tanner's eye with a sympathetic smile. 'News on the grapevine is that someone mistook you for a lump of wood?'

'It was Samuel Tunk,' came his unthinking response, leaving him staring off into space with a look of wistful confusion. 'No...' he continued, his muddled mind endeavouring to recall the recent events more accurately, '...it was Lord Blackwell's son, Jeremy.'

'Er...Jeremy Blackwell's dead,' came Vicky's stark response, her voice floating towards him as if through an impenetrable fog.

'Huh?' he replied, endeavouring to re-engage eye contact, only to find himself struggling to focus.

'Jeremy Blackwell's dead,' she repeated, in a gentle tone. 'Samuel Tunk as well. We found them lying next to each other, one with a broken neck, the other with a bullet through his head.'

'What about Lord Blackwell?'

'He's been taken to hospital.'

'But he's OK, though?'

'He's the one who called the ambulance.'

Tanner laid his head back down, closing his eyes to feel his mind instantly begin slipping into a fractured state of unconscious thought, only to be dragged out by the sound of Vicky's demanding voice.

'You need to tell us what happened.'

'I will, of course,' he replied, turning his head to see the paramedic attach a saline bag to a hook near the ambulance's roof. 'Did you know the children have been found?'

She nodded at him with a smile. 'News came over the radio on my way here. Are you OK to talk about Abigail?'

'Abigail?' Tanner repeated.

Vicky stared down at him with a concerned frown. 'The suspect – back at the station?'

Picturing the woman in question, Tanner nodded in response.

'The final forensics report came through for the other couple. The section relating to her DNA found at the scene concludes that the quantity was too small to prove she'd been on board. On top of that, the solicitor's saying that if her interview doesn't re-commence by half-past five this evening, he'll be filing a charge for wrongful arrest.'

Tanner lifted his hand to dig his fingers into his eyes, only to stop when he saw the tube leading out from the top of it.

'So anyway,' Vicky continued, leaning her head in towards Tanner's, 'I was just wondering if it might be best for all concerned if we made a statement to the press saying that it was Tunk after all, being that he's dead, and everything.'

'For Christ's sake, Vicky!' Tanner cursed, wrenching his head away in disgust. 'Our job isn't to do whatever it takes to placate the British press.'

'It isn't?'

'We're supposed to find out who's responsible, not just pin it on the most likely candidate.'

'Right, of course. Although, in fairness, how do we know it *wasn't* him?'

'OK people!' stated the paramedic, clipping a

monitoring device onto the end of Tanner's finger. 'I think it's time to wrap this up. You're welcome to continue, of course, but only after Mr Tanner is safely tucked-up inside a hospital bed.'

Vicky caught the paramedic's eye. 'Where's he being taken to?'

'The nearest. Wroxham Medical Centre.'

'Then I can come round in the morning,' she said, her eyes returning to Tanner's.

'You can, but I doubt I'll be there. As soon as I get the all-clear, I'll be heading home, so I'll definitely be at work tomorrow.'

'Good luck with that,' muttered the paramedic.

'My shoulder's fine,' Tanner stated, glancing around. 'It doesn't even hurt.'

'I could be wrong, but that's probably because of the lidocaine I injected you with on our arrival.'

'Don't worry, I'll be fine. I have a particularly high tolerance to pain.'

Hearing Vicky laugh in her sleeve, he decided to correct that last statement. 'OK, I don't, but that's what pain killers are for, right?'

'Of which you'll need a bucket-load if you think you'll be at work tomorrow,' the paramedic continued.

'I think I'm going to leave you two to it,' smiled Vicky. 'If I don't find you cursing with pain behind your desk tomorrow morning, I'll drop in to see you at the medical centre.'

'Don't worry, I'll be there!' stated Tanner.

'Don't worry, he won't,' retorted the paramedic, leaving Vicky shaking her head to climb carefully out.

- CHAPTER FIFTY FIVE -

'ARE WE READY to go?' the paramedic asked Tanner, in a condescending tone.

'All set!' he responded, offering her a broad toothy grin, only to hear his phone ring once again. 'Actually, I'd better see who that is first.'

Leaving the paramedic staring at him with a look of incredulous contempt, Tanner answered the call. 'Hello, yes, Tanner speaking!'

'Right then,' the paramedic was left to say, staring about as if searching for someone else to continue the conversation with. 'I suppose I'll see if I can find myself a coffee. Maybe you can give me a shout when you're ready?'

'Dr Johnstone!' Tanner continued, ignoring her completely. 'I thought you'd be safely tucked-up in bed by now.'

'If you didn't keep unearthing dead bodies for me to examine, no doubt I would be.'

'Yes, of course. Sorry about that. Anyway, I'm currently lying in the back of an ambulance waiting to be taken to hospital, so you'd better push on.'

'I'm sorry, I'd no idea. Are you OK?'

'According to the paramedic who's supposed to be looking after me,' Tanner continued, glancing up to realise she'd gone, 'I might lose an arm.'

'Nothing serious, then?'

'Not really.'

'That's a relief. Anyway, I was calling to give you an update on the body found at Braydon Marsh.'

'Oh – right,' Tanner replied, wondering why such news necessitated a phone call.

'Mainly to confirm that it was a boy, just not the one you were looking for.'

'I'm sorry?' Tanner questioned, struggling to focus his mind.

'It was the mud we found him in; as in it wasn't.'

'It wasn't...what?'

'Mud.'

'If it wasn't mud, then what was it?'

'Peat!'

'And what possible difference does that make?'

'Well, I'm not sure if you know, but peat acts as a remarkably effective preservative. The body had been there far longer than I'd first thought.'

Tanner shook his head, his mind struggling to understand what Johnstone was telling him. 'Are you trying to tell me that it isn't Edward Blackwell?'

'That's correct.'

'Then who the hell is it?'

'It took me a while to figure that one out, but I got there in the end. Its teeth match the dental records of Christopher Jackson.'

'Who?'

'The son of Sarah and Robert Jackson, the victims Samuel Tunk was originally found guilty of murdering.'

'You mean to tell me that his body was never found?'

'Apparently not.'

As the last few words Christine had said to him over the phone began replaying in his mind, a sickening knot began to tighten inside his stomach, leaving him wrenching himself up to begin staring wildly about. 'Thanks for your call, doctor, but I've got to go.'

Ending the call without waiting for a response, he frantically dialled another number to end up sitting on the edge of the makeshift bed, listening to the tone ring over and over. When it eventually clicked through to voicemail, he immediately called her again.

'For Christ's sake, Christine,' he eventually cursed, his heart pounding deep inside his chest. 'Pick up the bloody phone!'

- CHAPTER FIFTY SIX -

LEAVING CHRISTINE A garbled message, instructing her to call him the moment she picked it up, Tanner painfully removed the needle from his hand to lurch out through the ambulance's open rear doors. Once on the ground, he threw his jacket over his shoulders to see Vicky's car driving off, leaving him stumbling after it, his functioning arm waving madly in the air. Relieved to see it come skidding to a halt, he continued charging after, only to be brought to a standstill himself by the sound of the paramedic's sharp chastising voice.

'And where the hell do you think you're going?'

'Er...' he began, glancing sheepishly around to find her glaring at him from the back of the ambulance. 'I just need to pop over to see my girlfriend. I won't be long.'

'Like hell you are!' she exclaimed, stomping over.

'What *are* you doing?' came Vicky's dumbfounded voice, winding down her window.

'Looking for a lift,' he replied, skulking quickly over.

'I thought you already had one?'

'Hospital can wait. I need to get home.'

Skirting around her car's bonnet, he saw the paramedic come to a standstill, her hands placed firmly down on her hips.

'We're not waiting for you!' she called out, as

Tanner pulled open the passenger door.

'No problem,' he replied, offering her an amenable smile. 'I'll make my own way.'

'You do realise that if you carry on without sufficient fluids in your system your body will go into a severe state of shock, at which point all your major organs will fail and you'll die?'

'Yes, I know. Then my arm will fall off.'

'I'm not joking!'

'Honestly, I feel fine, and as I said, I won't be long.'

Before she could say anything else, Tanner ducked inside to close the car door, only to find Vicky staring at him in much the same way the paramedic had been.

'She does have a point, you know.'

'I'm sure she does, but I need to get home. Can you take me?'

'Of course!' she replied, shifting the gear lever into first to begin trundling the car forward. 'Any particular reason why?'

'Johnstone just called. The boy's body we found this morning; it wasn't Edward Blackwell after all.'

'OK, but – so what?'

'I should have realised when Christine called,' Tanner began, grimacing in pain as he pulled on his seatbelt. 'She told me that one of her colleague's had found the missing children. I assumed she was referring to the girls, but then she said she was going to take the other one home with her, which must mean that Edward's been found.'

'That's good news, isn't it?'

'Not if he's the person we've been looking for all this time. Certainly not if he's inside my home,' he bristled, clawing out his phone to dial Christine's number again. 'And not when my girlfriend is in the kitchen, probably making him a bloody pizza!'

'Haven't we been over this already?'

'That was before I thought he was dead.'

Vicky shook her head from side-to-side. 'Honestly, John, I really think you're wrong about this. The person responsible is back there, currently being stuffed into a body bag.'

'As I keep saying,' Tanner continued, his phone back against his ear, 'just because everyone thinks it was Tunk, doesn't mean it was.'

'Well, he was certainly a more likely candidate than a twelve-year-old boy; murdering his father out of spite, the woman he was with just because she happened to be there, and the other couple for no reason whatsoever.'

'Why the hell isn't she picking up?'

'Probably because she's now making him an apple crumble. Either way, I think it's somewhat unlikely that she's busy warding him off with a rolling pin, unless he didn't like the pizza of course, and wanted Chicken McNuggets instead.'

Seeing her smirk out of the corner of his eye, Tanner put the phone away to focus his attention on the road ahead. 'I'd appreciate it if you didn't laugh at me, Detective Inspector.'

'I'm not laughing at you, boss,' Vicky replied, blushing slightly. 'I just don't think it's very likely, that's all.'

'Then perhaps you could drive a little faster. At the rate you're going, it will be sometime next week before we ever find out.'

- CHAPTER FIFTY SEVEN -

ARRIVING OUTSIDE HIS riverside bungalow to find Christine's MX-5 parked in its usual place, he waited for Vicky to stop the car before jumping impatiently out. With his colleague doing the same, albeit at a more subdued pace, Tanner remained where he was, his ears tuned for the faintest of sounds. When he heard the clatter of a saucepan, followed by the faint but unmistakable voice of Christine cursing, he glanced over to see Vicky offering him a supercilious smile.

'That was either young Edward,' she commented, 'bashing Christine over the head with a frying pan, or you've got yourself a broken floor tile.'

Tanner gave her a dismissive scowl before hurrying over the driveway to the front door. Fishing around for his house keys, he nudged it open to be greeted by the sound of the TV, blaring out what sounded like a Star Wars film.

'Hello?' he called, creeping inside. 'Is anyone home?'

'I'm in the kitchen!' came Christine's normal welcoming response.

Relaxing a little, Tanner made his way into the living area to see her preparing something next to the sink. Another step inside presented him with the pale unblemished face of a thin dark-haired boy, staring at the TV with a look of apathetic indifference to the intergalactic battle being played out in front of him.

'Good God!' he heard Christine suddenly exclaim. 'What on Earth happened to your arm?'

'Oh, sorry,' he replied, turning to face her with an apologetic grimace. 'I thought I told you.'

'And I thought you were joking!'

'Is...er...everything OK here?' he continued, his eyes drifting back to the boy slumped back against the sofa, his chin resting on top of his thin narrow chest.

'Is there some reason why it shouldn't be?'

'And Edward?'

'As I said on the phone, apart from being starving hungry and in desperate need of a shower, he seems to be OK. You're alright, aren't you, Edward?' she asked, lifting her voice above the sound of the film.

Seeing him nod silently in response, Tanner pivoted himself around to make his way cautiously over.

'Hello Edward,' he began, gently lowering himself down onto the adjacent edge of the L-shaped sofa. 'My name's John,' he continued, reaching for the TV's remote. 'I'm a police detective inspector. You don't mind if I turn this down a little, do you?'

Without waiting for a response, he pointed the remote at the TV to do so, only to find the boy still staring at the screen.

'I was hoping you'd be able to tell me what happened on board your father's boat a couple of nights ago?'

With still no reply, Tanner glanced around at Vicky, looking for inspiration. But all she did was to shrug her shoulders at him with a particularly blank expression.

Rolling his eyes, he turned back to find the boy still transfixed by the film, just as he had been when they'd first walked in.

'Your father was on board,' Tanner continued, 'as was a friend of his. A young lady called Deborah. Did you meet her?'

Still nothing.

'Maybe you were already in bed when she came on board?'

By this time, even Christine had stopped what she was doing to quietly watch, appearing to be as curious as Tanner was as to how the conversation was going to unfold.

'Perhaps you heard them talking together?'

More silence.

'Maybe you heard them doing something else?'

The sound of Vicky clearing her throat had him glancing over his shoulder to find her glowering at him with a look of stern reproach.

'OK, well...' Tanner continued, 'do you know if anyone else came on board? Was that the person who took you away?'

With still nothing from the boy but unblinking silence, Tanner felt Vicky's hand rest gently against his shoulder.

'Maybe it's best if we left this till later,' she whispered discreetly into his ear.

'Give me a minute,' came his terse response, pushing her hand away.

'OK,' he heard her continue, 'but you *have* to tread carefully.'

Tanner again pointed the remote at the TV, this time turning it off completely.

Resting his elbows on his knees, he leaned slowly forward, hoping to garner a little more of the boy's attention. 'Edward, it's really important that you listen to me. We *have* to find out what happened on board your father's boat. Can you tell me anything – anything at all?'

The boy's eyes finally slipped off the screen to drift down to his chest.

'Did someone else come on board? Was that the person who took you away?'

For the briefest of moments he thought he saw the corners of the boy's mouth lift into an almost indiscernible smile.

Tilting his head to try and look into Edward's still lowered eyes, Tanner narrowed his own to draw in a delicate breath. 'Did you see what happened to your father?' he whispered, barely loud enough for the boy to hear. 'Was it the person who came on board your boat, after you'd gone to bed, or maybe...maybe it was you who killed him?'

As if rising from the depths of hell, the boy's dark hooded eyes lifted themselves up to glare menacingly into his.

'Excuse me!' came Vicky's mortified voice. 'May I have a word with you, Chief Inspector? In private!'

'It *was* you, wasn't it?' Tanner continued, daring to stare back into Edward's soulless gaze.

'*Now*, John!'

With a cold shiver running down the length of his spine, as if the Devil himself had stepped over his grave, Tanner forced himself up. 'I want you to wait right there, young man,' he commanded, pointing a portentous finger at him as his chin returned to resting grudgingly against his chest. 'I'm not finished with you yet!'

- CHAPTER FIFTY EIGHT -

WITH VICKY VIRTUALLY dragging him into the hallway, all the way down to the front door, she eventually turned on him with a furious gaze.

'Just what the *hell* do you think you're doing?'

'Questioning the boy about the death of his father,' Tanner responded, offering her an indifferent shrug.

'But he's only twelve!'

'And that means he didn't do it, does it?'

'Of course it doesn't. But you can't cross-examine a twelve-year-old boy in the middle of your sitting room, certainly not before having read him his rights and giving him the chance to speak to a solicitor. I'm fairly sure you're supposed to ask his parents for permission as well.'

'Yes, and I would have, of course, but one of them is dead, and the other is back at the station.'

'There's also supposed to be an appropriate adult in attendance,' Vicky continued, 'and frankly, I'm really not sure that either myself or Christine qualifies, not when I'm your work colleague and she's your girlfriend. If all that wasn't enough, you're not even recording the bloody conversation!'

'He did it,' Tanner whispered, the words hissing out of his mouth. 'I *know* he did!'

'Then you'll need to caution him, escort him down to the station, ask permission from his mother to interview him, and then wait patiently for both a solicitor and an officially appointed childcare officer.'

Tanner opened his mouth to bark back a response when a peculiar shuffling noise drifted its way down the hall, one that pricked at his ears with discomfiting unease. Distracted by the sound, he tilted his head to one side, listening with more focussed attention. It took him a full moment to work out what it was; the patio door being slid slowly open. Only when he heard his name being spoken in a short broken gasp did his heart pound with sickening dread.

'Christine!' he exclaimed, shoving past Vicky to plunge back down the hall.

Bursting into the living room, his eyes baulked against the scene his mind had already pictured: Edward Blackwell, backing out through the half-open patio door, the cold steel edge of a glistening blade held firmly against Christine's oh-so delicate throat. As Tanner's eyes met with hers, staring over at him with ever-widening horror, he felt his head spin as he came to an unsteady halt. 'Edward, you need to put the knife down and let Christine go.'

'Sorry, I can't do that,' came the boy's sultry response, 'but to be honest, I've never been very good at doing what adults tell me, especially when not one of them has ever given a single shit about me.'

'I'm sure that isn't true.'

'Really? My own mother tells me as much just about every time she opens her mouth.'

Tanner paused for a moment before re-opening his. 'What about your father?'

'You'll have to ask him that yourself. Oh, sorry, I forgot. You can't, being that he's dead and everything.'

'It *was* you, wasn't it?'

Edward narrowed his eyes to the point where

Tanner could barely see them. 'The bastard had been asking for it for years,' he eventually said. 'Did you know he used to beat me?'

'I'm sorry, I didn't.'

'Whenever he got drunk, which was pretty much all the time. When he wasn't he'd call me a retard. Actually, he'd call me a miserable fucking retard, but let's not split hairs. I'm fairly sure that was probably because I never said very much. I learnt early on to keep my mouth shut, especially when I was around him. Of course, I would have preferred to have stayed just about as far away from him as was humanly possible, but my mother had other ideas. She'd dump me on him whenever she wanted to go out, which was about as often as my father got drunk. So I'd be left abandoned on board his stupid boat, forced to listen to him doing the most disgusting things to whichever whore of a woman he was with at the time.'

'Was that what happened on Monday night?'

Tanner watched Edward's bottom lip tremble ever-so slightly.

'He told me a friend was coming over, and that I was to stay in my cabin. For once I had the courage to tell him that I didn't want to, to which he said I could either do what I was told or fuck off back to my mother's house. I must admit to becoming a little upset. I seem to remember asking him why he seemed to want to spend all his time with women who were only interested in his money, but never with me.'

As Edward's eyes began filling with tears, he removed the knife from Christine's throat to wipe at the first to escape.

'It was only later,' he continued, returning the knife to her neck, 'after I had to endure listening to them screwing each other for what felt like hours, that I heard what he said to her about me; that she should try and "make a man out of me". He then changed his mind saying it would be impossible, being that my dick was so small she'd need a search light just to find it, something they both seemed to find hilariously funny. So I went into the kitchen, pulled a knife from the drawer, slit the woman's throat whilst she was still sitting on top of him like a pregnant cow, then stabbed my father repeatedly in the chest, something he seemed unable to do anything about being that his hands had been tied to the light above his bed. What I didn't understand was why neither of them seemed to find it funny. Personally, I thought it was hilarious.'

Whilst talking, Tanner had been inching his way around the L-shaped sofa, hoping to get close enough so that if Edward removed the knife from Christine's throat again, he'd have the chance to pull her away.

'What did you do then?'

Edward lifted his chin to offer Tanner a defiant glare. 'I took their money, grabbed some food, and left. At first I was going to follow Weavers' Way. I knew it led to my grandfather's house. He was just about the only person who ever showed the slightest bit of interest in me; him and my uncle. But then I discovered my new calling.'

'And what was that?' Tanner questioned, edging himself inextricably closer.

'Helping others like me.'

'Others like you?'

'Well, not *exactly* like me. I'm beginning to realise that few people are. I found myself beside a quiet stretch of water where only a couple of boats had been moored. My original plan was to sneak on board each for some food. I didn't have any intention of hurting anyone. But then I heard a couple on board one of them start yelling and screaming at each other. At first I thought it was funny, but then I realised they had two girls, one who I saw being hit hard across the face. She couldn't have been more than six. The scene brought back memories of my parents arguing,' he continued, his whole face now trembling as fresh tears welled up into his eyes, 'each one telling the other just how much they *didn't* want me.'

As Edward sucked in a juddering breath, Tanner took another half-step closer.

'I knew how those girls must have been feeling,' the boy continued, tears now spilling freely down the sides of his face, 'to go to sleep every night knowing that nobody loved them. At least they had each other. I had no one! All I had to look forward to when I went to bed was to wake up the next day to go through the same thing over again – day after day – night after night – all the time wondering if it was somehow my fault – that I must have done something for my parents not to love me.'

For the first time since entering the house, Tanner saw Edward for what he really was; just a boy, desperate for the warmth and compassion only another human being could provide.

Stopping where he was, Tanner relaxed his stance to draw in a soothing breath. 'It wasn't your fault,' he eventually said. 'I can't imagine how any of it was.'

'*THEN WHY DID THEY NEVER LOVE ME?*' Edward suddenly screamed, as if his soul was being wrenched from his body.

As he began sobbing with uncontrolled emotion, his body slowly collapsed like a crumbling block of flats, leaving him sinking to his knees, the knife that had been held against his hostage's throat clattering harmlessly to the floor.

The moment it did, Christine leapt away, throwing herself into Tanner's beckoning arm.

With her body shaking against his, Tanner took an

anxious moment to examine her neck. Thanking God she'd been left unharmed, he held her tight to watch Vicky leap forward, kicking the knife from Edward's crumpled body to immediately dig out her phone.

'You're OK,' he whispered softly into Christine's ear, drawing a lock of hair from between her tear-soaked lips. 'You're safe now.'

As the words drifted effortlessly out of his mouth, he felt his mind slip suddenly to the side, as if he'd just stepped on a sheet of ice. Spinning around, he reached for Christine's arm. But she wasn't there. Nothing was. All that remained of the world was a spiralling chasm into which he fell, deeper and deeper, until there was nothing left to feel or touch but the cold embrace of never-ending darkness.

- EPILOGUE -

A SUDDEN JOLT had Tanner waking up to find himself gazing into the blurry eyes of a woman's vaguely familiar face, staring down at him with a look of cantankerous dispassion.

'Where – where am I?'

'You're in the back of an ambulance,' the woman replied, her arms locked over her chest. 'Strangely enough, it's the same one you were in the back of about two hours ago.'

Realising she was the paramedic who'd been looking after him before, a far more familiar voice came drifting over towards him.

'How's he doing?'

'Christine?' he questioned, lifting his head only to feel himself spin nauseously around.

'Hey, darling,' came her smiling face, hovering above his like a shimmering mirage.

'I – I can't see you properly,' came his panicked response.

He watched her send the paramedic a look of questioning concern.

'Don't worry,' the woman replied, peering at a monitoring device, 'it's a side-effect of his body's lack of fluids, but it's where it's supposed to be now, so his eyesight should be returning to normal.'

'And the rest of him?'

'Everything seems to be OK, apart from his arm, of

course.'

'He's not going to lose it, is he?'

'Why – does he need it?'

'Of course I need it!' Tanner stated, lifting his head again to help emphasise the fact.

'Then I suppose we'd better take a look. Can you move your fingers?'

'I – I think so,' he replied, staring down the length of his body with a look of focussed determination. 'Look, there, you see?'

'I meant the ones attached to your injured arm,' the paramedic replied, with a distinct lack of amusement.

'Oh, right. You should have said.'

'You *can* move your fingers, can't you?' Christine queried, taking hold of his other hand.

'Piece of cake,' he grinned, gripping hers back with ease. 'It was just my idea of a joke.'

'Oh, right. That was even less funny than normal.'

'How about you? Are you OK?'

'Pretty much.'

'And the baby?'

'Oh, he's fine,' she replied, offering Tanner a reassuring smile.

'He?'

'It's a guess based on how much he's started kicking me. I think you may have a footballer on your hands.'

'Can't he play golf instead?'

A short sudden blast from the ambulance's siren brought Tanner's mind whirling back to the most recent events. 'What happened to Edward?'

'Vicky looked after him until some more of your colleagues arrived.'

'And then?'

'She read him his rights and led him away, making

sure he was handcuffed first, which I thought was a little unnecessary, given the state the poor boy was in.'

'By "poor boy", you mean the young man who was threatening to cut open your throat?'

'If we'd had the childhood he'd been subjected to, that could have been either one of us.'

'What about the nature versus nurture argument?'

'Well, I suppose it's likely that he was born with some sort of mental imbalance, but if he hadn't spent half his life being rejected by his mother, and the other half being beaten-up by his father, I seriously doubt he would have ended up doing what he did.'

As the ambulance veered to the right, Tanner grimaced in pain as his weight was thrown onto his injured shoulder.

'That was the turn into Wroxham Medical Centre,' commented the paramedic, glancing through a window. 'Once inside, they'll be able to hook you up with some more pain killers.'

With the ambulance coming to a halt, the paramedic nudged her way past Christine to open the doors. 'Are you ready?' she asked, turning back to look at Tanner.

'I don't suppose you could give us a minute?'

'You're not going to do another runner on me, I hope?'

'I just want to have a quick word with my girlfriend.'

The paramedic took a brief moment to take them both in. 'OK, I'll let the driver know, just in case he heads off with you still inside.'

With her head disappearing around the door, Christine turned to look at Tanner. 'What's all this about?'

'I was thinking, back at the house, when that knife

was being held to your neck.'

'How much you'd miss my cooking if I wasn't around?'

'Something like that,' he smiled.

'OK, well, don't worry. There's no need to rush out to Sainsbury's to buy their entire stock of ready meals. I'm still here.'

'But you – you nearly weren't, though,' Tanner continued, a surge of emotion sweeping over him, 'and with the baby and everything, I was wondering...well, hoping really.'

With tears stinging his eyes, he took hold of Christine's hand.

'Hoping...what?' she asked, her own darting between his.

'For permission to ask your father for your hand in marriage?'

Tanner watched her first open and then close her mouth, the edges of her face flecking with colour.

'Just your hand, mind,' he added. 'He's welcome to keep the rest of you.'

Christine snorted with laughter. 'Are you sure?' she eventually asked, her eyelashes batting away at tears of her own.

'I've never been so sure of anything in my entire life,' he replied, 'apart from that time I bought a subscription to Yachting Monthly, of course.'

'Well, I'll certainly think about it. Meanwhile, I suggest we find a doctor to give you the once over.'

'You're not going to say yes?'

'Not until I know you're of sound mind and body. At the moment, I'm not convinced you're either.'

'I'm fine!' Tanner insisted. 'Honestly!'

'We'll see, but I don't even know if you're going to live long enough to make it inside the medical centre, and I'm fairly sure the phrase "till death do us part" meant slightly longer than five and a half minutes. And I know there's nothing in the Church of England's wedding vows about how many arms the groom is supposed to have, but I'd at least like to know before agreeing to marry him.'

'So that's a no, then?'

'No, that's a maybe. Now, let's get you inside before I change my mind.'

'Don't you need to have made up your mind before being able to change it?'

'Do you want me to say no?'

'Um....'

'Right then. Wait here, and I'll see if I can find that paramedic.'

'And then you'll say yes?'

'And then we'll have you checked over by a doctor.'

'And *then* you'll say yes?'

'And then I'll find a psychological evaluation form for you to fill in.'

'OK, so if the doctor confirms that I'm not likely to die anytime soon, that my arm isn't going to fall off overnight, and that your psychological questionnaire reveals me to be sane, at least relatively so, then you'll agree to marry me?'

'Well, yes,' she replied, 'but you're still going to have to ask my father, and I can assure you that he's going to be none too pleased when he finds out that you're only interested in my hand, so you may want to re-think that line on the way over.'

John Tanner
will return in
Bluebell Wood

- A LETTER FROM DAVID -

Dear Reader,

I just wanted to say a huge thank you for deciding to read *Weavers' Way*. If you enjoyed it, I'd be really grateful if you could leave a review on Amazon, or mention it to your friends and family. Word-of-mouth recommendations are just so important to an author's success, and doing so will help new readers discover my work.

It would be great to hear from you as well, either on Facebook, Twitter, Goodreads or via my website. There are plenty more books to come, so I sincerely hope you'll be able to stick around for what will continue to be an exciting adventure!

All the very best,

David

- ABOUT THE AUTHOR -

David Blake is an international bestselling author who lives in North London. At time of going to print he has written twenty-two books, along with a collection of short stories. When not writing, David likes to spend his time mucking about in boats, often in the Norfolk Broads, where his crime fiction books are based.